P9-DTV-009

Nado Reid

Audrey Thomas is gaining increasing recognition as a Canadian writer of consummate skill.

She has published six novels including *Mrs. Blood, Songs My Mother Taught Me,* and *Latakia.* This volume is a selection from two of her critically acclaimed collections of short stories, *Ten Green Bottles* and *Ladies and Escorts.*

Thomas' stories have also been published in the *Atlantic Monthly, Saturday Night,* and *Toronto Life.* Her awards include Second Prize in the 1980 National Magazine Awards, Second Prize in both the 1980 and 1981 CBC Literary Contest, and Second Prize in the 1981 Chatelaine Fiction Contest.

Born in Binghamton, New York, Audrey Thomas earned a B.A. from Smith College and an M.A. from the University of British Columbia. Except for two years spent in Africa, she has been a Canadian resident for more than twenty years. She presently lives in Vancouver and teaches creative writing at the University of British Columbia.

Audrey Thomas

Two in the Bush
and Other Stories

New Canadian Library No. 163

McClelland and Stewart

0-7710-9306-3

The Canadian Publishers
McClelland and Stewart Limited
25 Hollinger Road, Toronto

CONTENTS

IF ONE GREEN BOTTLE...

When fleeing, one should never look behind. Orpheus, Lot's wife. . . penalties grotesque and terrible await us all. It does not pay to doubt. . . to turn one's head. . . to rely on the confusion. . . the smoke. . . the fleeing multitudes. . . the satisfaction of the tumbling cities. . . to distract the attention of the gods. Argus-eyed, they wait, he waits. . . the golden chessmen spread upon the table. . . the opponent's move already known, accounted for. . . . Your pawns, so vulnerable. . . advancing with such care (if you step on a crack, then you'll break your mother's back). Already the monstrous hand trembles in anticipation. . . the thick lips twitch with suppressed laughter. . . then pawn, knight, castle, queen scooped up and tossed aside. "Check," and (click click) "check. . . mmmate." The game is over, and you. . . surprised (but why?). . . petulant. . . your nose still raw from the cold . . . your galoshes not yet dried. . . really, it's indecent. . . inhumane (why bother to come? answer: the bother of not coming). . . and not even the offer of a sandwich or a cup of tea. . . discouraging. . . disgusting. The great mouth opens . . . like a whale really. . . he strains you, one more bit of plankton, through his teeth (my mother had an ivory comb once). "Next week. . . ? At the same time. . . ? No, no, not at all. I do not find it boring in the least. . . . Each time a great improvement. Why, soon," the huge lips tremble violently, "ha, ha, you'll be beating me." Lies. . . all lies. Yet, even as you go, echoes of Olympian laughter in your ears, you know you will return, will once more challenge. . . and be defeated once again. Even plankton have to make a protest. . . a stand. . . what else can one do? "Besides, it passes the time. . . keeps my hand in. . . and you never know. . . . One time, perhaps. . . a slip. . . a flutter of the eyelids. . . . Even the gods grow old."

The tropical fan, three-bladed, omniscient, omnipotent, inexorable, churns up dust and mosquitoes, the damp smell of coming rain, the overripe smell of vegetation, of charcoal fires, of human excrement, of fear. . . blown in through the open window, blown up from the walls and the floor. All is caught in the fan's embrace, the efficient arms of the unmoved mover. The deus in the machina, my old chum the chess-player, refuses to descend. . . yet watches. Soon they will let down the nets and we will lie in the darkness, in our gauze houses, like so many lumps of cheese. . . protected. . . revealed. The night-fliers, dirty urchins, will press their noses at my windows and lick their hairy lips in hunger. . . in frustration. Can they differentiate, I wonder, between the blood of my neighbour and mine? Are there aesthetes among the insects who will touch only the soft parts. . . between the thighs. . . under the armpits. . . along the inner arm? Are there vintages and connoisseurs? I don't like the nights here: that is why I wanted it over before the night. One of the reasons. If I am asleep I do not know who feeds on me, who has found the infinitesimal rip and invited his neighbours in. Besides, he promised it would be over before the night. And one listens, doesn't one? . . . one always believes. . . absurd to rely on verbal consolation. . . clichés so worn they feel like old coins. . . smooth. . . slightly oily to the touch. . . faceless.

Pain, the word, I mean, derived (not according to Skeat) from "pay" and "Cain." How can there, then, be an exit. . .

8

a way out? The darker the night, the clearer the mark on the forehead. . . the brighter the blind man's cane at the crossing. . . the louder the sound of footsteps somewhere behind. Darkness heightens the absurd sense of "situation". . . gives the audience its kicks. But tonight. . . really. . . All Souls'. . . it's too ridiculous. . . . Somebody goofed. The author has gone too far; the absurdity lies in one banana skin, not two or three. After one, it becomes too painful. . . too involved. . . too much like home. Somebody will have to pay for this. . . the reviews. . . tomorrow. . . all will be most severe. The actors will sulk over their morning cup of coffee. . . the angel will beat his double breast above the empty pocketbook. . . the director will shout and stamp his feet. . . . The whole thing should have been revised. . . rewritten. . . we knew it from the first.

(This is the house that Jack built. This is the cat that killed the rat that lived in the house that Jack built. We are the maidens all shaven and shorn, that milked the cow with the crumpled horn. . . that loved in the hearse that Joke built. Excuse me, please, was this the Joke that killed the giant or the Jack who tumbled down. . . who broke his crown? Crown him with many crowns, the lamb upon his throne. He tumbled too. . . it's inevitable. . . . It all, in the end, comes back to the nursery. . . . Jill, Humpty Dumpty, Rock-a-bye baby. . . they-kiss-you, they-kiss-you. . . they all fall down. The nurses in the corner playing Ludo. . . centurions dicing. We are all betrayed by Cock-a-Doodle-Doo. . . . We all fall down. Why, then, should I be exempt?. . . presumptuous of me. . . please forgive.)

Edges of pain. Watch it, now, the tide is beginning to turn. Like a cautious bather, stick in one toe. . . both feet. . . "brr" . . . the impact of the ocean. . . the solidity of the thing, now that you've finally got under. . . like swimming in an ice

cube really. "Yes, I'm coming. Wait for me." The shock of
the total immersion. . . the pain breaking over the head.
Don't cry out. . . hold your breath. . . so. "Not so bad, really,
when one gets used to it." That's it. . . just the right tone. . .
the brave swimmer. . . . Now wave a gay hand toward the
shore. Don't let them know. . . the indignities. . . the chattering teeth. . . the blue lips. . . the sense of isolation. . . . Good.

And Mary, how did she take it, I wonder, the original, the
appalling announcement. . . the burden thrust upon her?
"No, really some other time. . . the spring planting. . . my
aged mother. . . quite impossible. Very good of you to think
of me, of course, but I couldn't take it on. Perhaps you'd call
in again next year." (Dismiss him firmly. . . quickly, while
there's still time. Don't let him get both feet in the door. Be
firm and final. "No, I'm sorry, I never accept free gifts.")
And then the growing awareness, the anger showing quick
and hot under the warm brown of the cheeks. The voice. . .
like oil. . . . "I'm afraid I didn't make myself clear." (Like
the detective novels. . . . "Allow me to present my card. . .
my credentials." The shock of recognition. . . the horror.
"Oh, I see. . . . Yes. . . well, if it's like that. . . . Come this
way." A gesture of resignation. She allows herself one sigh
. . . the ghost of a smile.) But no, it's all wrong. Mary. . .
peasant girl. . . quite a different reaction implied. Dumb-
founded. . . remember Zachary. A shocked silence. . . the
rough fingers twisting together like snakes. . . awe. . . a certain rough pride ("Wait until I tell the other girls. The well
. . . tomorrow morning. . . . I won't be proud about it, not
really. But it is an honour. What will Mother say?") *Droit
de seigneur*. . . the servant summoned to the bedchamber. . .
honoured. . . afraid. Or perhaps like Leda. No preliminaries
. . . no thoughts at all. Too stupid. . . too frightened. . . the
thing was, after all, over so quickly. That's it. . . stupidity. . .
the necessary attribute. I can hear him now. "That girl. . .

whatzername? . . . Mary. Mary will do. Must be a simple woman. . . . That's where we made our first mistake. Eve too voluptuous. . . too intelligent. . . this time nothing must go wrong."

And the days were accomplished. Unfair to gloss that over. . . to make so little of the waiting. . . the months. . . the hours. They make no mention of the hours; but of course, men wrote it down. How were they to know? After the immaculate conception, after the long and dreadful journey, after the refusal at the inn. . . came the maculate delivery . . . the manger. And all that noise. . . cattle lowing (and doing other things besides). . . angels blaring away. . . the eerie light. No peace. . . no chance for sleep. . . for rest between the pains. . . for time to think. . . to gather courage. Yet why should she be afraid. . . downhearted. . . ? Hadn't she had a sign. . . the voice. . . the presence of the star? (And notice well, they never told her about the other thing. . . the third act.) It probably seemed worth it at the time. . . the stench. . . the noise. . . the pain.

Robert the Bruce. . . Constantine. . . Noah. The spider. . . the flaming cross. . . the olive branch. . . . With these signs . . . . I would be content with something far more simple. A breath of wind on the cheek. . . the almost imperceptible movement of a curtain. . . a single flash of lightning. Courage consists, perhaps, in the ability to recognize signs. . . the symbolism of the spider. But for me. . . tonight. . . what is there? The sound of far-off thunder. . . the smell of the coming rain which will wet, but not refresh. . . that tropical fan. The curtain moves. . . yes, I will allow you that. But for me . . . tonight. . . there is only a rat behind the arras. Jack's rat. This time there is no exit. . . no way out or up.

(You are not amused by my abstract speculations? Listen . . . I have more. Time. Time is an awareness, either forward or backward, of Then, as opposed to Now. . .the stasis. Time

11

is the moment between thunder and lightning. . . the interval at the street corner when the light is amber, neither red nor green, but shift gears, look both ways. . . the oasis of pleasure between pains. . . the space between the darkness and the dawn. . . the conversations between courses. . . the fear in the final stroke of twelve. . . the nervous fumbling with cloth and buttons, before the longed-for contact of the flesh. . . the ringing telephone. . . the solitary coffee cup. . . the oasis of pleasure between pains. Time. . . and time again.)

That time when I was eleven and at Scout camp. . . marching in a dusky serpentine to the fire tower. . . the hearty counselors with sun-streaked hair and muscular thighs. . . enjoying themselves, enjoying ourselves. . . the long hike almost over. "Ten green bottles standing on the wall. Ten green bottles standing on the wall. If one green bottle. . . should accidentally fall, there'd be nine green bottles standing on the wall." And that night. . . after pigs in blankets . . . cocoa. . . campfire songs. . . the older girls taught us how to faint. . . to hold our breath and count to 30. . . then blow upon our thumbs. Gazing up at the stars. . . the sudden sinking back into warmth and darkness. . . the recovery. . . the fresh attempt. . . delicious. In the morning we climbed the fire tower (and I, afraid to look down or up, climbing blindly, relying on my sense of touch), reached the safety of the little room on top. We peered out the windows at the little world below. . . and found six baby mice, all dead. . . curled up, like dust kitties in the kitchen drawer. "How long d'you suppose they've been there?" "Too long. Ugh." "Throw them away." "Put them back where you found them." Disturbed. . . distressed. . . the pleasure marred. "Let's toss them down on Rachel. She was too scared to climb the tower. Baby." "Yes, let's toss them down. She ought to be paid back." (Everything all right now. . . the

12

day saved. Ararat. . . Areopagus. . . .) Giggling, invulner-
able, we hurled the small bodies out the window at the
Lilliputian form below. Were we punished? Curious. . . I
can't remember. And yet the rest. . . so vivid. . . as though it
were yesterday. . . this morning. . . five minutes ago. . . . We
must have been punished. Surely they wouldn't let us get
away with that?

Waves of pain now. . . positive whitecaps. . . breakers. . . .
Useless to try to remember. . . to look behind. . . to think.
Swim for shore. Ignore the ringing in the ears. . . the eyes
half blind with water. . . the waves breaking over the head.
Just keep swimming. . . keep moving forward. . . rely on
instinct. . . your sense of direction. . . don't look back or forward. . . there isn't time for foolish speculation. . . . See?
Flung up. . . at last. . . exhausted, but on the shore. Flotsam
. . . jetsam. . . but there, you made it. Lie still.
   The expected disaster is always the worst. One waits for
it. . . is obsessed by it. . . it nibbles at the consciousness. Jack's
rat. Far better the screech of brakes. . . the quick embrace
of steel and shattered glass. . . or the sudden stumble from
the wall. One is prepared through being unprepared. A few
thumps of the old heart. . . like a brief flourish of announc-
ing trumpets. . . a roll of drums. . . and then nothing. This
way. . . tonight. . . I wait for the crouching darkness like a
child waiting for that movement from the shadows in the
corner of the bedroom. It's all wrong. . . unfair. . . there
ought to be a law. . . . One can keep up only a given number
of chins. . . one keeps silent only a given number of hours.
After that, the final humiliation. . . the loss of self-control
. . . the oozing out upon the pavement. Dumpty-like, one
refuses (or is unable?) to be reintegrated. . . whimpers for
morphia and oblivion. . . shouts and tears her hair. . . . That
must not happen. . . . Undignified. . . déclassé. I shall talk

13

to my friend the fan. . . gossip with the night-fliers. . . pit my small light against the darkness, a miner descending the shaft. I have seen the opening gambit. . . am aware of the game's inevitable conclusion. What does it matter? I shall leap over the net. . . extend my hand. . . murmur, "Well done," and walk away, stiff-backed and shoulders high. I will drink the hemlock gaily. . . I will sing. Ten green bottles standing on the wall. If one green bottle should accidentally fall. . . . When it is over I will sit up and call for tea. . . ignore the covered basin. . . the bloody sheets (but what do they do with it afterward. . . where will they take it? I have no experience in these matters). They will learn that the death of a part is not the death of the whole. The tables will be turned. . . and overturned. The shield of Achilles will compensate for his heel.

And yet, were we as ignorant as all that. . . as naïve. . . that we never wondered where the bottles came from? I never wondered. . . . I accepted them the way a small child draws the Christmas turkey. . . brings the turkey home. . . pins it on the playroom wall. . . and then sits down to eat. One simply doesn't connect. Yet there they were. . . lined up on the laboratory wall. . . half-formed, some of them. . . the tiny vestigial tails of the smallest. . . like corpses of still-born kittens. . . or baby mice. Did we think that they had been like that always. . . swimming forever in their little formaldehyde baths. . . ships in bottles. . . snowstorms in glass paperweights? The professor's voice. . . droning like a complacent bee. . . tapping his stick against each fragile glass shell. . . cross-pollinating facts with facts. . . our pencils racing over the paper. We accepted it all without question . . . even went up afterward for a closer look. . . boldly. . . without hesitation. It was all so simple. . . so uncomplex. . . so scientific. Stupidity, the necessary attribute. And once we dissected a guinea pig, only to discover that she had been pregnant. . . tiny little guinea pigs inside. We. . . like children presented with one of those Russian dolls. . . were delighted. . . gratified. We had received a bonus. . . a free gift.

Will they do that to part of me? How out of place it will look, bottled with the others. . . standing on the laboratory wall. Will the black professor. . . the brown-eyed students . . . bend their delighted eyes upon this bonus, this free gift? (White. 24 weeks. Female. . . or male.) But perhaps black babies are white. . . or pink. . . to begin. It is an interesting problem. . . one which could be pursued. . . speculated upon. I must ask someone. If black babies are not black before they are born, at what stage does the dark hand of heredity . . . of race. . . touch their small bodies? At the moment of birth perhaps? . . . like silver exposed to the air. But remember their palms. . . the soles of their feet. It's an interesting problem. And remember the beggar outside the central post office. . . the terrible burned place on his arm. . . the new skin. . . translucent. . . almost a shell pink. I turned away in disgust. . . wincing at the shared memory of scalding liquid . . . the pain. But really. . . in retrospect. . . it was beautiful. That pink skin. . . that delicate. . . Turneresque tint. . . apple blossoms against dark branches.

That's it. . . just the right tone. . . . Abstract speculation on birth. . . on death. . . on human suffering in general. Remember only the delicate tint. . . sunset against a dark sky . . . the pleasure of the Guernica. It's so simple, really. . . all a question of organization. . . of aesthetics. One can so easily escape the unpleasantness. . . the shock of recognition. Cleopatra in her robes. . . her crown. . . . "I have immortal longings in me." No fear. . . the asp suckles peacefully and unreproved. . . . She wins. . . and Caesar loses. Better than Falstaff babbling "of green fields." One needs the transcendentalism of the tragic hero. Forget the old man. . . pathetic . . . deserted. . . broken. The grey iniquity. It's all a question of organization. . . of aesthetics. . . of tone. Brooke, for example. "In that rich earth a richer dust concealed. . . ." Terrified out of his wits, of course, but still organizing, still posturing.

(The pain is really quite bad now. . . you will excuse me for a moment? I'll be back. I must not think for a moment . . . must not struggle. . . must let myself be carried over the crest of the wave. . . face downward. . . buoyant. . . a badge of seaweed across the shoulder. It's easier this way. . . not to think. . . not to struggle. . . . It's quicker. . . it's more humane.)

Still posturing. See the clown. . . advancing slowly across the platform. . . dragging the heavy rope. . . . Grunts. . . strains. . . the audience shivering with delight. Then the last . . . the desperate. . . tug. And what revealed? . . . a carrot. . . a bunch of grapes. . . a small dog. . . nothing. The audience in tears. . . . "Oh, God. . . how funny. . . . One knows, of course. . . all the time. And yet it never fails to amuse. . . I never fail to be taken in." Smothered giggles in the darkened taxi. . . the deserted streets. . . . "Oh, God, how amusing . . . . Did you see? The carrot. . . the bunch of grapes. . . the small dog. . . nothing. All a masquerade. . . a charade. . . the rouge. . . the powder. . . the false hair of an old woman. . . a clown." Babbling of green fields.

Once, when I was ten, I sat on a damp rock and watched my father fishing. Quiet. . . on a damp rock. . . I watched the flapping gills. . . the frenzied tail. . . the gasps for air. . . the refusal to accept the hook's reality. Rainbow body swinging through the air. . . the silver drops. . . like tears. Watching quietly from the haven of my damp rock, I saw my father struggle with the fish. . . the chased and beaten silver body. "Papa, let it go, Papa. . . please!" My father. . . annoyed. . . astonished. . . his communion disrupted. . . his chalice overturned. . . his paten trampled underfoot. He let it go. . . unhooked it carelessly and tossed it lightly toward the centre of the pool. After all, what did it matter. . . to please the child. . . and the damage already done. No recriminations . . . only, perhaps (we never spoke of it), a certain loss of faith. . . a fall, however imperceptible. . . from grace?

The pain is harder now. . . more frequent. . . more intense. Don't think of it. . . ignore it. . . let it come. The symphony rises to its climax. No more andante. . . no more moderato . . . clashing cymbals. . . blaring horns. . . . Lean forward in your seat. . . excited. . . intense. . . a shiver of fear. . . of anti-cipation. The conductor. . . a wild thing. . . a clockwork toy gone mad. . . . Arms flailing. . . body arched. . . head swing-ing loosely. . . dum de dum de DUM DUM DUM. The orchestra. . . the audience. . . all bewitched. . . heads nodding . . . fingers moving, yes, oh, yes. . . the orgasm of sound. . . the straining. . . letting go. An ecstasy. . . a crescendo. . . a coda. . . it's over. "Whew." "Terrific." (Wiping the sweat from their eyes.) Smiling. . . self-conscious. . . a bit embar-rassed now. . . . "Funny how you can get all worked up over a bit of music." Get back to the formalities. . . . Get off the slippery sand. . . onto the warm, safe planks of conversation. "Would you like a coffee. . . a drink. . . an ice?" The oasis of pleasure between pains. For me, too, it will soon be over . . . and for you.

Noah on Ararat. . . high and dry. . . sends out the dove to see if it is over. Waiting anxiously. . . the dove returning with the sign. Smug now. . . self-satisfied. . . know-it-all. . . . All those drowned neighbours. . . all those doubting Thom-ases. . . gone. . . washed away. . . full fathoms five. . . . And he, safe. . . the animals pawing restlessly, scenting freedom after their long confinement. . . smelling the rich smell of spring. . . of tender shoots. Victory. . . triumph. . . the chosen ones. Start again. . . make the world safe for democracy. . . cleansing. . . purging. . . Guernica. . . Auschwitz. . . God's fine Italian hand. Always the moral. . . the little tag. . . the cautionary tale. Willie in one of his bright new sashes/fell in the fire and was burnt to ashes. . . . Suffering is good for the soul. . . the effects on the body are not to be considered. Fire and rain. . . cleansing. . . purging. . . tempering the steel. Not much longer now. . . and soon they will let down the nets. (He promised it would be over before the dark. I do not like the dark here. Forgive me if I've mentioned this before.) We will sing to keep our courage up. Ten green bottles standing on the wall. Ten green bottles standing on the wall. If one green bottle. . . .

The retreat from Russia. . . feet bleeding on the white snow. . . tired. . . discouraged. . . what was it all about any-way? . . . we weren't prepared. Yet we go on. . . feet bleeding on the white snow. . . dreaming of warmth. . . smooth arms and golden hair. . . a glass of kvass. We'll get there yet. (But will we ever be the same?) A phoenix. . . never refus-ing. . . flying true and straight. . . into the fire and out. Plunge downward now. . . a few more minutes. . . spread your wings. . . the moment has come. . . the fire blazes. . . the priest is ready. . . the worshippers are waiting. The battle over. . . the death within expelled. . . cast out. . . the long hike over. . . Ararat. Sleep now. . . and rise again from the dying fire. . . the ashes. It's over. . . eyes heavy. . . body broken but relaxed. All over. We made it, you and I. . . . It's all, is it not. . . a question of organization. . . of tone? Yet one would have been grateful. . . at the last. . . for a reason . . . an explanation. . . a sign. A spider. . . a flaming cross. . . a carrot. . . a bunch of grapes. . . a small dog. Not this nothing.

OMO

I don't know, I just don't know. But maybe it isn't such a good idea—letting Negroes in the P.C. At least without warning them it won't work—they can be as outstanding as hell back home but what happens when they don't stand out at all—not physically—and are so tuned in to the idea they're different they can't change even if they want to? And Walter did. Walter really wanted to change. In this whole mess that's the one thing I hold onto—am absolutely certain of. If he didn't know what he wanted to change—or whom—if he just struck out blindly like a little kid hitting the chair he's just tripped over—how does that make him different from the rest of us? Yet, for him, it will be different. Another two or three days, when the newspapers get the story, back home (God knows what they'll do with it here), the differentness of Walter will sell extras or at least late editions. If it had happened to me, it would be news—happening to him it becomes sensation. And what will I say when they reach me?—it won't be long. "Tell me, Mr. Jonsson, did this boy seem disturbed to you in any way? Was he depressed, did he show signs of being unbalanced?" Can I call on the Fifth Amendment? Can I refuse to answer on the grounds that my answer would be so complete it would run into column after column and give them something they will only smell the surface of? I will refuse to answer. Just monosyllables. For if I hadn't found the diary, and read it, I probably wouldn't have had the kind of answer I now hold—not even thinking back, and deeply. Or I could run. Or I would if I could. Not toward the city—but out toward the bush and Walter. Surely the bush is big enough here to hide more than one escaping slave? I know one thing. If I stay here any longer drinking this cheap gin and reading, re-reading, devouring his diary, I'll be in the correct maudlin state when they arrive, in rented cars with their tires screeching to a halt (I wonder if they'll miss the house because of all the corn growing). UP AP. BAM, BAM, BAM. "Open up Mr. Jonsson. We know you're in there." As though I were the fugitive. And maybe they'll bring along my mother—or Dad. "Open up, son, we just want to talk to you." Nice people—Mother in an exclusive drip-dry floral print and Dad sweating (I sweat a hell of a lot too—hereditary I guess), fanning himself with his hat, determined to look on the bright side. If I shouted at them through the mosquito netting—"Go away. No bright side now for your bright little boy. No right side either. All wrong, wrong, wrong. Nothing but wrong and stupidity and your dear son too busy with his own goddamn affairs to reach out his hand to his brother. Yeah—you heard me—his brother. Wasn't that what you taught me—isn't that what this farce is supposed to be all about? Walter—my brother, I—Walter's. Bullshit." Have another drink, Mr. Jonsson. Thank you, Mr. Jonsson, I will.

Once, when I was young, light-years ago, and sick in bed with mumps, my mother gave me old copies of some women's magazine. I cut them up, pasted food pictures, pictures of cars, animals, on sheets of white card—you know the sort of thing. Anyway, at the back there was one little bit for children, a picture of a naughty boy or girl doing something anti-social like teasing the family cat or splashing mud on a clean floor. There was a caption above and below, and two little birds, self-satisfied looking things, on either side. The caption read (above): THIS IS A WATCH-BIRD WATCHING A MUD SPLASHER; (below): THIS IS A WATCHBIRD WATCHING YOU. WERE YOU A MUD SPLASHER THIS MONTH????? Those birds really used to frighten me—fat, beady-eyed, approved by my mother's favourite magazine. I even dreamt about them sometimes. And now I sit alone—except for Walter's diary —and stare at the wall. Whereon is written, in Walter's writing (but only I can see it)—THIS IS A WATCHBIRD WATCHING YOU. The more I drink, the clearer it becomes. Six, seven years old, waking up in the dead of night, Walter watching me, E.K. Jonsson, mud splasher, cat teaser, convicted of a hundred crimes against humanity Why couldn't it have happened to someone else?

Walter in his diary: "To be a slave in the physical sense may be exhausting and degrading, but it is vastly preferable to that other condition—being a slave to onself. In the first case one can retain one's spiritual liberty, the only kind, after all, that counts." No, Walter, my buddy, my friend. A slave is a slave is a slave. And whatever kind of slave you want to make him, he has to sleep sometime. And when he sleeps, he dreams of his masters. That's why I mustn't drink too much—must stay awake. Watchbirds. Something you thought you had a monopoly on. If I go to sleep I'll see you, Walter—head, bird—Shape. I wish you'd go away or tell me what to do.

Have—another drink? Thank you, I will.

I first met Walter Jordan at Berkeley, when we were all training to come out here. Naturally we speculated about him—who wouldn't, under the circumstances? He was the only Yale man in our group and nobody could find out much about him. The girls thought he was handsome—he wasn't really—not in the face. I'd say he was too negroid if it wouldn't sound ridiculous. But you know what I mean. Lips too thick, brow too heavy. Not a Sidney Poitier at any rate. But he had a terrific build—tall, lean, could walk as if he didn't have bones but something else, supple and sponge-like, in his legs. And a terrific dancer. I've never met a Negro who wasn't a terrific dancer, but I don't think it's any "race heritage" thing. I'm sure there are plenty of Negroes who dance as badly as I do and who do as I do—stay off the dance floor whenever possible. Anyway, Walter never said much at bull sessions, or in the classroom, and so naturally we were all curious about him. Some thought he might be selected out because he was so quiet, but most felt he'd been sent on with the rest of us because he was a Negro and had volunteered and all that. It would've looked pretty bad sending him back. Sort of "stay out of our fight" kind of thing. So he went. Nobody (officially) ever said "Be nice to Walter" or anything like that; but we all went out of our way to do just that, wondering to ourselves just what made him join and whether we could live up to him. Yeah. That was another crazy thing—we all had this idea that he would succeed where we might fail. And the girls—of course—they went out of their way to be nice to Walter because he was so remote and romantic, and such a terrific man on the floor. Still, maybe their motives were more sincere than some of ours. I, personally, never had much to do with him back there, not because of colour but because he went to Yale. My father went to Yale, and my grandfather; but Yale put me on the waiting list and meanwhile I got a scholarship to a place in the Midwest and accepted it. Professional jealousy, you might say. Still, on the plane out he livened up a bit, brought out a guitar (which was not unusual, half the group carried guitars I should think) and played some great classical stuff (which was unusual, most of the others being of the "thrum-thrum" and a strong clear folk-song variety).

Then when we got here we discovered, Walter and I, that we had been assigned to the same school about 200 miles up from the capital. The group split up and headed off in various vehicles for their appointments, and Walter and I set off by plane for this place. The headmaster met us and explained that as accommodation was scarce we would share the same house outside the town. As far as I can recall Walter hadn't really said anything since we touched down at the international airport (what was I expecting him to do—kiss the ground? Burst suddenly into the vernacular? Cry "Mother!"?), but I remember he looked at the headmaster and then at me and then nodded, without smiling. I thought "Oh, God, he's embarrassed," and chattered away in the taxi like a damn monkey, trying to put him at his ease. He just looked out the window—great storm clouds were building up for the first of our many downpours—and smiled absent-mindedly in my direction now and then. This is what he wrote in his diary that night:

"So it seems I am to (literally) share my lot with E.K. He is not a fool, so why does he act like one? To put me at my ease? If so, he underestimates my patience. I think he is thrilled by the idea of actually living in Africa with an 'Afro-American' or whatever term people like E.K. use when they think, to themselves, about people like me. Does he expect my reactions will be different from his? Thus far I should imagine they are roughly the same: a sense of heat, and wet and greenness, of a slightly rotten smell in the air, of ears still tender from that Dakota. Still, I must not prejudge him. He wants very much to be friendly—as though he were the host and I were the guest. Asked me, with a smile (and he has a nice one—very straight teeth and very white), which rooms I preferred. He even said, 'preferred.' Then we had a beer (no filter here as yet, and the manual says filter and then boil) and went our separate ways."

23

This kind of minority pompousness was, I admit, never evident to me. Still, Walter writing was not Walter talking. I wrote a letter (he probably did too) and then was so tired I turned the light out and lay in the dark trying to unwind. The rain had stopped and the insects were just tuning up. Also the frogs. I could have been back at summer camp except that it was about ten times hotter and twenty times noisier. But the difference was one of degree really. I even had that first-night scared-elated feeling I used to get as a kid. Then I remember thinking, "Christ, you're really here. This is Africa," and fell asleep.

"This is Africa." You know, you try to look back on first impressions and of course it's impossible—you know too much later on—or you know a lot more, yet not enough. What I mean is, I'm not sure what I meant by "this is Africa." The house was really terrible-looking, pale pink stucco on the outside and every conceivable pastel on the walls inside—even a mauve in the bathroom. But we had a fan, and a refrigerator, and a real toilet and bath, all of which we inspected that first night. So "this is Africa" shouldn't have conjured up a vision of mud huts and natives. I guess the insects and the heat and the rain fitted in, though. I used to be a real Stewart Granger–Humphrey Bogart fan and expected these. Anyway the next few weeks are just a haze of colour and light and heat—and of course the rain. Our school was eight miles from the house, and we had to pay a taxi a really fantastic fare to take us back and forth. Another Peace Corps myth exploded. "Our boys and girls won't have cars or motorbikes, except in very remote areas. They will rub shoulders with the natives and enrich their experience."

Walter writes, after we'd been there several weeks: "Those executives in Washington who think that we will get to know the people by riding on their transport are very

24

much mistaken. Know about them, maybe, but that's not the same thing. And the idea of rubbing shoulders with *anyone*, in this heat, is repugnant to us. The lifts we get are mostly from Europeans, while the moneyed African passes us by going so fast, usually, that I doubt very much if he sees us as more than just another blur on the side of the road. Often we walk as far as we can and then take a taxi—for an exorbitant fee. Even E.K., who is very enthusiastic about meeting the real Africa (though he has yet to define this term satisfactorily to me), agrees. Yet once a week he dutifully climbs aboard a Mammy wagon—much the same way as once a week he writes his letter home—out of a desire to gather and immortalize local colour. Sometimes I go with him (sometimes not) and we jolt slowly, painfully, thigh against thigh, into town. Immediately we get to school E.K. retires to a corner of the staff room and jots down his impressions in a little notebook which, like his camera, he carries with him wherever he goes."

Moral of the story: never room with a guy who keeps a diary. But if you don't know? I never saw the thing until three days ago. He wrote it at night, I guess, in bed. He never mentioned it to me or Miranda or anyone else. Yet he thought I was funny, carrying my notebook around, and I, like the fool I am, read him bits aloud, toward some of which he was very complimentary. When I first read the diary I was in such a state of shock it really didn't bother me —all the patronizing comments about E.K. doing this and that. Then I got bitter, and now I'm just surprised. Still, if I taught English like Walter, instead of math, I'd red-pencil the whole thing. It's so damn pompous and patronizing. I mean, I can't say he was a hypocrite—he never said he admired me or anything. But he never said he didn't. That's a kind of hypocrisy, isn't it? To live with a guy for over a year and write down blasts against him when he's asleep across the hall? I'd rather he talked about me to someone instead of having this private joke with himself. If he came back now I'd knock him down—just once—to let him know I've read it. If he came back. No. Mustn't think like that. It's better this way.

We had breakfast together, Walter and I, and rode to school together (usually) and came home together (at first) and ate together. We complained to one another about the staff toilets, or lack of them, and how it wasn't right we had to use the cinema john across the road from the school. We talked a lot, really, when I think back on it—but mostly about safe stuff—externals-—like the heat and the price of beer and how much we could spend to paint the inside of the house. He showed me a picture of his family once, early on. Nice-looking mother and a real knock-out of a sister. His father had the same ugly-handsome face as Walter, but not the terrific body. He came from upstate New York some place and his father was a teacher. I asked him what made him decide to go to Yale and he said "scholarships" and dropped it. He had a way of dropping things he didn't want to talk about. He just turned himself off, if you know what I mean, and it was useless to continue. Once, I remember, two other volunteers stopped in on their way from the north (we always had visitors because we had a house, and that meant a free bed). One of this particular pair was a Southern girl, Ruth-Ann, whom I hadn't warmed to at Berkeley and didn't like much better when I saw her alone. Bright though —but nosy and a real thing about being Southern and in Africa. Her duty, etc., etc. Anyway, she was washing up in the kitchen and suddenly came out, hands all soapy, to look at us three in the sitting-room. (The other fellow was a Jewish kid from the Bronx. Very young and brilliant—a damn nice guy and a hell of a poker player.) Ruth-Ann stands there in the doorway and laughs her soft Southern-belle-type laugh. "I was thinkin' of why I came and won-derin' if you-all had motives as selfish as mine. I know why Larry came, we've talked about it; but why'd you come, Walter? Was it for a white reason or a black one?" I looked at her, a kind of scared feeling beginning in my chest; but then at Walter—hadn't I always wanted to ask him that myself? He just did the turning-off bit, laughed and took down his guitar. I don't know if Ruth-Ann really expected an answer or just felt that Walter expected, or deserved, the question. Anyway, answer or no, she could still write home to Mama that she all had a weekend with E.K. and Larry and Walter, the American Negro she'd told them about. I think that's all she wanted—to be able to write home that she'd spent the weekend at our place. Still, I was disappoint-ed that Walter wouldn't open up and give us some reasons. Even in his diary he doesn't comment on why he came. But he was writing to himself and already knew. It would have been illogical to put it all down there if he was sincere about it and wrote only for himself. Miranda knows. Miranda knows a lot of things and I must see Miranda soon and tell her what has happened if she hasn't already figured it out for herself. Maybe she knows and that's why she is staying away—in case he's here—and hiding. I'll have to get in touch with her tomorrow.

He has one entry which shows he was delighted with "old Africa" or whatever name he'd call it, so maybe he came, like me, just to look and see.

"Today," he writes, "I leaned against a wall for two hours and watched the women crossing to the old market. Bare-foot, unselfconscious, immense loads of yams, tomatoes, tinned milk, you name it, on their heads. Often a baby slung behind sleeping, like some small opossum clinging to its mother's tail—content just to be. And often a small child walking beside, it too loaded down with the day's goods, yet

27

it too with that intensely royal posture these women have. Miranda, if she had been with me, could, but probably wouldn't, have pointed out the signs of malnutrition, of early aging and incipient TB. But to me it was all gaiety and colour and purpose. I could have stayed all day, but the heat and the noise and the smells made me drowsy and thirsty. After I stopped for a drink I caught a lift home, where E.K. was, as I had promised myself, stripped to his waist, sweating profusely, already on his third bottle of beer and half-way through his weekly letter home. He types it single-spaced, on an air-letter, and often reads aloud bits which he has incorporated from his notebook. E.K. sees Africa as a picturesque ruin, not a living entity, something which you 'do' and then write up for the folks back home. Yet who is to say he is wrong?"

I can't tell here if he agrees or disagrees with what he thought was my point of view. Not that he understood it anyway. Of course I think it's "picturesque" here—you'd have to be blind or blasé not to think so. But a ruin? I don't know where he got that idea. Anyway, if it's being ruined, it's being ruined by the Africans themselves. But that's another story.

That's his first reference to Miranda, which is funny, because he mentions how we met her later on. I don't know when he went to the market, but the casual way he says Miranda would have shown him things sounds as though it was after we'd known her some time. Why didn't he put that entry first—the one where he describes our meeting? He must have left blank pages and then gone back and filled them up. Which is a funny thing to do. But Walter is or was —Christ which tense do I use?—a funny guy.

We met her in the third month, I remember that. And I remember the day. I was making one of my "dutiful journeys," as Walter calls them, and this time he was with me.

The Mammy lorry was loaded to the brim—crazy things they are—sort of crates on wheels and if you're travelling behind one you can see the women's bottoms bulging out the back. Chickens, yams, kids, anything, they pile it all in. We squeezed on somehow, but the damn thing (or so we thought at the time, not knowing we were going to meet Miranda) broke down just past the first roundabout. Nobody really cares when something like this happens— they've got an incredible talent for just waiting around— but I was cursing and swearing because we were supposed to get to school on time—set a good example and all that— and now we'd have to find a taxi. Off it all came—humanity and produce—and everybody arranged themselves and their belongings by the side of the road. I was looking up and down, trying to see a taxi, when one screeched to a halt (I don't think the average African realizes what brakes are for) and nearly knocked me down. I was about to try a few curse words in the vernacular when this pretty girl leaned out and asked if I wanted a lift. I thought she meant both of us—"do you want a lift"—but she looked a little surprised when I signalled toward the crowd.

"Not all of you," she said, and smiled. She had a really terrific smile. Then I realized—and I think it was the first time I really took it in—that Walter, at a casual glance, could be mistaken for an African. "No," I said, feeling stupid but determined, "just my room-mate, Walter," and she looked relieved. Probably thought I was some kind of "I won't ride while others walk" religious nut, which is not my policy at all. I'm too much of a materialist to go in for the missionary bit. And anyway, you should see some of the missionaries—the far-out Californian sects for example— whooping along in their Cadillacs, etc. She said she had to go to the hospital and would we mind a detour, Walter asked if she were ill and she said no, she was a nurse, flashing that fabulous smile again. You could almost see Walter thaw and I was feeling pretty terrific myself and trying to remember the name on that particular Mammy lorry so I could take it whenever I had the chance. I think it was "God Sees All" or something like that. They all have slogans painted on the back and some of them are really great—like "Next Time" or "Psalm 147" or "Too Late." Nobody seems to know why they do it. Anyway—we went up toward the hospital and let her off, but not before we'd found out her name and asked her to lunch on Sunday, whereupon, says Walter, "E.K. gave her so many directions as to how to find the house I'm convinced she will get discouraged—or lost." This is a later entry, where he says we'd met a "very pretty girl with a beautiful name." Actually, he's pretty amusing about my efforts to impress her. I was really keyed up and considering the fact I'd only just met her I guess I must've seemed a bit of a nut case. Particularly as I'm not usually a girl-chaser and kind of shy, really. Here's what he says:

"Since Thursday E.K. has been cleaning the house, trying on colourful shirts (finally deciding on white because she's English), and peering at a copy of *Escoffier* which he managed to borrow. He finally decided on *coq au vin*—this decision necessitating a hurried trip to the market for the essential *coq*, which he brought back, live, in a taxi. Very triumphant until he remembered that somebody was going to have to kill it. At first I refused, but after suffering his mournful face for half an hour (the bird meanwhile running wild in the kitchen) I suggested we *both* kill it and dress it, which we did, not very efficiently, E.K. holding and I cutting off the head. Neither of us could eat any supper and even now, after half a bottle of whisky, I can feel the warm blood pouring over my hands. The kitchen is thick with white feathers, but we've decided to leave it until the morning."

God, I remember that part. I'd never killed anything before, and neither had he, I think. I really felt terrible; but it was worth it, because Miranda thought the dinner was great —or said so anyway. I don't know what it was supposed to taste like but it seemed all right to me. Anyway I was too keyed up just having her here to care much about food. Walter doesn't write anything about that evening, but he had a good time too, I know it, and didn't turn himself off once. She stayed quite late and we sat around, with candles, drinking beer and listening to Walter play his guitar. God, she was easy to be with, right from the beginning. At peace, kind of not all keyed up and tense and trying to impress— like so many American girls. I tried to imagine her as a nurse (actually she's here training native nurses) but couldn't picture her being at all brash and efficient. She came out with some palm wine the next week and invited us to a party the nurses were giving. Both of us, though Walter tried to get out of it and said he was too busy. Anyway, we both went and had a good time—at least I did, and I think Walter did too, though he was obviously falling for her himself. I didn't keep it any secret from him—at first—how I felt about her. He writes: "I watch E.K. and Miranda dancing, E.K. not a very good dancer. [I accept that, I'm not.] Arthur Murray course or dancing school when he was young. [Both, and a fat lot of good it did me too.] When it is my turn I can feel E.K.'s eyes on my back, hating me as a moment ago I hated him. [I don't accept that. I felt jealous maybe, that she was dancing with him and that he was such a terrific dancer.] I realize that I've never held her in my arms before and suddenly I am all left feet and bandaged hands and cannot dance—really dance—at all. I take her back to E.K., and excuse myself on the grounds I have to go to the men's room. There I met a curious man—like a ghost. Miranda knows him and says his name is Omo. He's an albino."

Omo. I wish to God we'd never gone to that dance—or really that Omo had never gone. Miranda told us about him, but he gave me the creeps, right from the beginning. When Walter came back he said, "I've just seen a white man," and not knowing what he was talking about we looked at him as though he'd had too much to drink. There were other white men at the dance besides me—these African girls are really lovely, some of them, and terrific to dance with or watch doing the "highlife." It's a sexy dance anyway, and they wear these long, tight two-piece dresses—really colourful. "No," he said, "don't look at me like that. You and Miranda, you're pink. A really white man." And then of course Miranda laughed because she knew whom he was talking about. Omo. One of the anaesthetists. There are quite a few albinos about, now that I'm aware of them, but when Miranda pointed him out to me, I was quite shocked. It wasn't so much that he was white, with that fair, kinky hair. It was that he looked kind of poached, if you know what I mean. A sickly colour, and he was wearing dark glasses. He was short and sickly-looking, but he had quite European-looking features. Miranda also said he was a half-caste (but I don't see how this could be, myself) and nobody knew much about him.

After that we kept seeing him—almost as though he were following us—or haunting us. And I know he bothered Walter. He wrote several times—"We saw the albino to-day, the one they call Omo." "Today I was crossing the street just as Omo was coming from the opposite side." Again, "He always wears dark glasses. Miranda says the light must hurt his eyes." And once, scrawled across a page, just "Omo, Omo, Omo," and underneath—

"Alb
Albatross
Alcatraz

Albumen
Albigenses
Albert Jordan" [His father's name.]
You don't have to be literary to figure that out, and that the
guy was really bugging him. If I became conscious of Walter being black when Miranda first offered me a lift in the
taxi, I think maybe Walter first became conscious of it when
he called Omo a white man at that dance. He began to beg
off going out with Miranda and me. At the time I—stupid
bloody fool—thought it was to give me a clear field. I had
no real idea how he felt about her—I knew he liked her but
couldn't imagine (ironic as it may seem, for I was aware of
how special she was right from the beginning) anyone lik-
ing her or loving her as much as I did. One time he refused
to go to her place for dinner and I got sore—I wanted to be
alone with her, but thought her feelings would be hurt. I
never considered his. We'd gone a lot of places together—
the market, the zoo, the stool village, movies—before this,
and he has recorded it all, with no real comment, in the
journal.

"Miranda sends us a note, by a friend, to invite us to dinner Sunday night. I complain of too much marking and beg
off. But E.K. says I will hurt her feelings and if I don't want
to go I will have to write a reply, which he will deliver.
When I finish my note, all very friendly and polite, it occurs
to me that on the face of it—two pieces of white paper, hers
and mine, covered with the little footprints we call words—
there is nothing to show that in the one case the pen was
held by small white fingers, and in the other, by my own—
large, pink-palmed and black. E.K. came back late, making
lots of noise to attract my attention, but I didn't feel like
getting up and turning on the light."

Even if some place inside I knew that he was unhappy it
never occurred to me to think in black-white terms. I mean,

I guess I did know he was jealous—but Miranda treated us, then, so much alike I guess I was flattered by the idea that it seemed to him she favoured me when I couldn't see it. Maybe it never struck home that he could really want Miranda the way I wanted her—for keeps. Oh, there are lots of Africans with European wives (but mostly British) out here, and some whites with native wives. But Walter, black, was out here among blacks and I guess I thought if he went for anybody he'd go for a native girl—they're really lovely, some of them. No, that's not true, I didn't think about it at all. I was too tied up with my own problems. Like he mentions one incident I don't even remember. I mean, I remember the day, but not what he says happened.

"Linda, one of the prettiest volunteers, stopped in today on her way up to the North. She's been on the coast for the weekend and is one of those lucky blondes who tan so beautifully. We were playing Monopoly and drinking beer when E.K. said, 'You look terrific in that white dress. It makes your tan look almost black.' Embarrassed silence while I calmly throw the dice and land on *Chance*. 'Go directly to Jail. Do not pass Go. Do not collect $200.' Still, E.K.'s innocent remark (what else could it have been?—he's not subtle) opens up new areas for speculation. Coney Island in the sun. Thousands of pinky-white Americans blasting themselves with Skol and baby oil, trying to reach the point where the E.K.s of this world will say to them, in all innocence, on Monday morning, 'God, you're positively black.' Me, Walter, running out of the sea and shouting, 'Look, it's easy, don't go to so much trouble, I'll trade you my skin for yours.' Who would listen, I wonder, and agree?"

I'd better have another drink. I shouldn't really re-read the stuff, it's so bitter. But I never knew, not until the end, what was really bugging him. And I swear I don't remember saying that. I remember Linda (who wouldn't?) but not

34

the dress and not the crude remark. Or the "embarrassed silence." Surely I could remember such a thing? Some time after this, there was a terrific storm over the city and— which was not unusual—all the lights went out. Walter and I were up late preparing lessons when a hell of a bang went and then a crash, then darkness. We stumbled around looking for candles—which we didn't find until the next morning—then gave up and, with the flashlight which we always keep by the front door, went out to see the damage. After the bang, the rain seemed to slacken off, but we were still soaked through by the time we got through our little corn field and reached the main road. A bloody great tree seemed to be lying right across the road, and we were just debating whether to try to set up flares when we heard a sound— kind of an animal noise—practically next to where we were standing. Walter flashed the light around fast and then we saw it—a motorbike, all twisted, and underneath it something that looked like a man. By pushing and pulling we managed to raise the tree a few inches and twist the man free. It was really horrible. Rain and sweat in our eyes, and each of us taking turns holding this puny little light while the other pushed. And the body was all soft and broken like a doll or a dead kitten. I ran off for help and asked a Lebanese down the road who sent his car and driver back with me. How long Walter stood there in the darkness, guarding a man he couldn't see, I don't know. It must have been worse for him than for me. At least I was doing something. Anyway, Walter picked up this fellow and carried him to the car—a really immaculate new Chrysler, and we were a mess. We went along in case the police wanted a statement, holding the man across our knees so he wouldn't get bumped too much. The hospital has its own generator, and the light, after all that darkness, made our eyes hurt. An intern put the man on a stretcher and we just stood there in the hall, dripping wet and covered with red earth and twigs, waiting for somebody to question us. The driver waited outside in the car. The injured man made another whimpering sound, and then a sort of gargle. And died. Walter turned to me and said, "You have blood on your hands." I looked down and saw that I did. I suppose that he did too. But the blood and this guy on the stretcher and nobody else around suddenly got to me and I was sick all over the corridor. Then we heard a voice and there was the albino. I don't know. It all fitted somehow. Walter looking like a tramp with his torn shirt and dripping clothes and me with vomit all over myself. And the dead man on the stretcher. Then this Omo, this albino, coming. I remember thinking, relieved, it's all right now—just a nightmare, none of this is really happening. But of course it was. Miranda had told us he worked at the hospital so I shouldn't have been shocked, but I was. He didn't say much, just looked at Walter, then me, and then went over to the dead man. "Was he a friend of yours?" he asked, and his voice was as queer as his looks—rather high-pitched and effeminate, but with a Scottish burr almost. We told him what had happened—or I did—I remember now, Walter didn't say anything and I did all the talking. Omo told us to go home, took our address, and said the police would get in touch. So we walked away down the corridor, leaving the dead man and Omo, and the driver took us home. We didn't even try to take baths or anything. Just rooted around for the whisky and went to bed. I can't remember that we said more than two words then, and the next day, when we saw Miranda and told her (I mentioned Omo, I think), it sounded as though it had happened to someone else. The tree remained for over a week, with just a narrow piece, the width of a truck, sawn out of the middle. Then they came with a fork lift and took the rest away. I was glad, because I couldn't bear to look at it.

Walter doesn't say much in his diary: "Yesterday there was an accident. A man died and Omo and I came face to face once more." And then, "E.K. is a brave man, but why did he suggest going for help? Is he a kind one, and quick-witted as well? Coming out of the darkness I might have been attacked as a thief." I thought nothing, consciously. But maybe he's right, maybe I knew no-one could question my motives. No, it's not true. His poison infects me. I thought nothing. I didn't know how to think—then. Anyway, Miranda told us some village had finally claimed the body—we were worried at first and wondered if we should arrange to bury him if nobody answered the ad in the papers. And life goes on, you've got to give it credit for that.

On Walter's birthday Miranda gave him a beautiful African cloth—something he'd wanted but hadn't bought. They're pretty expensive. He didn't try it on (she came to dinner that night and it was just like old times—we were all, I think, very happy) but went into his room and hung it up on the wall facing his bed. I don't think she meant him to try it on and she seemed very touched by his gesture. It really was a lovely thing—woven in four-inch strips as they do it here—all green and gold and scarlet. I must admit I wondered where she got the money for it—it must have cost her a lot—and I was a little jealous at the magnificence of her gift as compared with mine (I gave him a record of the Swingle Singers). Still, it was a happy evening, though Walter doesn't say anything in his journal. There are several blank pages after the accident and then he writes about a dance we all went to at the City Hotel (this was about three weeks later).

"Tonight, to impress Miranda perhaps, I wore the cloth she gave me for my birthday. It has been hanging on my bedroom wall where I can open my eyes every morning and without moving my head breakfast on the warm colours, stalk imaginary tigers in the jungle of reds and greens and yellows. We did 'highlife' at the City Hotel—even E.K., after he'd had a few drinks and forgotten he was shy. E.K., moving his hips self-consciously but surely among the shaking shoulders and melon-like bottoms of the girls was something to see. Because he is white, an 'Obronie,' he never lacks for partners if he feels like dancing. But Miranda wouldn't dance. She said she was tired and was content to watch. E.K. didn't like this too much but accepted it. He looks at her with what can only be described as dog-like devotion. And would I not be her devoted dog? She is the most charming person I have ever met and should be happy with E.K. if he ever gets the courage to ask her.

"About midnight, carried away by the noise, the beer, the scent of Miranda beside me, E.K. and his efforts, I decided to demonstrate my own prowess. Moving on to the floor without a partner, I hunched my shoulders and danced to the music until I felt it inside me and knew I could lead it, was a part of it. People stopped dancing—I could feel them stop and circle me though I kept my eyes nearly shut. Then my cloth fell off, revealing me in T-shirt and khaki shorts. Great laughter and applause from the crowd. I was sick, furious, and stumbled outside with my cloth to begin walking home. I heard E.K. and Miranda behind me, calling, so I ran until I found a taxi. And I have thought E.K. childish and absurd."

We ran after him but couldn't catch him. I was worried—I knew he felt humiliated but Miranda said he'd be better off alone. So we went to her place and talked—not about Walter, just life-in-general kind of things—and then I went home. There were no lights on and I wondered if Walter had come back. So I tried his door which was open and there he was all huddled up in bed as though he had the fever. The cloth was back on the wall. I didn't know what to say so I just got a couple of beers and sat on the edge of the bed, drinking. (I never saw his journal—it must've been under his pillow or in the drawer.) Finally he said, very far away, "It's all right," or something like that, so I left him and crossed the dining-room and went to bed. A few days later I got really drunk, after a particularly horrible day at the school (it was gradually dawning on me that I was not cut out to be a teacher, not a math teacher anyway, and the students had been giving me a rough time), and told Walter I wanted to marry Miranda.

"In a drunken 'heart-to-heart,' E.K. reveals to me what I have known all along—he plans to marry Miranda and will ask her at Easter. We sat on the edge of my bed (whoever designed the couch in the sitting-room didn't do so for comfort) while he chatted away about 'the marriage of true minds,' how wonderful she was, and so on. He kept trying to make it sound reasonable, almost sexless—a good arrangement—while all the time he blushed and stammered like a young girl, the virgin I suspect he is. After he had gone back to his room I rolled myself in my cloth and lay on the floor. I woke late, wet with tears and semen." He made fun of me to himself. That's what really shakes me. I know now a lot of it was just a cover (I sometimes wonder if he didn't write his journal to convince himself he was ironic and detached about everything). But I don't know if I can ever forgive him for making fun of me. If he came back, would I knock him down, or would I be too glad to see him? I need another drink to tell the next part. Have another drink, Mr. Jonsson. Thank you, Mr. Jonsson—may I have two or three? Be my guest.

Christmas came and went. We were both thoroughly fed up with the school, for different reasons, and celebrated by getting tight most of the time and taking Miranda to the movies. The garbage we sat through! Epics of this and that, crazy Indian love films, B or C grade, old Westerns. Christmas Eve I decided I wasn't going to wait to ask Miranda to marry me, but would ask her as soon as the ring was ready. I was having a special design made by a goldsmith in town, with all the local symbols on it. But he took his time—nobody hurries here except the taxi drivers. Meanwhile, on Christmas Day I went to the market. Miranda was coming to dinner that night. But I met her, then Walter. . . . Let Walter tell it.

"Miranda walks through the crowded market, her new sandals obviously hurting her, for every now and then she pauses, stands bird-like on one leg and rubs her foot. Each time she stops the line of children following her (in the hope of getting a penny) stops too. This goes on along the line of stalls, and I watch, unseen. E.K. comes around the corner, puffing heavily—it is very hot—his camera in one hand and a fistful of money to bargain with in the other. She sees him, halts, and they walk on together, the children following behind. As they pass the stall where I am busy bargaining for a string of prayer beads, I turn my head away; but Miranda calls, 'Here's Walter as well,' and forces me to walk along with them. The thing begins to look like Farmer-in-the-Dell. Miranda is looking for some presents to send home—she has been too rushed to want to shop before. She buys a huge straw hat for her brother, a Northern smock for her sister, who is expecting a baby in March. She holds the smock against herself for size—blue with gold embroidery—and smiles. I try to imagine her in a blue smock, swollen with E.K.'s child, and turn away. We pause to examine a table filled with the giant snails which are considered such a delicacy here. Still alive, they move carefully over the damp leaves. Then the man Omo appears, from nowhere, and nods curtly to Miranda. She has told us he doesn't like Europeans, but now, filled with Christmas, she touches his

40

arm and asks him to wait. We are introduced, and he gives a strange high-pitched giggle and says, 'Oh yes, the two young men from America. I didn't recognize you.' We can't see his eyes because of the thick glasses, but his mouth is thin and cruel. Miranda asks him what he's buying and he giggles (there is no other word for it) and says, 'Snails.' E.K. looks sick and we smile and move on. I felt his eyes following us, and why not? Even the children at school make remarks about our strange trio. Yet they are not wicked. This man gives off what can only be described as a scent of wickedness and decay. Or am I exaggerating?

"Dinner a success. E.K. is now an admirable cook."

Omo. Dinner was a success. Omo and snails. Even while I ate I kept thinking about Omo and the accident—and snails. I didn't think about Omo and Walter. Why should I? To me, then, there was no connection.

Last week the ring was finished. I dressed up for a surprise visit to Miranda. I showed the ring to Walter and he said it was beautiful and wished me luck. You know all these crazy things about walking on air, etc., that the crooners used to sing about back in the forties. Well, that's the way I felt, as though I were walking on air. At 7.30 (it was already dark) I set off for town. At 2.30, with the ring in my pocket, I returned. I was surprised to see a light on, but figured Walter was waiting up for me. I didn't really want to see anyone, just then, not even Walter, so I sneaked around to the back and let myself in the kitchen door. Then I heard voices and realized Walter had company. The other voice, without the face, I didn't recognize at first.

"It wasn't hard to find the way," it said, "since you were kind enough to give me your address. Or,"—it giggled—"your friend was kind enough." And Walter's voice, resigned, quiet.

"Why don't you get out?"

"But I came to see you, my friend. We are friends, aren't we? Almost brothers, you might say." Then the terrible giggle. I was too shocked to move. And curious, too. Yes, I was that all right. Curious.

"Almost," said Omo, "like brothers."

"I don't know what you mean."

"Oh come, come, come. You're not stupid. I know quite a bit about you, you see." Then, sharp and quick, "You'd like her, wouldn't you?"

"Don't you dare talk about—"

"Miranda? Why not? Isn't she your friend, and your friend's friend?"

"This has nothing to do with you. Please go."

"But I've come all this way just to see you! I saw him get out of the taxi and came right out to comfort you." Then, softly, "what do you suppose they're doing now, eh? Talking about mathematics? Or perhaps in bed? That's more like it, isn't it? In bed, maybe. No sheets on a hot night like this."

I found I had moved forward, then stopped at the sound of his voice, pitched even higher.

"No! You wouldn't hurt me. Sit down. I said, sit down— White Man!"

I couldn't move now. Walter's voice sounded very far away.

"I tell you, I don't know what you mean."

"And I tell you not to be so stupid, White Man."

I could feel him lean forward, almost hissing.

"Isn't that what you want to be, with your white friends and your long trousers and your fancy degree? Omo, like me. You know why they call me Omo, don't you."

"I know."

"Whiter than white. Your wash is whiter than white with Omo. It is not my name."

"It is not your name."

Walter, hypnotized in the sitting-room, I, hypnotized in the hall. The voice went on and on in little hiss-like sentences.

"Alastair's my name. Alastair Campbell. The man they call Omo. Would you like to know something about me? No? Too bad. Mine's an interesting story. My father was a missionary, a man of God. My father, man of God that he was, and with God on his side, made many converts—among them Comfort Mensah, who felt, perhaps simultaneously, the hand of the Almighty and the hand of my God-fearing father. But my father was an honourable man. He married the girl and had many brotherly-lovely children before he died of yellow fever. Many lovely children—all brown, and the pride of the mission. And one freak, Alastair, who killed his mother and broke his father's heart. When they took that white body out of that black, black womb, I think he considered it a judgment of God. He sent me away, back to his home in Scotland, paid for my education (where he got the money I'll never know). And when I wrote I wished to go into medicine he agreed without a murmur. All this done by letter; for never once did he—or anybody—come to see me. As a child at school I found I could only imagine him as a long tanned arm ending in a hand holding a fountain pen. A hand for signing cheques —not for writing letters. I wasn't popular at school. How could I have been? A freak with weak eyes, a boy who wore sunglasses, even in Britain, a boy who never received a brown paper parcel full of home-made cakes, or a few sweets. And in the end, a boy too weak to go on and study medicine."

"Why are you telling me all this?"

I had forgotten Walter, but now I, too, wondered why.

"Shut up and listen. So I trained as an anaesthetist and

came back here, to claim my 'inheritance' as it were, to be one of my mother's people—an African. I do my work well, speak the language now like the native I am, mingle with what your friend would probably call 'the people.' But I am set off by my skin, that white skin you covet so much, from a satisfactory relationship with anyone, black or white. The superstitious African views me as something special, a natural freak, and therefore endowed with supernatural powers. He shuns me as a friend, not because he feels I am lower than he is, but because I am higher, more powerful, closer to the gods—or devils." He laughed again, and each laugh hammered his words into my brain. Coffin nails. Why didn't I stop him? I don't know.

"The European cultivates me out of curiosity, tries to take my picture when he thinks I'm not looking. I frighten him. And I shun the European because for fifteen years the European with whom I should have had the closest ties existed for me as nothing more than a hasty signature. My father, the God-fearing man, the apostle of brotherly love."

"I'm truly sorry—"

"That you can't change places with me? Is that what you were going to say?"

"No."

"Well, it should have been. Don't be sorry for me, be sorry for yourself. Aren't you, eh—just a wee bit?"

"Will you have a drink?"

"It's about time." A giggle. "I wondered how long I'd have to wait."

My heart stopped. But whisky and glasses were in the sideboard and a decanter of water was on the table. They need not come out to the kitchen.

"That's better," said the voice. "Now you are showing some true brotherly love. Shall I tell you a story?"

"If you have to, and then I really must—"

44

"What?" Giggle. "Lie in bed and wait for your friend to come back? What will you think about, eh? He won't be back tonight. Forget it."

"Tell me your story." Walter's voice was deep and terrible and resigned—like the voice of somebody in terrible pain. I wanted to go to him and kick that little white fink down the front steps. But I couldn't. Anyway, I didn't.

"Have you ever killed?" he asked.

"No."

"I have, this afternoon. One of your kind—a white woman. A stupid bitch who shacked up with an African while her husband was on leave, and then discovered she was pregnant. Amusing, don't you think? The issue could hardly have been passed off as her husband's child, now could it?"

"But why?"

"You're too impatient, black boy. I'm coming to that. Why? Because she tried to get rid of it herself, and as is obvious from her original adventure—she was a bungler. They brought her in this afternoon for an emergency operation. I administered the anaesthetic."

"You mean you—"

"SHUT UP, BLACK BOY. I 'mean' nothing of the sort. I simply told her something as I leaned over and put the needle in. I whispered, 'Now you are going to be paid back for meddling with those who are not your own kind. I'm going to give you another present from a black man. I'm going to kill you, swiftly and efficiently, now, and in front of all these people.' She cried out, once, and then she died. It will be written off as a massive hemorrhage and heart failure due to shock."

The hairs rose on the back of my neck.

Walter said, "You frightened her to death."

"That's it. I frightened her to death." Giggle. "Aren't you shocked that someone as weak as I could do something as

45

strong as kill?"

I heard Walter get to his feet.

"What's the matter, White Boy, don't you believe me? It's only begun for you. The hate and the bitterness that make you choke on your own bile. But it has begun. That's a step in the right direction, isn't it? Think about your friend, eh? And the girl. . . ."

"Get out." Walter was shouting. I heard the door slam. "Don't come back here, ever. You're mad. I'm not like you —I hate no-one."

"Love me then, black boy," said Omo, from outside the door. He began to cry. "All I want is some love, that's all." I heard Walter stumble, as though he were drunk, and then the heavy inner door slammed into place. Omo rapped on the door softly, then louder, but Walter had turned out the lights and gone into his room. I waited until the footsteps had died away, and then I inched down the hall and fell asleep with my clothes on.

When I awoke it was nearly noon and I thought Walter had gone on to school without me. The shock of Omo's appearance at our house, plus my own misery at being refused, however nicely, by Miranda, kept me drinking until late afternoon. When Walter didn't come home that evening I began to get worried. I looked in his room and all his books were on the table. His bed hadn't been slept in, but this journal was lying face-down on the floor. The last entry, the one with which I began, said "Must find Omo." Nothing more.

Three days ago they found him, his head bashed in from behind, in some bush behind a café. The proprietor, the papers said, could tell the police no more than that the man who was called Omo was sitting with a young African until they both got drunk. He thought they left together.

And Walter? He hasn't come back yet. I left food in the

46

refrigerator and the door open, and hired a car (I told the school I was sick with fever). With an interpreter I traced him to the north, driving day and night, and finally to a small village near the border. The village only remembers him as a strange young African, nearly naked, who squatted in front of their fire and tried to tell them something in a language they didn't understand. So I sit here and drink. Miranda may have been and gone—if she has seen the papers. She would know about it anyway; but how much did she know about Walter? How much did any of us? Anyway, I think I'll stay here now, for a while, and wait. For one thing the interpreter was sure of. The elders, when questioned, were certain that before he left he had told them one thing. He had told them he was going home.

THE ALBATROSS

We hid in our tiny bathtub and waited for the footsteps to move off down the path. Hugging each other from necessity, the curtain drawn as though we are simply waiting for the floodlights to go on—hero and heroine caught in the classic clandestine clinch. Rocking with silent laughter. Have you ever had to sneeze in church, been seized by insane giggling in the public library? It's very difficult.

"I know you are in there, my friends. Hello, my friends, are you at home?" A gargling under water way of pronouncing his words. "I told you it was Hermann," she hissed. "Shut up." How does he know? This is one window he can't peer into. Maybe he has rubber-soled stilts. No, keep quiet. He's only guessing.

Then the baby woke up, so we stepped gracefully over the rim and went to let him in.

"Well, Hermann, you're out late. Business pretty good, eh?"

"Business is not so good. I am thinking of getting out. Nobody buys these days." Nobody but bloody fools like us. Got your fat foot in the door that time, didn't you?

"Never mind, Hermann; have a cup of coffee. Margaret was just going to put the coffee on, weren't you, Margaret?"

Loosens his tie and eats up all the cakes. "You see my belly?" No, Hermann, we don't see it—sack of pudding with a head at the top. "I have lost some weight. Nearly ten pounds. I have taken nothing but soups and salad all day."

"Have another jam tart, then, Hermann."

"Thank you, they are very nice. Margaret must make for my wife the receipt."

Dank you, dank you. You're a tank you Hermann. One of these days too many jam tarts will make for your wife de widow. How much insurance do *you* buy, old chap?

"Well, what brings you out at this hour, Hermann?"

"The Book. I was to myself wondering how the Book is coming on?"

"Well, Margaret's very busy with her term paper just now, aren't you, Margaret?" Vigorous nod. Hermann looks dejected. Margaret begins to wear her can't-put-a-dog-out look. Idea.

"Would you like to hear the last bit again? When the fuse blew we never got to replay it. Of course *we've* heard it several times since then, haven't we, Margaret?" Another vigorous nod. Funny how she lures them here and then clams up. Worth investigation. "You know, Hermann, you really need a dictaphone and secretary, doesn't he, Margaret?" Margaret weakening. My jellyfish wife.

"I don't mind, really, but the term paper and the baby keep me rather busy at the moment."

"It will make for us our fortunes. I know myself a man in Hollywood." Hermann knows a man everywhere, but his collar is frayed and he eats up other people's cakes.

I fiddle with the knobs and Hermann's voice, like Hermann's bulk, fills the little room. He beams and listens to himself. Solemnly. Over a second cup of coffee.

"I went to Greece by mistake. I was in the general hospital in Alexandria with an infection of the neck. My neck was full of pus. You know, you walk in the desert and the desert, it is very bad. And you sweat and the shirt begins to get stiff. Then you had the sandstorms, and the sweat and the sand become one crust. Each movement that a man makes, it is like he is in a suit of armour. I think that most of us were infected, some more, some less. And they ask me when the pus is all gone, do I want to go back to my own unit? And they are very nice; they don't tell me that my unit is already in a poor spot. Because it was then the end of April and Greece collapsed two weeks after I arrived. I suppose it was on about the twentieth of April.

"In any case, the ship I am on went over there, and when I arrive everybody says, 'Why did you come? Everyone's retreating. Why did you come?' A mess.

"So—we retreated, and the retreat was no fun. We went down first by train, and every five minutes we were bombed —the planes coming down as low as they could. And it was like this all the way to Kalamata. And there the stories really start, for at once we were taken prisoner. And our own particular unit had the dishonour to be taken by Max Schmeling. Do you know Schmeling? He was a boxer who got knocked out by the late Max Baer. Well, Schmeling was a parachutist, I think a captain, maybe, and my unit was taken prisoner by this man. They bombed us for several days, and then we are ordered to go down to the jetty, where the Navy will pick us up and take us to Egypt. Around midnight we heard the ships—destroyers—coming in, and we are told to throw everything away, kit bags, guns (we were supposed to destroy our guns), gas masks—everything.

"And then they move out without us. I never find out why. They move out without me, and without my company, and that is that. There we were, still standing on the jetty. Our major and lieutenant disappeared, and after a while they come back, both crying like babies. They told us we should have faith in God and the King and some other things similar, and that our brigadier had surrendered. Naturally I, being of Austrian birth, was very unhappy about

51

that. So I take my paybook—my identification—and destroy it. And I keep the gun. You might say that for legal purposes, such as being a prisoner of war in a German camp, Hermann ceased to exist."

Excited in spite of ourselves. Strange names, the exotica of war, Max Schmeling, bombs. Better than the late-late movie. Hooked again by Heroic Hermann. The tape runs out with a wistful pizzzz. "Come again, Hermann. Any time!"

"Thank you. Next time I will tell of how I move from the village to Larissa. Very exciting stuff. My friend in Hollywood will eat it up." Like cakes.

Mrs. Pilkinson, spreading her aura of expensive cheap perfume, never takes off her hat. Same hat always, three plastic cherries on black straw. You'd think she could be a little more adventurous, a plastic pumpkin perhaps for autumn, a small snowman at Christmas, a slice of plastic watermelon in summer.

"Excuse me for mentioning such a del-ee-kate subject, my dear, but does your husband use a deodorant?" Only after you've been here, lady. Five minutes with the Air Wick—after I check that the kid's still breathing. "Yoo-hoo, Avon Calling." Either my wife has a basic speech defect or she can somehow tune herself out.

"Why don't you say 'no' to these people once in a while?"

"Why should I?"

"They waste your time and that one wastes my money."

"They're interesting."

"Mrs. Pilkinson is *interesting*?"

"Yes, she is. And she's had a hard life. It can't be much fun going from door to door like that."

"Can't be much fun for all those husbands who have to come home to a house smelling like a 50-cent brothel."

"How do you know what a 50-cent brothel smells like?"

Touché. Never marry an intellectual. Or not one who's an aural nymphomaniac.

But then there's Hermann. Who could deny that Hermann is interesting? In Hermann my wife has found the jewel for her collection. Heroic Hermann, sucking the past like barley sugar. Hermann with a future like a cancelled stamp. Pilkinson can stuff herself for all I care, but Hermann has something. Sometimes.

". . . then I begin to get terribly sick from the malaria." We prick up our ears. Pavlovian reaction to Hermann has begun again. He should really be on "Zis Is Your Life." Wasted on us. And why should such diseases have these delightful names? Malaria, diarrhea, carcinoma, syphilis, beri-beri. Allow me to introduce my little daughter Diarrhea. Like characters in a Greek tragedy.

". . . a very high fever and couldn't walk. We had no quinine, no nothing. So they carry me into the church and the priest he puts all the holy icons around me and pours buckets of holy water over me. My three companions, they nearly die with laughing. I thought I too would die—but not from laughing. And then an old man comes with one of those straight razors—you know—that they use to shave with. So he, the priest, cut me in the centre of my forehead. A careful observer can still see the scar." Observe carefully. Hermann tips his round forehead upward to the light. The landlady's lampshade casts a rosy glow. We make ourselves believe that we can see it. My wife swears afterward that she can see it, so it must be there.

"First of all the blood came out—it looked as black as India ink and as thick"— tick, tick, tick, we watch the blood ooze out and hold our breath—"like syrup or molasses. He had put some kind of container under my head and asks me then to lean myself over so that this blood would drop into it. And after maybe ten, fifteen seconds, when this black blood had oozed out of the ugly wound, red blood came and I felt myself much better.

"Then the second thing he does is to knead my belly— to give me a kind of massage of the abdomen. I did not have a belly at that time, but let us say he kneaded the part where my belly is today." Don't have to ask us to observe carefully where your belly is today, do you? "It was very painful— but in the end Hermann did not die of malaria."

"I really wish he did." Sleepy murmur from the heap of blanket called Margaret.

"What—die of malaria? So do I sometimes."

Upright now, shocked and hurt. "Had a friend in Holly- wood. You knew what I meant." Tomorrow I will buy my- self one of those straight razors. You know ze kind?

"Won't you have some more potato salad?" asks the con- sumptive young man who is building a cabin in the woods and paints huge canvases on Mexican themes. They have been to Mexico, and as we eat our delicatessen dinner, they tell us about the colours, sights and smells.

"It is the smell of Mexico I really wish to capture."

Their twin girls eat with us, sitting on little wooden home-made potty-chairs. Clever idea, I suppose, but I don't think we'll stay for dinner next time. The wife wears Ber- muda shorts and has a haunted look. She confides to Mar- garet that after she had the twins she spent two months mentally incognito. Doesn't remember a thing. Wish I could forget that plonk-plonk in the middle of a forkful of potato salad. Must ask her how she did it.

At home we turn the television on without the sound. And

without turning on the lights. However, Hermann doesn't come.

Jesus keeps falling off the fuzzy-felt board, but the young man in black never pauses, just picks him up and rubs him gently back in place. They have declined tea and coffee. "I'm sorry, but it's against our rule." So we finish our coffee stealthily and I light a tentative cigarette.

"Oh, I come from New York State," says Margaret. I must have dozed off.

The two young men (are there really two or am I getting tired? Maybe they have to travel in packs, my brother's keeper kind of thing—make up for Cain) are very interested. Almost excited. One says, "Then you must have seen the place where he had his vision?"

"No," says Margaret regretfully, "I'm afraid not."

"It is my great dream," says the other (or is it the same one?), "to go to New York State and stand on the spot where he had his vision." Margaret argues theology with them. Discusses is maybe a better word. I watch her. Like the landlady's lampshade, she casts a rosy glow on all these people. Saint or nut—I wish I could make up my mind.

Jesus falls down again and is carefully picked up. I feel neglected.

"How long do you have to do this sort of thing?"

All three looked at me, startled, as if they had heard the voice of God walking in the garden.

"I don't, ha, ha, mean talking to Margaret and myself here. I mean travelling around to people's homes to explain your doctrines."

"Two years." They answer in unison. "And then we hope to go to Salt Lake City."

"After you go to upstate New York, of course."

Margaret glares at me. Not the voice of God after all.

The serpent. I hood my eyes and stare innocently back. They laugh modestly and show us the little book which explains the whole thing better than they can. "I really don't think —" Margaret gives them each a tube of Avon silicone hand cream as they leave. Bicycling all over like that and winter coming on. What the hell, we can spare it. What's a couple of tubes of $1.69 hand cream between friends. I put the book on the bottom row beside this month's *Watchtower*. Then I notice they've forgotten one of the disciples and have to go running down the road after them.

This sort of thing has got to stop.

"He searched us, and by some stupidity we had about three, four German pistols on us, so this gives them a very clear indication that we must have killed some Germans in order to get the pistols. So naturally he got mad." (Hermann, for Christ's sake, don't stop now, get on with it. The recorder whirrs softly as Hermann helps himself to another brownie.) "And took the machine gun from the armoured car. And as there was no wall he stood us against nothing in particular." (I do, too, Hermann. I wish you had a friend in Hollywood.) "And wanted to shoot us to kill us. And for why? Because we had German pistols. Well, he was ready for the execution, and we more or less figured that was the end of the story. I was thinking how stupid I was not to shoot somebody instead of giving myself up like that. To be caught and shot for nothing. To shoot back and be killed, at that time, is not so important. At least we would have defended ourselves and have wounded them. But to be shot like that? Like cattle?

"But before he was ready comes a small car with an officer. And the officer he started to argue with the NCO about the execution. And so, of course, in the end, we are ordered to get into the truck as he wants to find out where we get the pistols, from whom, etcetera. Once you are into the red tape procedure—the chances that you will then be shot are practically nil."

Hermann has done it again. We breathe a sigh of relief and Hermann beams like a harvest moon.

"You like it?"

"I don't think," says Margaret, mopping her forehead

with the dress she is mending, "that 'like' is the right word."

"You think it will sell?"

Oh Hermann, Hermann the Austrian German, victim of the Great American Dream. But your story should have been written twenty years ago. You've sold us, Hermann. What is more important, you've sold me. Isn't that enough?

"How's business, Hermann?"

How in hell can he do any business when he sits around eating Margaret's brownies and drinking our coffee 80 per cent of the time? Hermann, my friend, to help you and to help ourselves I zink we'll have to do the bathtub bit again.

"Do you think we're using him?" says Margaret, drying the coffee cups.

"The question of who's using whom is an interesting one. And when are you going to finish that term paper if he keeps dropping in?"

"Any day now." She will, too, that's the trouble.

"Speaking of term papers, there's an English boy in my seminar. . ."

"No."

"How do you know what I was going to say?" She examines a cup carefully.

"I do know what you are going to say. There's an English boy in your seminar and he has nowhere to go for Sunday

57

dinner. . ."

"Christmas dinner."

"Correction. Christmas dinner. And you thought it would be nice as there's only you and me and the baby and it's our first Christmas away from any of the family. . ."

"I'm so glad you see it that way. I was afraid you might object."

In the end he comes, with a big bag of apples and no pyjamas. I eat an apple, nude, sitting up in bed and listening to him snore away happily in the sitting-room. The aunts all send us thank-you letters for the Avon cologne and Margaret's sister writes from Boston that little Timothy hangs his turtle soap around his neck every night before he takes his bath. I wonder what little Timothy's going to think when that turtle's all melted away and he's left with a dirty great piece of rope.

We don't see Hermann over Christmas, but one night (must've changed to crepe-soled shoes, the bastard) he arrives with something that looks like a portable typewriter. Business, she must be looking up.

"I thought I would see what you think. The company has lent it to me." We settle down. Rather disappointing, I must say. No hair's-breadth escapes tonight. Hermann is up to somzing.

"You will sit here. And you, my dear Margaret, will sit yourself please here." Hermann adjusts the coffee table. The machine opens up and Hermann switches off the light.

"You see my friends, a record player-slide projector." The inside of the case is lined with some white stuff and Hermann settles himself between us. He throws a switch. A voice, not Hermann's, begins to speak.

"Here is a picture of John and Mary Doe and their two lovely children." (Gay Kodachrome of John and Mary smiling toothily at each other in tastefully furnished sitting-room. Children reading *Playboy* or something in the corner.)

"Ping."

Margaret jumps. "What's that curious 'ping,' Hermann?" Hermann has stopped the machine. We're right on cue.

"The 'ping' it tells me when to change the picture. Clever, no?" We resume.

"John and Mary and their two fine children live in a fine house on a fine street in Blankville." (Picture of fine house —exterior view—on fine Blankville street.)

"Ping."

"One morning John kisses his wife goodbye." (Kiss. Chaste close-up.)

"Ping."

"And sets off, as usual, for his office downtown." (Cut to John behind the wheel of his fine car.)

"Ping."

"Suddenly out of nowhere." (Car obviously out of control, not John's.)

"Ping."

"Comes a car." (Closer shot of nowhere car.)

"Ping."

"John swerves." (Picture of frantic John frantically turning the wheel.)

"Ping."

"But it is too late." (Nasty picture of two cars on top of one another.)

"Ping."

"Mary and the children are devastated."

"Ping."

"After the sad formalities of the funeral, Mary discovers that John has no insurance and her widow's pension is very small."

"Ping."

"The fine house in Blankville must be sold." (They goofed on this one; sign comes out as Ǝ⅃AƧ ЯOꟻ.)

"Ping."

"Mary must go to work."

"Ping."

"She moves from apartment to apartment with her two growing children." (Picture of sleazy apartment kitchenette with open milk carton on the table and the two kids with sad eyes eating peanut-butter sandwiches.)

"Ping."

"But it didn't have to be like this. Let us go back to that fatal morning when John kissed Mary goodbye for the last time." (Picture of John kissing Mary goodbye for the last time for the second time.)

"Ping."

"Yes, John crashed." (Same old crash.)

"Ping."

"And of course Mary was devastated."

"Ping."

"Ping."

"But after the sad formalities Mary found she had a friend." (Enter friend with a sad but toothy smile and bulging briefcase. I'm not sure Margaret should watch this sort of thing. Might give her ideas.)

"Ping."

"Her friend is the man from Transatlantic and he tells her that John has thoughtfully provided for her and the children." (Picture of Mary looking touched as she gazes at a cheque made out for $10,000.)

"Ping."

"The fine house in Blankville does not have to be sold." (Somebody took down that crazy sign.)

"Ping."

"Mary does not have to go to work." (Mary, slightly bored, reading a book.)

"Ping."

"The children do not have to be neglected." (Children smiling toothily over another issue of *Playboy*.)

"Ping."

"And all because John looked ahead and talked things over with the man from Transatlantic." (Picture of picture of John on mantelpiece of fine house. Children and Mary all gaze at him worshipfully. If John could look ahead, I wonder why didn't he take a taxi?)

"Ping."

"Mary's friend can be your friend too. Why don't *you* let the man from Transatlantic into *your* home?" (Picture of the man from Transatlantic smiling toothily at You and Me.)

Ping. Ping. Ping. Music.

"Do you think it will sell?" asks Hermann anxiously.

"It's certainly very novel." Trust old Margaret. I'd like to write a letter to the public about the man from Transatlantic. He'll help you to look ahead all right—sell you $10,000 worth of life insurance you can't afford and eat up all the bloody brownies in the house.

"Just great, Hermann." Margaret gets up. "Will you stay for coffee?" The man from Transatlantic loosens his tie and folds up his little machine.

Spring. The baby stands up for the first time, the landlady promises a new coat of paint, we plant a garden (much too early and nothing comes up but parsnips). The voice of the turtle is heard in the land, mingled with the voice of the tape-recorder as Hermann spends more and more of his time at our house, escapes from a moving train head first, lives with some shepherds on olives and cheese, is captured

61

again, escapes, tries to set sail for Crete and is captured again. I run out of tapes and have to buy some more, but the story goes on and on and on. And not just Hermann's story, but the story of the others—the old Greek woman who drops a precious egg into his hand and walks away before he can thank her in his faltering Greek—the famous brigand who had killed 23 men and lived as a proud and terrible outlaw in the hills. Our heads spin like the two reels on the tape recorder.

" 'And,' he said, 'when the war is over and you go back to your fatherland and your general says, "Where have you been all this time, during the war," what are you going to say?' So I said, 'It depends where I was.' So he says, 'You are going to tell him you are the whole war with me, that's what you're going to tell your general. And your general will say, "What man is this?" And do you know what you are going to tell him?' I said, 'Well, I would tell him, he was good man.' He said, 'Yes. You will say, "He was a *very* good man," that's what you are going to tell him. That's what you are going to say to your general.' So we were sitting there drinking. What could happen to us, after all? More than the killing of us, and we had been faced with that before! So he said then, 'After that, you will say to your general, "Don't you want to do something for this very good man?" And what will you tell him?' 'I will tell him yes.' And he said, 'Do you know what you have to do for me? You will tell your general to tell your king to tell the fucking bastard king we have here in Greece that all those mountains, where my sheep are, belong to *me* and to nobody else.' And I said, 'If my general asks me I will tell him.' But he never did."

This time it was little felt steps with names on them. The hierarchy of the church. Elders, deacons and what not, with

God at the top, of course. The little steps kept falling off. I was tired. It had been a bad day. The baby was teething and had eaten up some of Margaret's footnotes; we'd had a polite row about Mrs. Pilkinson's spring catalogue. ("If you think I'm going to support that bloody woman by ordering a dozen Castile Easter bunnies you're very much mistaken." That sort of thing.) I was also tired of watching those little steps fall down—and I wanted a beer.

"Say," I said to the earnest young man. "That fuzzy-felt board seems to be giving you a lot of trouble. Have you ever thought of trying something else, something really up-to-date and modern?" They looked at me politely. "Well, maybe modern isn't exactly the kind of word you'd take to."

"Oh no," replied one of the twins. "We pride ourselves on the fact that our church has something to say to a modern society." Dangerous word, pride. Pride goeth before an etcetera. I wonder, if you interrupted them in the middle of a sentence, would they have to start again?

"Well, I have a friend who has a dandy little machine. It's very light and could be easily carried in your bicycle basket. It looks like a typewriter, see, but when you open it up it's a portable phonograph and slide projector combined. While the record gives the spiel, slides flash on the screen—which isn't really a screen at all but the back of the box painted white. You could have pictures of Upper New York State, covered wagons, Salt Lake City, maybe the elders standing around on the steps. And it goes 'ping' when it's time to turn the slide. Could be a big seller." I gave them Hermann's card.

"I suppose you think you're funny," said Margaret's back, as the two bicycles disappeared down the road.

"Well, I think I'm funny-ha-ha and not funny-peculiar like some people I won't mention. But it could put a little life into their routine, couldn't it?"

"Once upon a time there was a Man." Picture of earnest man gazing at fertile farmland in Upper New York State.

"Ping."

"This man had a vision." Out-of-focus sunset or something like that. I'm not quite sure how one would work out the vision bit, but it could be an interesting problem.

"Ping."

"An angel descended with some tablets from the Lord." Picture of angel zooming in for a perfect three-point landing with tablets strapped on his back.

"Ping."

SLAM. Anyway, the baby laughed.

"The trouble is," he said, "the colour of the wall detracts from the colour of the canvas." Watch your step, buddy, I mixed that colour myself.

"Well," said Margaret, "I'm afraid I don't see where else we can hang it. But I do agree, the wall doesn't do justice to it. Are you sure you want us to have it?" Careful, Margaret, always look directly at the person to whom you are speaking.

"Of *course* he wants you to have it," said the haunted wife. "And if it's worth something some day, you deserve it for encouraging him." We'd deserve it for looking at it.

We all sat down for tea. I looked at the twins uneasily.

"They don't seem very happy on the sofa. Perhaps they'd like to sit on the floor?" They sat on the sofa. What the hell, it's the landlady's sofa and maybe they only react to wood. The huge canvas loomed over us. Portrait of an Unfortunate Tortilla.

"I haven't named it yet," he said. "It seems to detract from the canvas to give it a name. Limits one's aesthetic reaction, or channels it, I should say."

"He never signs his pictures," the wife confided to Margaret. I should bloody well hope not.

"We have a remark-ay-ble new mascara stick," confided Mrs. Pilkinson, helping herself to another sausage roll. "It not only colours the lashes, but tiny filaments in the colouring agent make the lashes longer than they really are. It comes in forest green, Mediterranean blue, sunset mauve and jungle brown."

"Ping."

Picture of Mrs. Pilkinson leaving our fine little rented house with bulging tummy and full order book. When Margaret looks at me I tell her she resembles a whisk broom.

The earnest young man takes out a little black notebook.

"And shall we put down June thirtieth as the date of your total immersion?" Stunned silence.

"I'm afraid," says the voice of the serpent, "that there's been a misunderstanding."

"Ping."

"Then you wouldn't give your child a transfusion even if it were dying?"

"The Bible says we must eat no blood."

"They usually give it to you in the arm, my friend, not in a teacup."

He wants his magazines back.

"I gave them to the baby. She's teething again. There's nothing in the Bible that says you can't eat newsprint, is there?"

"Ping" and Fade Out.

"Mrs. Pilkinson, my wife is lying down."

"Well, I'll just nip in and—"

"No, you won't just nip in and—Mrs. Pilkinson, this is a small house. There is only one chest of drawers, Mrs. Pilkinson. The chest of drawers is already full of your products and there is no room for my underwear." I move closer. "As you know from my wife, Mrs. Pilkinson, I do not use a deodorant. And because I do not use a deodorant I need to have a large supply of underpants and vests. If I have to cut down I'll get *smelly*. You wouldn't want me to get smelly, would you, Mrs. Pilkinson?" I move one step closer.

"Ping. Ping. Ping."

"So I will just fit this piece of muslin over the intake-hole and away we go." The vacuum cleaner pries into all the secrets of the sofa, runs along the carpet and up the walls. He dumps a large amount of dirt on the landlady's flowered carpet.

"You look like a decent clean-living young couple. Now can you sit there and tell me you want that pretty baby of yours to grow up in all this *filth*?"

"Yes. And I'll thank you to clean up that mess you made before you leave."

"Ping."

Hermann opens the boot and stands back as though he is about to show us the crown jewels.

"Well. Well. That *is* interesting, Hermann. Ah—are you going to do some sculpture on the side?"

"You do not recognize it?"

"Well, to be honest with you, Hermann, I don't." He beams and struggles to pull the immense block of stone onto the lawn.

"Here, Hermann, let me help you with that." Oh God, it's some sort of present. Cornerstone from a building he blew up single-handed. Where in hell are we going to put it?

"Thank you. I am not so strong as once I was."

The three of us stand there and Margaret practices appreciative noises in her throat.

"You do not understand? Good. I have gone into business for myself. I have decided the only way to succeed in this country is to go into business for oneself. You notice the finish?"

The blank surface of the stone catches the last rays of the sun.

"Well, it's very shiny. You must have been working hard to get it so shiny." I knew he'd go crazy in the end. Poor guy. My heart goes out to Hermann the German and his crazy block of stone.

"Ha," remarks Hermann slyly. "I did not polish her. She polishes herself!" Then we lift the stone back into the boot and Hermann carefully covers it over with old rags.

"Morpheus Memorial Markers," says Hermann, striding toward the door with energy and purpose in every step. "Morpheus Memorial Markers. You like it—no?"

Hermann eats the last chocolate-chip cookie. "You see, my friends, many years ago I had given to me a secret formula for cast concrete. 'So what,' you will say, 'cast concrete has been around for a long time.' But have you ever heard of the cast concrete which *polishes herself*?"

We hadn't.

"It looks like granite, the stone?"

It looked like granite.

"Well, I decided to get some samples made up and now I am no longer the man from Transatlantic, I am Morpheus Memorial Markers. You like the name?" This addressed to Margaret—one poet to another.

"Very suitable."

"The classical reference, the alliteration—the Canadians will eat it up."

"How many have you sold so far, Hermann?"

67

"Well, that is the trouble. The stones I can get made, but I need a chiseller. At a reasonable price. The stones I have arranged. The chiseller I have still to arrange."

"You mean a man who will chisel the epitaphs?"

"That is it."

"Margaret has a friend who's an artist. I could give you his address."

"He's a painter, dear. What makes you think he could use a chisel?"

"I'm sure he could use a chisel a damn sight better than he can use a paintbrush. Anyway, it's worth a try if Hermann wants somebody cheap. And look how clever he is at carpentry—building that cabin and those potty-chairs and all that." I give him the address.

"Say, Hermann, how much are these memorial markers going to sell for?"

"I had thought of $49.95. The Canadians, they like the 95." He looks at us wistfully. "I don't suppose you'd care to...?"

"Well, Hermann, unless I get fat on all this baking Margaret does, or murder somebody, or something like that, I don't think I'll be needing one of those for a long time. But it's a great idea, Hermann, really great. I guess you'll be pretty busy from now on—getting the new business started up and so forth."

"I am never so busy as to neglect my friend and his charming wife. Besides, there is the Book."

"Oh, yes," (foiled again by Hermann-never-take-a-hint), "of course, there's the book."

"I suppose we could have kept it in the garage."

"Next to the painting?"

"Ping."

We stood in the bathtub and waited for the footsteps to die away.

"Are you there, my friends? My friends, are you in there?" (Oh no you don't, Hermann. Not this time.) "Please, my friends, I am desperate. I wish to use your bathroom."

We step gracefully, and in unison, over the rim.

"Well, Hermann. This is a surprise. Margaret was just scrubbing my back." (What in hell is he wearing? Been to a masquerade or something?) "We thought you had forgotten us."

"Excuse me, please, for one minute." A Hermann resplendent in gold braid goes quickly into the bathroom and shuts the door. Margaret yawns delicately and puts the coffee on.

"What is he wearing?"

"Don't worry, we'll soon find out."

"I am sorry to trouble you, my friends. I am now commissionaire at the Olympia. Until business is better. You like the uniform, no?"

"Terrific, Hermann." (Why, you poor bastard, won't they even let you take a pee on the house?)

Margaret comes in with coffee and tomorrow's breakfast rolls.

"You look wonderful, Hermann. And you've lost weight, haven't you?"

"You think so?" Hermann beams and takes off his hat with the patent leather visor. I switch the recorder on.

"Did I ever tell you of how the Italians became our servants?"

"No, you didn't."

"Well, at Corinth there were always about four, five thousand Italian prisoners, plus the Greeks, in the same barracks. They were supposed to be released. But for some unknown reason, the Germans didn't release them. So they were supposed to be free, but were still prisoners. Both of us were prisoners you might say...."

No, Hermann, we can't ping you. I put my arm around Margaret while the tape recorder whirrs on... and on... and on....

A WINTER'S TALE

Some memories are butterflies, swift, graceful, leaving behind a sense of summer and contented hovering. The delicate, fluttering ones. No harm in these. Some are cathedral windows, butterfly wings on a solemn scale. Crimson, emerald, sapphire. Jewelled truths. Cold, perhaps, because reflections only, but leaving behind a thrill and terror of organ music and the smell of grapes. Communion. Or memories like bats—unseen and only sensed in the dark and dusty corners of the night. No voice speaks, and nothing is heard but the silent, terrible scream of the sleeper, struggling to awake. Or luna moths, soft and veined like thighs. Night thoughts. Or wingless completely—maggots in rotting meat.

Which is this, then—or none—or all? You judge. I remember the snow which fell like a blessing on our shoulders. I remember his words—but not the sound of his voice. "Is it all right to call you darling in bed?" I remember the sleeping town, crumbling yet strong in its granite unconcern for the lovers it had seen before and would see again. I remember it all, as though it were today.

It is easier to conjure up a fairy tale (which is what I could do right now and write it down correctly, according to the rules) than to put one's finger on the pulse of truth. In the tale it is all so easy. I, the princess, and he, the prince. We meet and of a sudden fall in love. There are dragons, of course, and wicked dukes and many other dangers; but these can all be banished, crushed or conquered. We mount the milk-white steed, ride off into the silver dawn. No sequel; nothing sordid. When the storytellers say "The end" they mean it. Never the names of Cinderella's children. Yet he and I were once upon a time (but only once) like the prince and princess. He woke me with a kiss, freed me from chains of loneliness and dragons of despair—if only for an evening. For what he woke me to, and what he freed me from, I should, I suppose, be grateful.

One night, once upon a time. That's all. One silent winter's night it was, when the snow fell in great flakes until the whole sky seemed to be alive with wings—the ghosts of a million butterflies or moths.

It was, I suppose, on the morning after, when I woke early and remembered, "You're twenty-one and still a virgin!" that I opened the door (or at least unlocked it) to the events which were to follow. Not that I hadn't considered the fact before. But it was usually as a form of parlour game with other girls at college.

Someone would start—"I wonder how many of us are really virgins." And some would proudly boast that they were not (often the liars), while others would laugh uneasily and proudly boast they were. Still others would turn away and smile. Yet most of us agreed it wasn't worth it—degrading, somehow, to have no control; "Unless, of course," someone inevitably added, "you're really in love." But that's the trouble, isn't it? Songs, mothers, friends and guidance counsellors: everyone assured us we would know—and we believed them. The very young still dream of shining knights who will awaken them with kisses from their innocent, tormented dreams. And desperate, heavy-thighed with spring, they allow themselves to be awakened in a dark car or a deserted lane by someone who, in the long daylight of Later

On, which stretches before them like a northern winter, turns out to be neither a prince, nor charming. I hadn't allowed that to happen—avoided the cars and the lanes. I all but avoided the spring. I was not only prudent but afraid—afraid of the dark, masculine laughter and the promise of new delights. I prided myself on my fear and knew I was right.

But now I wanted nothing more, on this winter morning in this strange mediaeval town, than to be that which I had shunned before. I was cold in a new way—not cold by choice but rather (why hadn't I seen it?) cold by destiny. I lay wide-eyed and shivering in the wet dawn; my roommate, only the top of her pale hair showing from beneath the mound of blankets, was asleep. She slept the sleep of the uncomplicated —and the beautiful. If I ever were to write my fairy tale it is she who would be the princess. Beautiful and good and innocent. It is a truism, I suppose, that the pretty girl chooses the plain girl for her friend; but the reasons are not so simple, or so selfish, as one might think. Often the pretty needs the plain not as foil, but counterfoil—an official sign that there is more to her (the pretty one) than meets the eye. She was uncomplicated, yes, but passionate, forever in love—it seemed to be a necessary condition to her survival. Yet the passion would soon die down and she would move on to a new partner, still searching and still innocent, and still (this was something to marvel at) untarnished. Still a virgin. We had known each other more than two years and were the best of friends, although her reasons for virginity—a deep, religious repugnance to something she felt was so unsanctified and therefore sinful—were different from my own. She was not cold, but simply committed to a dream. And now I reflected that her chances of finding it, and of losing her virginity, were infinitely better than mine.

I was never beautiful—not even as a baby. But as a child

—and later—I believed that I would, of necessity, become so. Then, somewhere around my seventeenth year, I had realized, and accepted, that this was not to be, and I laid that dream aside, firmly but with regret, the way one might lay aside a favourite dress which has suddenly become too shabby or too small. I took refuge in the fact that I was not, at least, ugly and might even become, with time and perseverance, attractive. I also took refuge in my intelligence. And this was a great bond between us, my roommate and me. (For the good fairies of our childhood had, with her, left nothing out.) We could discuss things—not just men—together. Together we discovered the world of books: philosophy, history, fiction; and together thrilled to their voices: now angry, now sad, now gentle, now morose. We even felt, sometimes, we had grown up together (which perhaps we had) and could often read each other's thoughts, anticipate each other's reactions. A marital relationship if you like, but one which exists most often between two women or two men. That morning I was glad she was asleep when I woke up hearing that "still" so loudly in my ears. "Twenty-one and still a virgin." I was terribly conscious of my body, warm beneath the many layers of blanket, and for the first time conceived of my "maidenhead" (such a poetic term!) as something already drooping on the stem. Suddenly I wanted to be something else than "still a virgin," wanted to give myself, that was it, to give *myself*, that is to say my body, to someone else. It was no longer a question of avoiding being taken. I wanted to know it all—what it was like to hesitate and then succumb, what it was like to be roused to such a pitch of wanting that all scruples, reservations, built-in checks would be lost upon my body screaming to be touched and touched and taken. I wanted to know what it was like to fall asleep and waken to the pressure of another person in the bed. I wanted everything.

My precious intelligence said not to be so foolish, that the words which had been spoken so mockingly (and they had been spoken to me, not about me, flung down as a careless challenge I could pick up or ignore) should be received as they were given—lightly, as a jest. He had, after all, been tight. And so had I and so had everyone else.

I can see him still, leaning against the mantelpiece, observing the others (an after-play party and many still with their make-up on: Lonnie Donnegan filling the smoky air with his pulsing voice, the nervous, overexcited chatter which was a symptom of relief and relaxation; Macduff jiving with Lady Macbeth; the fat girl who had been prompter telling everyone how she lost the place at a crucial moment, demanding her share of attention and drinking too much and too quickly). I thought, "If the devil were to show himself on earth he would look like this man: intelligent, tall, lean, somehow sulphuric and dangerous." I knew who he was, of course (who didn't?), knew his girlfriend too, a shy dark-haired girl who wore no make-up, and yet was beautiful, as beautiful as my golden roommate—Rose-red to Snow-white. Knew also that they were lovers, although she did not live with him, but with three other girls in a flat not far from our boarding house; had seen them together at parties, she rarely speaking, he always, or usually, surrounded by a group of admirers, male and female. For he was brilliant, and when drunk would let forth a flow of words, of speculations and pronouncements which took one's breath away by their very simplicity and power. And although she was beautiful, many said (both male and female, particularly the hangers-on), "What does he see in her?" I had wondered myself, for he did not look the type who would seek out goodness, deliberately, unless it were to destroy it—certainly not to establish anything so permanent as the relationship which they so obviously had. Then one day I had seen them, sitting on a mound above the battlements of the ruined castle (the castle which had made the choice of the play so obvious, once someone had suggested it). It was late October and cool; but the sun was making a wan attempt to warm the earth, looking somehow sad, convalescent, in the blue-grey sky; and few had left their books or gas fires to come out and watch the rehearsals. They sat there, he leaning back on his elbows, his face tilted upward, eyes closed, somehow more arrogant than ever, while she read a book.

Suddenly he leaned over and whispered something to her. She got up, put her book down carefully, marking the page with a bit of paper. Then she gathered her scarlet gown around her and rolled, like a child, over and over, down the slope to the bottom. She ran back up, her pale face flushed with delight, and he took her in his arms and kissed her. Then she picked up her book and they walked away. I knew, then, what he saw in her, and why, although I kept silent (I had been an unknown witness after all) when the inevitable question was raised.

Yet this evening he was alone, without her, offered no explanations, simply came in late and took up his stand by the mantelpiece, leaving it only to get another drink from time to time. I too was alone, had hurried home to wash off the make-up (I was not enough of an exhibitionist to wish to appear as a witch at a small gathering with no audience-actor barrier to separate me from my friends and fellow-students). My roommate had come with her latest knight, a young doctor, and was very gay (and very beautiful) across the room.

That he and I should speak to each other was inevitable, for I was sitting on the floor directly below him, and, like him, observing. He looked down and then said:

"You were very good."

"It is hardly a part at which one could fail." I smiled up

76

at him, for he was interesting, if, from my point of view, unapproachable, and not only because he "belonged," if that is the right word, to someone else.

"You're wrong, you know. There are witches and witches. You made me feel that you were not evil, which is the standard interpretation, but inexorable. And," he added, somewhat inconsequentially, "I liked your hair." (They had silvered it for the part; but I had washed it before coming out —even at the risk of a cold. It reminded me of death, I suppose, though that might not have occurred to me then.)

"Well, I didn't. Perhaps for the play. A 'secret black and midnight hag' would look silly with red hair."

"You flatter yourself. Your hair is not red, it's brown." I was annoyed. Even a plain girl usually has one feature of which she is proud, or at least relies on to feed her feeble vanity. Mine was my hair.

"It's red."

He sat down, then, next to me, crossing his long legs tailor-fashion. "Perhaps I haven't really looked at it." Right then I felt as I would if a window had suddenly been opened directly behind my neck, that I would want to—wanted to —move away.

Then, "Are you a virgin?" Very low. In the smoke and dimness it was difficult to tell if he were smiling.

"Yes," I said, and stood up, searched frantically, looking for someone who could serve as an excuse for a graceful, if hurried, exit. No-one. I stood there, and he laughed, mocking me.

"How old are you?"

"Does it matter?" I was angry with him, with myself, with the dark-haired girl who should have been by his side.

"In your case I should think it does."

"I'm twenty-one."

"Twenty-one and still a virgin!" Then he laughed again,

got up abruptly and left the party, saying goodnight to no-one, walking through the crowd like a displaced god.

On the way home, alone and in spite of my damp hair, I wandered toward the ruined abbey, one of my favourite spots in a town so steeped in history and fable the very damp oozed mystery. On the left stood the battlements of the once forbidding castle—where we had played *Macbeth* that very night, in spite of the cold and the wet. Farther along and up, a cross, marking the death of their first student martyr, was built into the street. A small dog walks, they said, six feet above the pavements, ghosts making no allowance for sub-sidence. Wherever one turned one was met with Romance; but of it all I loved the abbey, and its nun, the best. Nothing was left but one broken wall and if you chose at midnight you could put your hand in through a grille and feel her ghostly fingers touching yours. They said she killed herself for love, was beautiful but true. A fable probably, but I went back that night to see if she could give me reassurance. I leaned my face against the rough stone and touched her hand. I was terribly troubled—too much excitement, little food and too much drink. I touched her hand (I think), but nothing happened. No sense of kinship, of principles glori-fied, only a sense of something dead and dull.

From there I wandered to the sea, which guards and threatens the old town. The moon was out, and through the mist I could see quite clearly the line between earth and water. But the night sound of the waves, in which I usually delighted, did nothing to calm me and I turned toward home. My roommate was asleep when I got in—asleep when I awoke. I caught a cold, which was to be expected.

When I was better and about again I heard the story of why he had been alone that night. (And all the time I lay in bed I wondered if he had asked about me. I felt it was his fault

78

I had a cold, his fault I was so restless, couldn't read, could barely carry on a conversation. And yet I wouldn't ask about him—couldn't.) He'd had a row, or so the story went. I was somehow relieved—his mockery was not, after all, directed at me alone. But such was his unique place amid our circle (the circle in which I was included not only because I was my roommate's roommate but because I was new and therefore "interesting") that no-one knew more than that. And when, a few days later, the two of them were seen walking together, as usual, there was nothing more said except (with varying degrees of jealousy or satisfaction depending upon the speaker), "They've made it up."

And so, although he had awakened something in me which would not now sleep, the something remained general—an undirected longing, a sense of myself as a cup (a family heirloom, perhaps? I mocked) waiting to be filled.

I went to dances (plain girls who are intelligent and brave make it a point of honour to be good dancers); parties (plain girls who are intelligent make it a point of honour to be witty without being coarse, to learn to drink without getting drunk—to be, if not "in demand," at least worth inviting); studied hard and had midnight discussions, over beef tea or coffee, with my roommate (I was beginning to wonder if the young doctor were not, perhaps, her knight after all) and with my fellow boarders. We solved questions of life, religion, politics one night, only to destroy the solutions, as a child will destroy the sand castle he has built, the next. In other words I participated and was content—at least until the final goodnights were said, my roommate was asleep and I was left alone with my twenty-one years—and my virginity. I dreamt, but my hero, when there was one, remained faceless or out of focus, simply The Hero, perhaps the old god Thor. Naturally I saw *him* at parties, public lectures, dances, in the tea rooms, on the street. Saw him and her I should say, for they were one in my mind. They were a relationship rather than two separate individuals. I made sure I never got too close, although I did not think he would repeat his words, realized (in my intelligent part at least) that he had probably forgotten them. Our eyes never met, although we said the usual "hellos," made the necessary social gesture of formal recognition when the occasion called for it.

And so it might have gone on, and there would have been no memories and no story, if it had not been for one fact, one circumstance which blew away my safety, my carefully constructed castle, as surely as if a cannon had been fired point-blank. For, as well as being plain, I was poor. One thinks of Americans in Europe as being at least reasonably well-to-do, but this is not always the case. I was not unique, for there were, and are, many others like me, who through their own efforts—or those of their parents—have begged, borrowed, worked summers, evenings, done God knows what to follow the still-fresh American dream of Europe as a Mecca of culture and tradition. Wasn't that part of the charm of this particular place? The scarlet gowns, the ruined castle, the abbey, the local ghosts, the grey buildings which had a patina of history, like old silver, on their stony sides? Romance—that is what we lack in America and what we seek among the spires of Oxford, the studios of Paris, or in my case the cobbled streets of a Scottish university town. We call it "education," or "broadening one's outlook," but its real name is Romance. Yet if one is poor, and one manages to get there at all, one has to, at some point, compromise. My compromise was painless but necessary: I would not travel during the Christmas "vac," and then, in the spring, my roommate and I would go south, to Spain, for two weeks. She was going skiing at Christmas with some of the people from the boarding house (regretting already her

80

departure, however temporary, from the young doctor, but at the same time anticipating Austria—and another chance to travel). She did not offer to lend me money, for she knew, without being told, that our relationship would never be the same if she did, even if I refused (which she knew I would). And I could have gone somewhere—had invitations to London, to a friend in Dundee, to people from the boarding house itself, who were "going down" for Christmas. I did not refuse out of a sense of martyrdom; but the idea of Christmas with a family other than my own (and, even with my own, Christmas was always something of a strain—a too-hectic renewal of outgrown relationships, festivity as flushed as fever, overeating, too many questions and I with inadequate answers) distressed me. I said I had work to do (which was true) and, in a way, was relieved when they all left and I could be alone. I went out of the station, and turned, not toward the way home, but down to the beach, walking aimlessly—no thoughts, just a sense of freedom and an awareness of sound—the damp sand's suck-suck at my shoes, the great inhale-exhale of the sea, the "mee-mee-mee" of the gulls, like spoiled children fighting over toys. I found a bit of stick, wet, washed up by the sea, and dragged it behind me as though I had a companion who walked on one incredibly pointed leg. Then I stopped and drew a figure in the sand, again aimlessly, hardly aware of what I was doing, a stick figure, neither male nor female, simply a sign (to whom? the sand? the great North Sea?) that someone had been there. I stood and watched the waves run up to it and then, afraid, run back again on their silver feet, up, back, up, back, finally touching it, then pouncing on it quietly, quickly, giving it little cat-licks, until it disappeared. It was only then that I felt lost rather than alone, and I hurried back toward the town and the security of the boarding house.

That evening, I took a hand mirror (the only one there

was, unless I went down the hall to the bathroom) and examined myself, naked and shivering in spite of the gas fire which hummed merrily at the end of the room. I could see my toes and a bit of my calves, then part of my legs and my knees. And so on up to my face, my plain, sensible, intelligent face. Yet of course one could not be objective. The me I saw, or the fragments of me which I could summon with a flick of my wrist downward or upward, had no external reality. I wondered what I would look like to someone else, standing naked, flat-bellied, straight-legged on the worn carpet. I tried to imagine myself pregnant, my flat stomach swollen with importance, sharing its secret with anyone who cared to stop and look. When I was a child and exchanged scraps of knowledge (overheard, misinterpreted, mangled by ignorance and innocence) with other children, I had received with delight the information that babies came out of your bellybutton. It was an exciting idea, and a pleasant one. I would swell and swell until one day, "pop"—my child would fly out like a genie summoned from a bottle. When I told my older sister (for the knowledge and wonder, the beautiful simplicity of the thing, needed to be told to someone else) she laughed and gave me the correct—and to me, infinitely less romantic—version. I did not attempt to argue, did not doubt that what she told me was true; for I was learning that the nasty explanations in life were usually the true ones. Yet I felt cheated somehow, and ashamed, and kept the terrible secret, for once, to myself. I looked back on that child now with a certain amount of awe. For even after what my sister had told me I had never doubted that some day I would have a baby, just as some day I would be beautiful and married. "Twenty-one and still a virgin!" I said to myself as I turned off the gas and prepared for sleep in my neat and narrow bed.

Several newcomers had arrived at the boarding house when the halls closed for Christmas—bits of flotsam and jetsam, thrown up like myself by the tide of the great public holiday.

The African next door, lips protruding from his face as though they had been added later, after the head had been modelled, as a child adds features to a head made of clay or plasticine. He had brought a portable phonograph which he played at night (I knew, for once I knelt down and peeked under his door), in the dark, while he was asleep or lying down. French lessons, lessons in British history, and once the great bell-boom of Dylan Thomas, *A Child's Christmas in Wales*. I was intrigued by the African, but he never answered my greetings with more than a swift and soon-extinguished smile, a smile like a skilled arpeggio upon a keyboard. Someone had probably told him to smile at all the Whites before he left the tropics, poor thing. He ate his meals out and once I was disloyal enough to wonder if he ate with his fingers; and once I wondered, but only casually, scientifically you might say, what it would be like to knock on his door one night and walk in naked, walk over to his bed in the dark and turn the records off. I had a feeling he might scream, for he looked very serious. There was a French girl, whom I already knew by sight, studying for some external degree, teaching primary school and hating it. She descended to the dining-room every morning, always cold and discontented, with great red chilblained hands. She ate quickly, muttering to herself, devouring sausages the way she devoured knowledge. The landlady had asked me to be nice to her, and I had invited her to my room one night for a drink; she had poured out her hatred of the place, her homesickness for France, her need to distinguish herself. And, although I had listened sympathetically, or tried to, her ugly, square figure, her sullen face, her general atmosphere of dissatisfaction made me uneasy. She was older than I and reputedly very brilliant, and I could not help seeing certain parallels, however tenuous—myself in a boarding house ten years hence, chattering away about a thesis to someone, anyone who would listen and pretend to admire.

One other room had been let to a young Indian medical student, who uncoiled himself for breakfast, lunch and tea, then coiled himself up again to the thick books on anatomy, physiology, God-knows-what, lined up precisely on his mantelpiece. He had a slightly out-of-focus picture of his wife and child back in India, which he showed me once, in a rare moment of friendliness. I admired it, of course, although to me it was just an exotic blur. He said the picture helped him to study better, then whispered a polite, "If you will excuse me," and went down the hall to his room.

They were all so serious, so dedicated; I the hypocrite among them, carefully displaying my books for the day on my little table, leaving my door open so that they could see, if they stopped to look, how busy, how equally serious, *I* was; and putting the same books away, unread or unremembered, each night when I closed the door. Except for my sex I was not unlike the drone—a drone among the workers— yet my humming gas fire and my bent, studious back gave the illusion that I was what I was not. My restlessness, after the first few days, drove me back again and again to the sea, where at least I felt unashamed of my idleness, too insignificant to be regarded as anything—much less an idler. It was when I returned from one of these expeditions, these purgings of guilt for not making good use of my time, that I discovered him in my room, leaning against the mantelpiece, just as he had leaned that night. He saw me in the doorway and said peremptorily:

"Have you got a shilling? The fire's gone out." I went to the bedside table and opened the cigarette tin in which we kept the shillings for the meter. I handed him one and he stooped down, quickly lighting the fire, and said over his shoulder, "There's a trick to these, you know. I used to use the same shilling over and over in one place I lived."

"It would have shown up on the meter."

He stood up. "There's a trick to that too, a more elaborate one. It involves the landlady or," (he smiled) "her daughter." I stood there in my coat, wondering why he had come, what he wanted from me.

"Aren't you going to ask me in?"

"You are in."

"Only technically—I can see that by your face."

"Please sit down. I'm sorry, I'm just surprised to see you."

"You mean surprised that I'm still in town or surprised to see me here?"

"Both."

"I've been to Edinburgh for a few days, but I had work to do, so I'm staying here over the vac."

"Of course. You take your degree this year."

"Take it with honours, I hope." He stretched his long legs out to the fire, and leaned back in our one and only easy chair. It seemed only natural to offer him a cup of tea, to methodically hang up my coat, take the electric kettle to the bathroom and fill it, come back and plug it in, sit across from him (but on the floor) waiting for it to boil. He had closed his eyes and I was shocked to see how tired he looked —shocked and gratified; it made him, somehow, more human. When the kettle boiled I found two mugs, a tin of milk, sugar and a packet of biscuits. I thought he had fallen asleep, he was so still; so I sat there helplessly (but not discontented) with the biscuits on the floor between us.

He opened his eyes. "Milk, please, and no sugar." I held out the mug to him and he acknowledged my hospitality with another of his strange smiles (they could hardly be called "grins," yet I had the feeling that that was what they were, that he was mocking me).

"Are you always prepared for any emergency?"

"What do you mean?"

"The type who always has a shilling for the meter, a kettle that works, milk, sugar, biscuits—the lot."

"I would like to be."

"You wouldn't find it boring?"

"How could it be boring? One would be so busy trying to anticipate all the emergencies, in order to prepare for them, one wouldn't have time to be bored."

"And if one found, in the end, that one had shelves and shelves of useless stuff—that one had never encountered any of the emergencies for which one had prepared. . . ?"

"You're mocking me."

"Not at all. I'm just pointing out to you the deadliness of such a philosophy." He reached over and helped himself to another biscuit. I noticed his nails were bitten, and relaxed.

"Suppose I were to ask you out tonight, would you be prepared for that?" I realized, then, that this was exactly what I had been anticipating, preparing for, since I first entered the room—and perhaps before?

"I couldn't go."

"Couldn't because you can't or couldn't because you won't?"

"Does it matter?"

"Yes, as a matter of fact it does." And a look passed between us as silent and swift as stolen money exchanging hands.

"Because I am, as you would probably put it, 'taken'?"

"It would be dishonest."

"That depends on your definition of honesty. If I tell you honestly that I am bored and restless and lonely, and that I want to spend the evening with you, who are also bored and restless and lonely, is that dishonest?"

"To tell me, no. For me to take you up on it—yes."

"So you would rather stay here and pretend to read all these attractively arranged tomes," (he gestured toward the little table) "than come out with me."

"I didn't say I would rather; I simply said I wouldn't go out with you."

It had grown dark and I stood up, surprised to find that I ached with tension. I had thought I was managing so well! Everything seemed a bit far away, as though I were coming down with flu. When I switched on the light he closed his eyes. "Don't." I switched it off again.

"Tell me," he said, "do you believe in God?"

"Is it important?"

"Possibly."

I went to the window and stared out, other windows casting little paving stones of light along the dark street.

"I like to believe there was a God."

"What happened to him then?"

"He made the world—and then he died." (A cat and a mouse, casual, playing with words in order to retreat, advance. If we could keep on talking!)

He laughed, "Of what? Of overwork?"

"Of loneliness. You see, it was very beautiful, but imperfect—like all beautiful things. He couldn't, being perfect himself, being perfection rather—get down."

"Down to earth?"

"Exactly."

"And so he died?"

"Wouldn't you?" (I turned and watched the fire. Little, cold, blue fingers playing on the flame.)

"And what did this curious God of yours ever do for you?"

"I told you. He made the world."

"And that's enough?"

"That's all there is."

"Come here," he said, and when I sat down beside him he opened his eyes and looked down at me.

"If God is dead, and you are grateful to him, then why are you afraid?"

"Of him?"

"Of him—and me."

"You see a connection then?" I was too tired to refute him.

"I think I see. You wish that you could wait for some perfection—one moment, at least, to offer him, to make up to him for what he lost."

"I'll disappoint myself if I do not."

"You love me?"

"No." (Not love, no—what burned in that room was not love.)

"You know I don't love you?"

"Yes." We were not playing now. I shivered.

"And you think that things—worlds—situations such as what could occur tonight—should be created out of love?"

I struggled valiantly (I thought then) to return to the game. "I never said he created the world out of love."

"But that's what you meant."

"Not exactly. I don't know why he did it. I've often wondered. Bored perhaps—or lonely."

"But I am bored and lonely—and so are you. Can't we create a world? Wasn't the whole trouble that there was no-one to share his loneliness?" Heaps of words, pebbles collected on deserted beaches. Arrange them in curious designs. Use them for windows and doors, for stately paths and promenades. If one is interested in the moment, what does it matter that the tide is coming in or that a small child runs along the beach and kicks the castle in? We stood up together and I got my coat.

"Don't be afraid," he said, and I closed the door quietly.

We went down the stairs, moving against the accusing silence of the shut doors of my studious, serious neighbours.

"Where are we going?"

"To my flat."

It was nearly dawn when we returned, and the snow muffled our footsteps as though it, too, were a conspirator. At the corner, under the streetlamp, where the great white flakes, like moths, hurled themselves against the light, he kissed me, lightly, and was gone.

"No regrets," he had said and, "No regrets," I had achingly replied. Then I turned and walked slowly toward the house. I never saw him—alone—again.

SALON DES REFUSES

Toot-toot woke suddenly, jerked upright as though she had been pulled by an invisible string. The pale sunlight of a winter dawn, cold as a false smile, sidled through the bars and deposited small parcels of light on the floor. Toot-toot lay down again, stuck her head over the edge of the bed and watched the little squares of light. She reached out her pudgy hands and tried to coax the sunlight to her, wanted one of the little boxes to open and to play with under the thin blanket. "Toot-toot," she whispered softly, "toot-toot." Her pigtails stuck straight out from her head, as in a child's drawing. She reached too far and fell off the bed in a tangle of blanket and sheet. Snow thudding from the steep roofs in a winter thaw. Toot-toot did not care; her hands had reached a square of light. She lay happily, fondling the light, a royal child playing with building blocks of gold. "Toot-toot," she crowed happily from her tangled nest, a small cockerel greeting the false dawn. Eleanor La Douce, her black eyes shooting around the room like hot coals and coming to rest on the small figure playing on the floor, jumped out of bed and snatched the blocks of sunlight, ran screeching around the room. "You're a whore," she shrieked at Toot-toot. "You're a whore like all the rest of them. Fiends fiends fiends," she muttered, staring at her empty hands. "They have stolen from me my diamond brooch, my string of pearls, my son, my château on the Loire. Has it come to this, that the wife of General La Douce should be forced to steal from such as you?" Her skinny arm snaked out and slashed the air with a sound like wind in broken branches. Toot-toot cried quietly upon the floor. "Fuck you," said Eleanor La Douce.

Mother Brown heaved herself up the hill from the bus stop, the wind stinging her eyes, darting obscenely under last year's coat, playing tunes with icy fingers up and down her fat thighs, blowing down her neck with a rude kiss, howling away like a whole mob of naughty schoolboys. If the storm kept up tomorrow she would have to take a taxi. She thought resentfully of the taxi fare, of spending money. Wops and kikes, all of them, take the longest way round and fill their pockets with her hard-earned cash. Her resentment warmed her and she made it up the rest of the hill and across the compound without difficulty. Perhaps she could claim for taxi fare, being a widow and all that, and the varicose veins. It wasn't as if they had people standing in line to work there. Still, she'd have to go carefully—fifty a week was nothing to sneeze at. She thought of her account at the First City, swelling slowly and methodically like a woman great with child. And she thought of the brochures on Florida and California. Her anger melted like snow in sunlight and she was smiling happily as she waddled through the glass doors, pausing to stamp her feet and polish her bifocals, which had misted up in the sudden warmth of the building.

"Well, Mrs. Brown," said the gold-rimmed Director as he signed her in, "you look like the cat that swallowed the canary." On the wall behind the desk was a huge map of the compound and, in the corner, a globe. The desk was a jumble of papers, with pink and yellow memos stuck, like pastel butterflies, on spindles. She was about to tell him about the long walk from the bus stop, but two policemen came in the office, a grey little man swaying between them, so she went out, her galoshes making a suck-suck sound as she padded across the hall and turned the key which would bring the elevator down. She was early and there was no-one else waiting. A huge aluminum Christmas tree preened itself in the centre of the hall and the janitor had already turned on the light wheel underneath. The grey metal branches turned pale and pretty shades of blue, red, yellow, green. Very nice and of course they couldn't take a chance on fire, but she preferred the real thing herself; bet it cost plenty though. She thought of the taxi again and frowned. Throwing their money away on foolishness. State-controlled, of course. Always plenty of graft in a state-controlled institution. Still—fifty a week. She patted her black plastic handbag. She'd have to nip up and see when Cynthia was off for lunch. She wondered what she'd think of the brochures. Of course if two went in together on a thing like this it would be even cheaper. Still, Cynthia was a Catholic and she didn't know if she could stand all that business about the Pope and the BVM. Not that she didn't believe in God, but there was something queer about having an old geezer over in Italy— probably couldn't even speak English either—telling them what they could and couldn't do. Maybe she'd better not suggest anything to Cynthia just yet. Invite her around one evening and see what happens. No good getting tied up with somebody she wouldn't get on with. With a start she realized that the indicator above the door was pointing to M, so she unlocked the door and got in, pressed the button for the third floor, got out and proceeded down the hall toward a heavy door marked "88." Selecting another key from the collection which jangled around her ample waist (or where her waist would have been if she'd had one), she carefully unlocked the heavy door and listened as it closed behind her with a satisfied click.

Caught like a rat in a trap. Trapped like a caught rat. Mrs. Marsden struggled feebly—felt the soft hairs sprout like spring grass upon her body—felt her teeth grow long and pointed, felt her eyes grow small and sharp. She should have known the cheese was tainted—hadn't it been full of holes? She picked up the remains of the cheese in her small sharp claws and stared through the hole, but she could see nothing except the cruel teeth of the trap. The trap grinned at her suddenly and she screamed—but it came out as a squeak, and before she could scamper away the teeth snapped down and click, click bit her in two. Her tail twitched for a moment and then she was still.

Nurse Primrose heard the click, popped her head around the corner of the staff room, where it floated for a minute like a balloon, the features under the starched white cap as colourful and meaningless as the features—painted eyebrows, painted mouth, circles of rouge, stiff glued blond curls—of a child's doll; like a balloon it disappeared. "It's all right," she said, lighting another cigarette, "it's only Mother B." The hawk-faced night nurse finished her coffee in one gulp, took the mug over to the sink and rinsed it carefully, leaving a damp ring of moisture on the table. She dried the cup on a towel marked "88" in indelible ink and put it back on the shelf above the sink, lining it up precisely with the row of green glass mugs already there, each one initialed in nail polish. Then she yawned widely, showing her gold teeth, and picked up her coat and bag.

"See you tomorrow," she said to Nurse Primrose as she went out the door and down the long hall, past the Negro trusty who was busy washing the floor with savage strokes and muttering curses under her breath. The night nurse stepped daintily along the slippery aquarium-coloured linoleum, peering in two of the side wards as she passed. "Jesus," she said to herself. "Why the hell can't they sleep in the night-time?" She nodded curtly to Mother Brown as she passed, but Mother Brown, still lost in the warmth of Florida sunshine and desirable waterfront residences, barely noticed the other woman. Two sets of wet tracks, the night nurse going out and Mother Brown coming in, ran parallel but in opposite directions the length of the long green hall. The trusty looked at the tracks and cursed them musically in a strange, excited tongue. Then she took her wet mop and danced slowly up the hall and back erasing the tracks and laughing to herself at some hidden, apocalyptic joke.

"You miss all the fun," said Nurse Primrose with what she took to be a wry expression.

"What's happened?" Ladling two spoonfuls of Instant Maxwell House into her mug, Mother Brown poured boiling water from the electric kettle and helped herself to several lumps of sugar from the flowered bowl. She sat heavily and gratefully, warming her hands against the mug, and waited. Nurse Primrose wasn't high hat like that other one, thought Mother Brown. Always let you have a cup of coffee before beginning work and didn't put on airs because she had a white cap with a couple of bands and you were only a PN. Nurse Primrose was all right. Pretty, too, with her yellow hair and trim figure. Wonder why she doesn't marry again. Still—once bitten twice shy, and the other one had certainly been a rotter—walking out on her just because she had an abortion and didn't tell him. Why should she have children if she didn't want them, and she had said that with the world in such a dreadful state, it really wasn't right. Mother Brown, no fool, had agreed verbally with the last part of the argument, but had thought of Nurse Primrose's trim figure and the memory of her own confinements, had smiled a little knowing smile to herself. Still Nurse P. was

95

all right. She took a cautious sip of the coffee, singed her tongue. "What's happened?" Nurse Primrose lit another cigarette from the butt she held in her long white fingers.

"Well, I only came on at five of course, so I didn't see or hear it all, but apparently some of the Shocks on 92 got loose—you know the insulin didn't come up on yesterday's plane?" (Mother Brown hadn't known, but she nodded anyway.) "And they tied up Nurse Little and locked her in a closet. Then they went around smashing and screaming until Hilda," (this was the hawk-faced nurse who had nodded to Mother Brown as she went out) "heard the racket and called the Director. It took ten men from the male wards to calm everything down and Mrs. Little has resigned. Had hysterics when they let her out and she's under sedation at her sister's." Her voice dropped to a frightened and delighted whisper. "You see, they couldn't find her at first, what with her being bound and gagged and locked in the broom cupboard, and she had to lie there listening to all the noise and feet and they kept yelling they'd kill her, but they'd dropped the keys somewhere and couldn't get at her—the Shocks I mean. And then the door had to be broken down before they got her out."

The smell and sound of a steam table came rolling down the hall and Nurse Primrose ballooned her head out at the end of the sentence. "Just leave it at the end of the hall—we'll be there in a minute." She popped back in.

"Mark my words," she said in a soft, satisfied voice, "there'll be hell to pay and probably a lot of State Inspectors down from Albany. If Beatrice Little hadn't resigned. . . ." She left the sentence hanging in the smoky air as she adjusted her cap and washed her hands at the sink. Mother Brown ruminated, digesting the news slowly and carefully, her coffee forgotten. "But how did they get loose in the first place?" she ventured, not quite sure of her ground. After all, these nurses stick together. Kind of a union, you might say.

"Exactly," replied Nurse Primrose, crackling out of the room in a flash of starched skirts and yellow hair. "Somebody—naming no names—slipped up."

Thirty-two women, two and thirty ladies, twenty plus twelve creatures on whom the labels lady, woman, person hang uneasily, sniffed the hot steam and recorded the fact, for they cannot be said to have known anything—day or night, sunrise or evening star, Monday or Friday, winter or spring—that they were about to be fed. The continual muttering in the long ward grew louder, rumbled like a vast stomach as the orderly casually ladled porridge into plastic bowls, tea with milk and sugar into plastic cups, stacked up in small towers the toast that had been made three hours before and margarined hastily before dawn. Had anyone wished for an alternate menu, for tea without milk, with milk but without sugar, with lemon perhaps, or toast without "butter," how in the vast web of their verbal confusion could they have found the right words, and would anything have been changed? Porridge and tea and toast with margarine, vitamins in fluted paper cups. After all, it was nourishing—and there were always scrambled eggs (made from powder kept in huge tins in the kitchens) on Sundays. Could they tell it was Sunday by the scrambled eggs? Could they orient themselves in any way by the different palatal sensation (if there is one) between porridge and scrambled powdered eggs? Nurse Primrose and Mother Brown, each starting at one end of the room, coaxed, wheedled, pushed, shoved, threw the food in the thirty-two mouths, or thirty-one, for Mrs. Marsden in spite of the coaxing, wheedling; in spite of firmness which bordered on physical violence, lay still as a stone, her body rigid under the thin blanket, her hands turned up with the fingers curled like claws. Only the faint pulse at her temple

97

indicated that she was alive and listening. Nurse Primrose smacked her playfully on the cheek. "Little girls that don't eat, won't grow up to be big and strong." Nurse Primrose pried open the thin mouth with her crowbar fingers. Mrs. Marsden bit her. Hard.

Rose cried out, but someone smacked away the scream and no sound came. She ran terrified around a room with no corners, a bare room with no cupboards to hide in, no windows and no door. The man ran after her, clumsily, drunkenly. She dared not turn her head but she could hear the heavy thump, thump of his boots upon the floor and smell the hot whisky breath of his coming. Round and round they ran and the room grew smaller and smaller until there was no room, no room to run, no room in the roomless room. He jerked her to him, flung himself upon her, pressed her against the wall. She could feel his hot metallic mouth upon her face, his tongue thrusting against her teeth. "Rape," she cried frantically—but no sound came and as she opened her mouth his tongue forced its way in and his hot saliva dribbled down her chin. "Well, there's one that'll always open up," said Mother Brown with satisfaction as she moved off down the ward.

An orderly came in to help them make the beds. Together with Aunt Jemima, the Negro trusty, the four of them paired off and worked quickly (roll the patient over, swab the rubber sheet, put on the draw sheet with a quick pull, rolling the body to the other side, plump the pillows, arrange the coarse muslin nightgown—everything stamped with "88" to make sure nothing was lost or sent to the wrong place—the blanket drawn up, the body tucked in and folded precisely, as though it were an important letter— order out of chaos). The nurses retired for a break while

Aunt Jemima, her hooded eyes revealing nothing, immersed in her own particular dream, chuckled musically to herself and began cleaning filth off the iron-grey beds.

Mother Brown plugged in the electric kettle, and Nurse Primrose lit a cigarette. "I don't know," she said thoughtfully, looking at her bandaged finger. "Sometimes I wonder why I don't ask for a transfer. They think we have it easy up here—all these dear little old ladies and all in bed—but I'm sick of the smell of shit," (Mother Brown winced inwardly. She always referred to it as "Number Two") "and bed sores and trying to jolly up a lot of vegetables." She stared at her finger. "Sometimes I think I'd like to quit the whole deal and get married again, but I suppose that's the same thing really—work your fingers to the bone—except you don't get paid for it."

Mother Brown clucked sympathetically. "What you need, my dear, is a holiday or a little trip. A change is as good as a rest they always say." She wondered if she should show Nurse Primrose the brochures, take her mind off her troubles—probably just her period—what's she got to worry about on her pay and at her age? She decided against it and sipped her coffee in what she hoped was a sympathetic manner.

Nurse Primrose patted her yellow curls and blew a smoke ring. "I suppose that's it. Of course it's really the responsibility that cripples me. All this book work, signing for drugs, check and double check, and those bitches from the Grey Ladies waltzing in every week with their crap about 'brightening up a dreary life' and 'musical afternoons' and that kook doctor hanging around with his 'while there's life there's hope' jazz. Sometimes," she said, looking at Mother Brown with her doll-baby eyes, "I envy you PNs. *You're* not responsible if one of the old dears falls out of bed and breaks her hip. *You* don't have to talk to the relatives if one of them kicks the bucket. I wouldn't be surprised," she said spitefully, "if that PN on 92, what's-her-name, your friend—didn't have something to do with all the hoo-hah last night. Didn't tie 'em down tight enough or something. But *she* didn't get locked in the cupboard—oh no!"

Feathers ruffling, Mother Brown said icily, "My *acquaintance*—" she underlined the word with the tip of her pink tongue "—my acquaintance, Cynthia Goodwood, to whom I've no doubt you refer, is a highly trained practical nurse. I'm quite sure she. . ."

"Forget it," said Nurse Primrose. "I was only being bitchy." Mother Brown accepted the apology with a hurt nod of her head, but their relationship was cool for the rest of the day.

Eleanor La Douce danced the shimmy in New Orleans with a sailor named Joe. Eleanor, the sweet young thing, danced the shimmy on Canal Street with a sailor named Tom, a sailor named Dick, and Harry the drummer who sold ladies' lingerie and told her tales of tall mountains in the West and tall tales of buildings in New York. Eleanor shimmied and shook with longing. Eleanor strutted and stuck her little bottom out. "Gimme a break, sister," said Harry, Tom and Dick. "My last night in port," whispered the sailor whose name she had forgotten. "How much you willing to pay?" said Eleanor, and she and Tom and she and Dick and she and Harry and the sailor shimmied across the floor and through the beaded curtain at the rear. "Has it come to this?" shrieked Eleanor La Douce, as she rummaged in her pillowcase with frantic hands. "You have stolen my jewels, my château on the Loire, my baby with the raven curls. Whores, villains, hags and harpies." She spat a mouthful of feathers into the air where they floated dreamily onto the green floor.

You are wrong, you philosophers, we are not the sum of

all our yesterdays, but the product of all the tomorrows which never came. Wrapped in our dreams we only wake to yesterday and madness and damnation.

Mother Brown, somewhat surprised at her boldness, announced, and did not ask, that she would take her lunch at 11.30. The idea of the cold walk across the compound made her wish she had packed a lunch, but, hugging her black plastic bag full of Florida oranges and palm trees and a pleasant breeze from the sea, she ventured forth, the cruel wind waiting for her just outside the door. Head down, she waddled briskly toward the canteen. Cynthia was already there, her little finger crooked daintily around a chipped and flowered teacup. Mother Brown picked up a plastic tray and took her place in line.

"I suppose you've heard about last night?" asked Cynthia, taking a dainty sip of tea. "Yes," replied Mother Brown rather curtly, her mind on other things. She attacked her stew, chewing the meat with difficulty and pleasure. The warm food made her feel more cheerful, and as she pushed her plate to one side and began on the cottage pudding, she smiled at Cynthia, whose voice had been tinkling away for some time.

"Well, it's nothing to smile about, my dear. You wouldn't have liked it to have happened to you."

"But it didn't happen to you, did it?" The words came out muffled in crumbs and custard.

"It didn't, but it might have. I tell you, I've been feeling *queer* all day, and could only take tea and toast for lunch." She looked accusingly at her friend's tray. Dropping her voice to a whisper, she leaned across the scarred table to Mother Brown, squeezing her words out carefully, like toothpaste.

"You-know-who asked me to work the night shift yesterday, but I said, 'No thank you, dearie, not I, I have social commitments this evening and cannot possibly get back here by midnight.' " Cynthia was fond of her social commitments, although their nature had not as yet been revealed to her new friend. " 'I realize,' I said, 'that I am relatively new here, and only a lowly PN, but the Goodwoods are not used to being pushed around. The Goodwoods,' I said to her, 'practically own the bank in East Orange, New Jersey.' " Believing, by now, that she really had said all this, her thin face was flushed with righteous indignation. "And if I had *stayed* —!" She gave a delicate shudder. "I feel a migraine," (she pronounced it mee-grain) "coming on. I know I shall have a sick headache by tonight, just *thinking* about it. Perhaps," she said tentatively, "I should do what George and Eunice have been begging me to do all along and move in with them." She looked as though she might cry. Mother Brown seized her opportunity. "What would you think," she offered tentatively, "of coming to Florida or California with me? A few more months and I should have enough to put a down payment on a cottage, and with Harry's pension and my social security I think I'll have enough to live on. Naturally both kids want me to live with them when I quit, but I think young people should be by themselves, don't you?"

"Oh, I *agree*," replied Mrs. Goodwood thoughtfully, as she turned the idea around, examining it for flaws as one might examine a ripe peach or a cantaloupe. One could almost see her picking it up and smelling it. "But Florida—I don't know. So many Jews down there, aren't there, and of course there are my social commitments to consider. And the children would be *devastated*, if their Mama went so far away."

Mother Brown patted her bag, then glanced at the clock. "Well, you think it over. I've got some lovely brochures from different places—but of course I can always find someone else. I just thought, seeing as how you don't like it here very much, and with your husband having passed over, you might feel a bit lonely and at loose ends."

"Oh I'm never *lonely*," interjected Cynthia with a tinkling laugh suggestive of too many, rather than too few, acquaintances. "Still, it might be nice. A change and all that. This climate is certainly bad for my sinus. The doctors' bills I've had to pay for drainage!"

"I'll tell you what," said Mother Brown casually, picking up her coat and adjusting her galoshes, "why don't you come around to my place some night and we'll have a cup of tea and a chat about it. That is, if your social commitments would allow it." Cynthia glanced sharply at her friend's face, but Mother Brown was the picture of innocence as she fastened her plastic rain scarf over her cap.

"Well, I *couldn't* get away this evening, but perhaps tomorrow night?" Mother Brown left her two of the most attractive brochures and her address as they parted at the elevator. The aluminum Christmas tree, exotic and immortal, shimmered gaily in the hall. But Mother Brown was again lost beneath the palms and failed to give it the attention it deserved.

A male nurse, virginal yet virile in his white uniform, travelled downward, passing Mother Brown between the third and second floors. In one hand he carried a large tin can, under his arm a crudely wrapped brown-paper parcel. He hated working in the OR at any time, but this morning had been terrible. The two doctors, like second-rate comedians, with their endless stories of the golf club. And that kike doctor, Weinstein, was the end, with his bit about the daughter and her private dance. Think they're pretty cool—donate their time and collect it back on the income tax. Charity. Services for one amputation and one. . . . Usual fee. What would the usual fee amount to? Something in three figures anyway. Not nice to think about, though, all that chopping off of this and that. The RCs have to keep it all, I think. Can't stand up at Judgment Day if so much as a toe is missing. Still (he brightened), he'd drop these off on his way over to lunch. That fat-assed bitch in pathology would have a treat. "Listen, sweetheart," he'd say to her, "which would you rather have, the drumstick or the breast?" Whistling, he got out.

Dinner consists of minced spam and mashed potatoes, custard-powder custard—and tea with milk. Everything minced and mashed, chopped and creamed to facilitate its easy mastication by tired or toothless jaws. Equality and custard-powder custard for all. Mother Brown and the orderly move efficiently up and down the rows. Thirty-two old ladies in rows of eight. But one extra bowl, for Mother Brown, taking no chances, never pauses by the bed of Mrs. Marsden. Aunt Jemima scoops up the extra dinner with her fingers, squatting on her haunches in the corner. "White trash," she mutters, "goddamned white trash." But whether this referred to the food or something else she does not say. Steam trolley rolls off on its rubber-soled feet and Nurse Primrose returns, flushed and pretty from the cold, to give the afternoon sedation. Then the recreation room is tidied, although it is never used on 88. Visitors' Day, and you never know who might peek in. On one wall of the room is a reproduction of Van Gogh's *Starry Night*; across from it a dusty print, slightly out of focus, of a young girl with a muff. The walls are the colour of milky tea and porridge, a colour not recommended by the best interior decorators, but cheap and serviceable, the colour of No-Hope and muddy rivers. An empathetic colour and perhaps more suitable than the state would understand or realize. There are a few benches running along the walls, as though an amateur performance might be about to begin, and one or two sofas with sagging springs covered with faded chintz. Here the potted plants will be placed at night, and the cut flowers, pushed anyhow into jam jars or the occasional, donated, vase, will wither and fade in the damp, overheated air. The flowers and plants sometimes would be returned to the ward the next morning or, more often than not, would stand neglected and unnoticed until the next Visitors' Day (Monday Wednesday Friday four to five and by special permission of the Director in cases of extreme emergency). Unnoticed, except by an old Negro woman, who would shuffle in when no-one was looking and reach out tentative and trembling hands toward the blooming memory of warmth and colour and long ago. Recreation room—but why should we be concerned with recreation in the case of thirty-two old ladies? They would neither understand nor appreciate. Better left in their beds, where they can bloom like hothouse flowers amid their fantasies of past and future. Mother Brown closed the door behind her as she went out.

The visitors leaked in, not very many, for the weather was cold. Not very many ever, for the ladies were old. They deposited their offerings at the Staff Room and went shyly and slowly into the ward. What, after all, does one say to a crumpled face, a blank or furious stare? "Hello, Mother. Well, here we are again. Everything all right? Can you hear me, Mother? Are they treating you well? She looks well, doesn't she, Dad?" Conversation trickles off into little drops of "hem" and "well, well, well." How does one converse with madness? For the sane it is impossible, and the insane do not care about each other. "Well, I think she knew we were there," they say hesitantly to Nurse Primrose as they shrug their way back down the hall. "You'll tell her we came, won't you?" "Certainly," replies the painted and professional smile. "I'm sure she appreciates your visit." She hurries them along with her cheerful, clattering chatter. The occasional priest or minister. The occasional minister's wife. "Come unto me all ye that labour and are heavy laden. . . ." A few prayers—a feeling of having done all one can. Perhaps a word of remembrance after the Sunday sermon. Mentioning no names of course. "Whew," says Nurse Primrose, lighting her cigarette, "I'm glad that's over." The wet shoes and boots have left puddles of melted snow along the rows and down the corridor. She frowns at this disorder.

Mother Brown took off her galoshes and stood them carefully on the classified section of yesterday's paper. She changed her stockings and turned up the thermostat. Waddling across the doily-covered room in her carpet slippers, she went into the little kitchen, lit the gas under the kettle, and took a package of birdseed from the pantry shelf. Carefully she opened the cage, and the little bird, head on one side, peered at her inquisitively and hopped out onto her thick finger. "There's a good boy," she said, and with her free hand she drew out the soiled paper and the empty cup. "Did you miss me?" she crooned, admiring his pretty feathers and bright eyes. The bird flew over to the mantelpiece and perched below a faded picture of a young woman and man on their wedding day. The woman was plump and coyly smiling. The man was thin, and not much taller than his partner. He looked as though something had disagreed with him. Holding a silver paper horseshoe, they stared fixedly at Mother Brown as she cleaned the cage and put fresh water in the little cup. "What do you think, Petey?" she said lovingly, "I've brought you a present." And from her handbag she produced a little mirror which she hung by a string from the top of the cage. She put the bird back gently, fastened the door, and sat down with a cup of tea before the television set. She wondered sleepily, before the sound came on, if Cynthia had a canary. "The children will be devastated!" Still, Cynthia *was* refined and it would cut down on the mortgage. She supposed Cynthia would want the property under a joint name. Well, they'd have to see about that. Wonder if Cynthia has an account of her own. Must find everything out. Wouldn't do to get mixed up with her unless the whole thing was clear. The picture on the television screen attracted her attention and she forgot Cynthia in the excitement of her program.

Eleanor La Douce, her fingers busy, quickly and gleefully braided strips of bed sheet into a long, firm plait. The night nurse dozed over her *True Confessions* as Eleanor scrambled out of the room, her nightshirt flapping crazily around her skinny legs. She climbed on top of the washbasin and quickly and efficiently hanged herself from the steel light fixture. Swaying gracefully, as though to an old and lovely melody, Eleanor waltzed slowly toward the waiting arms of General La Douce.

Mother Brown turned heavily once and went back to her cottage. Hands tucked under her fat cheeks, she dreamed of oranges and slept the sleep of the just.

AQUARIUS

They had been warned what to expect; yet the explosion—
what else could you call it?—and the quantities of water
which leapt at them—for as the whale descended the water
did, indeed, seem to leap, as though it had almost taken on
the shape, or at least the strength, of the great beast which
had violated its calm—there was a collective "aaahh" from
the little group of spectators, and a band of elementary-
school children drew in closer to their teacher and shrieked
in fearful delight.

"Brian, Daniel," called out the honeyed, public voice of
the teacher, "Settle down now; come away from the side."

The man started, as if he had heard a voice calling to him
from a dream. He felt disoriented, his glasses spattered with
water—as though he were looking out from the lower port-
holes of the whale pool, not in and down from outside—
and his head still echoed to the sound of the whale's re-
entry into the pool. And disoriented in another way as well,
for something had happened to him as the whale leapt up
toward the sound of the keeper's whistle: like the water, he,
too, had felt the shape and thrust of all that energy and had
been strangely thrilled by it and strangely envious. Standing
there now, still only vaguely aware of the schoolteacher,
the children, the other spectators, blinking as he rubbed his
glasses clean, terribly conscious of his thin body and his pale,
scholar's hands, he felt abandoned, cast down from some

unimaginable height of strength and brute beauty and thrust. Wished, for a moment, to be one of the children who could close up, like delicate petals, around the tight bud of their teacher's serenity. He felt his separation from the whale. "O Ile leape up to my God," he remembered, "who pulles me downe?"

As if in answer he heard his wife give a low laugh and murmur something to her neighbour, an American who was worriedly examining the water-splashed lens of his camera and paying no attention to the whale who was now circling the pool, faster and faster, just below the surface of the water. Occasionally a brief island of dark, rubbery back would rise up above the surface and then disappear again, as the whale plunged deeper and deeper into the heaving water. The attendant, perched on his little platform like a circus artist, explained through a hand mike that the whale could reach speeds of up to 30 miles an hour. Mentally he went round and round with the rushing whale, faster and faster, five, ten, fifteen, twenty—he riding the slippery back as though it was the easiest thing in the world, waving his hand to Erica as he passed, casually, as one might wave to an old, almost forgotten friend seen suddenly from a taxi window; then up and up with the whale, out away from the blue water of the pool, which burned upward after them like transparent, ice-blue fire. A triumph against gravity, captivity, everything. "O Ile leape up to my God."

Erica laughed again. Before the performance began she had moved around to the other side of the pool, almost directly under the platform so that she could be in front of the whale as it leapt. He took off his glasses once more, nervously, for he did not need his eyes to see her: long hair tied back artful carelessly with a bright silk scarf, the top button of her cardigan undone, a mannerism he had observed in her for almost twenty years. He knew the shape of her neck as it rose from the cardigan, and the texture of that neck, with its tiny orange mole, like a rust spot, and the texture of her pale, coarse hair. She would be smiling up at the attendant, of whom she had already asked one or two extremely intelligent questions, amused no doubt by the boy's look of amazement and respect. How could *he* know the way her mind worked, or the extraordinary talent she had for seeming to know more than she really did. He had watched her leaf quickly through the paperback on whales which had been on display in the souvenir shop as they came in. But the boy was not to know this, or to know that years before she had typed for him an article on the reality factor in *Moby Dick*. She would look up at him, leaning back a little, and ask her questions with an air of polite apology, as though only too aware that *everyone* knew the answer except her; and the attendant (or museum guide or gallery official) would regard her with a kind of wonder—as if he had heard a flower speak. Yet sex was not really her game—not in these casual encounters at any rate; she simply wanted, had to be, always, on the side of the professionals.

And that, he thought, (his mind reflecting, ruminating, while his body still unconsciously swayed slightly in a circle, in time to the rhythm of the whale), was precisely where he had failed her. A serious poet—a new Eliot if not a wild, new, apocalyptic bard—was one thing; a scholar who wrote poetry for a hobby was quite another. What was this fellow's name? Perry or Percy—something like that. The little mini-skirted girl had announced him at the beginning of the show. Something Frenchified and out of keeping with his T-shirt and sneakers and buckets of raw herring. What had his mother been thinking of when she gave her son that name? Perhaps she hoped he'd grow up to be a poet. His name should have been Harry or Dan or even just Red.

"Now I'll get Skana to give me a kiss," the boy said, descending from his perch and standing next to Erica, but in front of the low glass breakwater. He blew his whistle twice.

The whale stopped circling immediately and sped over toward her master, lifting her great blunt head up toward his inclining cheek. They touched and the spectators "aaahhed" again. Then the young man held up a fish directly over the whale's head, so that her mouth gaped open and her 44 teeth, blunt and sawdust-coloured ("George Washington must have looked like that when he smiled," he thought irreverently) were exposed. The boy patted her on the head and gave her the herring. She thrust her head up again and the audience duly chuckled. He gave her another fish and another friendly pat.

Again the watching man felt a strange thrill of identification and envy. There was nothing patronizing in the boy's attitude: he and the whale were a team—they complemented one another. The boy explained that the teeth were used only for holding and grasping. The man felt his tongue move almost involuntarily in his mouth, trying to imagine the tactile sensation of a mouth full of those quaint, wooden-looking molars, trying to imagine the stress of those molars against something they had chosen to grasp and hold. And suddenly he remembered the feel of Erica's teeth that first time, and how something had willed him, just for a moment, to set his teeth against her determined seeking, a something that had been almost immediately forgotten in the great conflagration of his desire.

Tipping the rest of the bucket into the water, the attendant thanked them all for coming, switched off the mike and prepared to walk away. The older man, on the other side of the pool, watched his wife touch the boy lightly on the arm (just one more intelligent question for the road). The man moved back toward the door where he stood idly, used to waiting, rubbing his index finger against his thumb and still feeling that terrible sense of loss. He decided he would have to come again, without her, and try to define more explicitly what it was he really wanted from the whale. For he wanted something, that much he was sure of: maybe a new poem; maybe only reassurance; maybe something more. As his wife turned he noticed that her sweater and the front of her slacks were wet. He was annoyed—not because she would insist upon going home, but rather because she would stay, moving unconcernedly and triumphantly amongst the curious. And she would have a story to tell the children or her friends.

"My dears, I was nearly *swallowed up*, like a female Jonah or Pinocchio or someone!" and still later he would watch her bury her face in the wrinkled clothes, inhaling the faint aroma of her triumphal morning, before she tossed them in the hamper. Suddenly he was thoroughly disgusted and decided to ignore her smile and wave (was he mistaken, or was the redheaded young man beginning to look just a trifle bored?), moved out with the last of the stragglers, back into the aquarium proper. Now just Erica and the boy were out there by the pool. Erica and the boy, and somewhere below them, Skana, the killer whale. The children, pulled along by their teacher's authority, as though by an earnest tug, had long since disappeared to look at other things.

Had Erica experienced a genuine thrill when the whale leapt? She might have, once. And the creature was powerful and female, sleek and strangely beautiful—like the woman herself. He had always associated her, too, with the sea—because of her name and her pale blond hair and cold blue eyes. When he first loved her he even saw himself as something Scandinavian, a Siegfried, and exulted in her restrained, voluptuous power and her ice-blue eyes. ("Except for that one moment," he thought, "when I set my teeth

against her thrusting tongue. Strange I had forgotten that.")
Later, because the Siegfried role was not his true self-idealization, he allowed himself to be mothered by her. She had been lonely when he met her and he sensed she needed to be needed. She had taught him all he ever knew of sex (he never asked her where she got her knowledge), and cooked for him thick homemade soups in a huge copper kettle she had discovered at the Salvation Army shop. And she it was, too, who willed him to be a poet, encouraged him, made do with bare floors and tipsy, mismatched chairs. She was afraid of nothing, neither accidents nor poverty nor death. "I am terrified only of the mediocre," she told him once, and he had thrilled to hear her say it, wrapped in his old dressing gown, drying her long, pale hair by firelight. It had all been heaven then: the thick soups, the crazy chairs, the bottles of cheap wine, the crusty bread, the basement flat which—with her incredible luck—had contained a fireplace and a priceless, abandoned, Hudson Bay "button blanket" on the wall.

She had seemed the ultimate in womanhood, the very essence of female with her full, Northern figure and her incredible self-assurance and practicality, so different from the flat-bosomed, delicate foolishness of his own well-bred female relatives. And what excited him most, although he would never have admitted it, and indeed felt actually ashamed, at first, even to himself, was a certain sluttishness about her—the top button of her inevitable cardigan always left undone or missing, her legs crossed thigh over thigh, quite casually—his mother and sisters had always crossed only at the ankles. Her strange desire to make love when she had her period. But even more than this, the things she said. Once, in the very early days, she had run her hands along his thin flanks and kissed him there and laughed with delight at his thinness.

"I will fatten you with kisses," she had cried. And indeed, he could feel his body firmer, fuller, where she had traced her fingers and her lips. Then suddenly she had grabbed his head between her hands, kneading his scalp in her beautiful capable fingers and licking his face with her warm tongue— as though he were her kitten. He had already grown a beard, even then, and she had whispered, rubbing her cheek against him, "Your beard is all soft and springy—like pubic hair." So that his face flamed up at her bold words and for days he found it difficult to go outside, to expose his face to others, so deep was his sensual delight, so wanton his happiness.

He walked slowly along the illuminated displays and admired the care that had been taken with the lighting and accessories of each exhibit. Shells, sand, gravel, anemones and kelp: like with like or near-like. Everything conspired to give the illusion of a real beach or cove or lake or ocean home. It was spacious, tasteful, and most effective. Yet he felt cold and claustrophobic in the aquarium, as though it were he who was shut in, not the fish and other specimens. An iguana observed him wipe his forehead with a cynical, prehistoric eye; the octopus flattened his disgusting suckers against the harsh reality of glass; the alligators slept with tourists' pennies clinging to their heads and backs. The wolf-eel, however, looked as if a mere quarter-inch of glass would not stop *him*. "Fishermen will sometimes cut the line," he read, "rather than handle this fish." He believed it. The thick, sensuous lips, the small eyes, the conical front teeth convinced one that here was evil incarnate, a creature who would not hesitate to attack. Erica, he thought, would have laughed loudly and squatted down with her nose against the glass, grinning, daring the eel to pit his aggression against hers.

He read that they had been captured up to a length of eight feet. Taller than a man. Imagine finding *that* on the end of your line! Where was Erica?

Had it all been a trick, her violent lovemaking which somehow was in keeping with her Nordic looks—a love like waterfalls and mountain torrents, a love that suggested terrible deeds to be done for love or hate or kinship, quite in contrast to his own, soft, dreamlike attitude. But in those early days she could rouse him up until he forgot that he was thin and lank and weak of vision; and he would take into himself her passion and her fury until the little flat rang with their cries, like the harsh, triumphant cries of eagles or giant sea-birds, and he thought his heart would burst from excitement and exertion. He was transformed, transfigured, under her incredible shaping hands. He entered her as Siegfried leaping through a wall of fire. He lived.

But she had never been able to rouse him to the heights of poetry. All his best work was done before he met her. He felt, now, that this was as much a failure in her as it was in him. Vampire-like she had renewed herself with his passion; and then, having won him and worn him out, she had begun to cast him off as worthless—to shed him as a snake might shed its winter skin. On the strength of the acceptance of his first book they had married. When his second group of poems had been repeatedly rejected she initiated her first affair. Her children, tall and blond like her, came to take the place of the poems she had urged him to create, just as her anonymous lovers (sometimes he could even smell them on her skin—what a bitch she was!) had taken his place in her body. It was as if, after the first wild, dreamlike years when he made poetry all day and love all night (she blond and buxom, like a seventeenth-century genre painting then in her spotless kitchenette, with the first child, round and rosy-cheeked, hugging the backs of her knees; and at night a rich dim honey-coloured nude), it was as if

116

she had peered down into a well, assessed the amount of liquid remaining there, and then, with a practical shrug of her shoulders, had shut up the cover and gone elsewhere for her water.

And the water in the well became stagnant, scum-covered, undrinkable. Noises from outside filtered down, as distant as summer thunder—and as deceptive. When he tried to write about his anguish he found that he was no longer interested in the old preoccupations with beauty and order and truth. He could only dryly mock himself, forsaken merman, and mocking, failed again. The money from his mother's estate, the small advance from his first book: these vanished even more quickly than his dreams. He had always taught part-time, to guarantee they wouldn't starve. Now Erica suggested coldly that he apply for a full-time job; and he, with a sinking heart, accepted his defeat. He began to see himself as a man walking slowly toward the exact centre of a low-walled bridge. He had not yet reached the centre but it would draw him on and on and someday—over. He taught reasonably well, but he was always tired; and the mountains just beyond the city, mountains which had always thrilled him, began to oppress and even frighten him. They seemed to be growing larger, hemming him in against the sea. A worrisome phrase kept running through his mind: "with one stride came the dark." Often, lately, he had had to leave his class for a few minutes and light a cigarette in order not to weep. Sometimes he wished that Erica were dead.

"Open water fishes," he read, "are darker above than below." To fool the enemy. Not the wolf-eel though. But is an eel a fish? And where was Erica?

But the paleness might be a camouflage, not a symptom. Like Erica's pale hair and honeyed skin. "The good heroines of the Western world are always blond and fair," he

117

thought, "like Erica." But the Vikings were blond too, or red-haired and fair. The "Rus." And destructive. Ravenous in appetite if not appearance. "The fish's pallor is a mask," he said to no-one in particular. Where was Erica? Not making love to the young attendant, even if he had turned out to be a novice marine biologist. Oh, no. Her taste ran now to higher things: historians, art critics, young writers (especially poets) on fellowships. A boy in a T-shirt, whose hands smelled of herring, would no longer physically excite her. And he remembered again, "The only thing I'm afraid of is the mediocre."

He hesitated in front of the Mozambique Mouth-Breeder, attracted by its name. Were the young fry snug or struggling—which?—behind the closed gate of their mother's teeth, coming awake in the slimy warmth of their mother's mouth? How did she eat without swallowing them? How catch her food? Or did she not eat at all while she carefully manoeuvred the African waters, aware of her incredible mouthful. He had always felt the aloneness of his own infant children, had carried the first strapped to his back in a harness of his own devising—his unique example of mechanical inventiveness. He had told her it was to save money—for he had been slightly afraid of her, even then—and she had been very proud of him. They had been, he reflected now, naïvely picturesque as they padded along the busy streets on Friday mornings. Friday had always been a day of reorganization for them, of doing the weekly shopping and changing the bed and answering any letters. Later she would wash her long blond hair while he worked on the latest poem, the child asleep on his lap. They were poetic about their poverty too, acting out the romantic role of the artist and his barefoot wife, for she had given up shoes (at least indoors) long before it was fashionable to do so. And had named their first child Darius. It was all so transient:

money and fame were not beneath them but just ahead of them; and they accepted their poverty with style and good grace because they knew it was only temporary, accepted it the way the wise accept the bitter winter, knowing of the spring.

But it was not to be. Wherever he sent his work it came back rejected: first (on the strength of his book) accompanied by a kind and sometimes helpful letter, later by the now-familiar oblong of paper or card, clipped to the upper left-hand corner. Thank you for your submission. Thank you for giving us the opportunity to read. . . Thank you but no thank you. He couldn't believe it. Eventually he had to. Once he had received his manuscript back with a letter, quite a long one, only to discover it was from a fellow-struggler who had received the two manuscripts clipped together under a single message of dismissal. The writer of the letter was ironic and amused; but he was furious, and felt publicly exposed in front of this stranger from Brick church, New Jersey, USA, who had also offered inadequate libations to the gods. He even thought of writing to the editors. Surely there was an ethical principle involved? But in the end he didn't—it was too humiliating.

And so, finally, she took a lover and he a full-time job. That night he had shaved off his beard in a fury of bitterness —a mask for the wrong dance. Why had he ever let it grow again?

He looked at his watch. Where the hell was she? Surely she couldn't be *still* talking to that boy. And he was bored with all these strange, slippery creatures that surrounded him, lost in their own dream-like, antiseptic coffins. The vague bubbling noise and shifting light had given him a headache. And it was nearly lunchtime. She would want to go to Chinatown and have a meal, knowing he hated the kind of restaurant she always chose—the dirtiest, tackiest one she had not yet tried, with peeling, musty oilcloth-covered tables and slimed menus, where the lukewarm soup was served in heavy, cracked white bowls and the smells from the kitchen made him gag. "Ahh," she would exclaim, giving him a wicked smile, "Now this isn't one of your bloody tourist traps, my darling; this is the real thing!" She would enjoy watching his discomfort, would eat quickly and with great show of appetite, scooping the liquid up toward her bent, blond head, almost lapping it up like a cat, in her haste to get on to the next course (which was usually a revolting and expensive something that was not on the regular menu), afterward licking the film of grease from her upper lip with one sweep of her tongue. He couldn't bear it, not today. He'd have to find some excuse.

She always laughed when he told her such places disgusted him—"You weren't always so discriminating!" And it was so. He felt a physical revulsion now for anything that smacked of foreignness or dirt or unclean, hidden things. Three nights before she had unexpectedly thrown her heavy, blue-veined thigh over his as she was getting into bed, and had cried out in triumph, "Look how thin you are getting! I could crush you!" And his sudden leap of desire had been quenched by a smudge of lipstick on her teeth. He couldn't bear it if someone forgot to flush the toilet.

He was beginning to feel a little giddy, and turned back toward the fish, as if seeking some answer or relief. Perhaps she had simply gone home without him? She liked to mock him, now, in front of their nearly-grown children, and she had to work out the story of her wet clothes. "Darlings, I was nearly drowned! This morning—at the aquarium— you nearly lost me!" She was afraid of nothing and she despised him. The Pacific prawns, delicate as Venetian glass or transparent drinking straws, moved gently just ahead of him. How beautiful. He wondered at their strange reversal of sex and envied them their beauty and, for a long moment, their eternally ordered environment. He and Erica had had a reversal too—but ugly, unnatural. She had dominated him always, more and more, had emasculated his body and his soul and having done so, cast him aside, an empty shell. Even this trip to the aquarium was her suggestion. He had wanted to cross the bridge and drive out to Horseshoe Bay, have a quiet lunch beside the water. It appeared to him now that even the exhibits he had seemed to choose at random had been chosen first by her, as living illustrations of her strength and his incredible, female, weakness.

He remembered how she had told him, captive, everything about her labour during the birth of their third child. Had described it in such detail he had sickened and begged her to desist—this in the semi-private room at the hospital, while the woman in the other bed remained an implied smile behind the plastic curtains. She had raped him—truly —as the Vikings raped their conquered women. And she had desecrated him and everything he dreamed of. That night, while he sat wretchedly with his head between his knees, she talked of herself and the young doctor who assisted her as if they had been lovers who created the child between them. And he had visualized the gloved hands of the doctor reaching forward between her bloody thighs to draw out the thing that was *his*, and had fallen from the chair and onto the coolness of the hospital floor. That story was one of her best ones.

He decided to go home. Let her walk or take the bus. Let her disappear forever. Let her get knocked down by a taxi cab or knocked up by the chairman of the Symphony Committee: it was a matter of indifference to him. But out in the corridor he saw the door to the pool was standing open and felt irresistibly drawn to the dark shadow of the whale, floating down there somewhere below the surface of the water. No-one was about. A bucket of fish and the big pink plastic ball stood ready beneath the empty platform. The red-haired boy was nowhere to be seen. He was vaguely aware, through the glass, of the back of Erica's cardigan and her bright scarf near the counter where they sold the shells.

At the water's edge he hesitated, peering down uncertainly, then stuck his fingers in his mouth and whistled twice, a high, thin sound that came back to him out of his childhood, a sound that would reach down and pierce the heavy blanket of the water and draw the big whale up to him. He inclined his cheek, waiting. "Skana," he whispered, "Skana." But the surface of the pool remained a calm, indifferent blue. The whale did not hear or did not choose to answer.

He got up, slowly, awkwardly, and went to join his wife.

JOSEPH AND HIS BROTHER

Joseph was our cook-steward—a kind of legacy to us from our friends Tom and Sheila who had been out there for two years and had left a few weeks before our arrival. As we bumped up the road from the coast to the university where we were to live, I took his picture out of my passport case again and again—"my" cook-steward. He grinned at me, a handsome, gap-toothed man. "Lucky you," said my English mother-in-law. "Fancy having servants." I looked at his picture again, then out the window. Women in beautiful bright-coloured cloths stepped off the road and stood staring at us as we passed. Ragged children appeared at the edges of villages, shouting and jumping—"Bronie, Bronie, Bronie." Two men, barefoot, their cloths slung over their left shoulder, stood talking seriously at a crossroad. Each had a Singer sewing machine on his head. Joseph spoke English, could read and write a little, was an excellent cook. In the photograph he wore a white sports shirt, not a traditional cloth. He would have his own quarters. I tried to imagine myself giving him orders. The huge trees of the rain forest towered above us on either side. Our children, in spite of warnings about bumps, stood up on the back seat, waving out the window. Lorries honked merrily and sped past us on blind curves, their sides bulging with people. Most had signs painted across the back. "God's Time is Best" "Psalm 100" "Mind Your Own. . . ." Rusty wrecks nearly hidden by giant ferns littered the sides of the road. "Take it slowly at first," said a man on the boat, "Africa can eat you." If we opened the windows the red dust flew in at us, covered our skin and hair, even our eyelashes, like paprika. What were the children feeling? What did they think of all these black people, the heat, the forest through which we were passing? What would they think of a cook-steward? Near the end of the journey, outside the big town where we would do our shopping, I saw scrawled on a blackboard easel, in front of the Agip gas station, these words:

REX 8.30 TONIGHT
PAY UP OR DIE

I clutched my husband's hand. We were surrounded by taxis, lorries, walking figures, noise. The strangeness caught at my throat. Rex. 8.30 tonight. Pay up or die. What if he didn't like us and put something in our food. It was only the next day, when I asked Joseph about the sign, that I found out that Rex was the name of the local cinema. I laughed but was ashamed of my original interpretation. There was a rich smell of baked bread and ground-nuts roasting in the oven.

The white man is ashamed to be afraid of Africa and yet the shame does not completely obliterate the fear. That first night, children asleep under musty-smelling mosquito netting, we lay awake holding hands and listening to the drums. They were faint but seemed to come at us from all directions—dadada/dadada/dadada. Only recently the University watchmen had carried lanterns and bows and arrows. Some strange creature screamed over and over again from a distant tree. We laughed and kissed each other and laughed again. We had arrived to find Joseph standing grinning

124

shyly on the doorstep. The children ran to him at once. "Hello Joseph. Hello. We've brought you presents." He patted each blond head and laughed. Did a cook-steward protect you against the darkness and the drums? Rex. 8.30 tonight. Pay up or die.

Joseph was everything that Tom and Sheila had assured us he would be. At six in the morning he came in from his quarters next door, began peeling and chopping grapefruits and oranges and paw-paw for the morning salad. All the fruits were green here. There was no such thing as yellow lemons or yellow grapefruit or orange oranges. Only the bananas remained their familiar selves, but smaller. Joseph chopped while the kettle boiled, mixed the fruit with a little sugar, then put it in the fridge to chill. (Fridges had locks here—stewards were thieves, the other women told me. You couldn't be too careful.) At six o'clock he brought us up our morning tea. "Cock Cock Cock Cock Cock." He always announced himself instead of knocking. We sat up in bed and listened to the Overseas Service of the BBC. The children woke, rubbed their eyes, ran in for a quick kiss and downstairs to find their beloved Joseph. They sat on the kitchen table eating thick slices of bread and marge while Joseph fried eggs and made toast. "Madame," he called me, my husband, "Master," in spite of all our egalitarian speeches. After breakfast he waited at the side of the road with other stewards and nurse-girls, each with one or more charges, for the little school bus which made the rounds of the compound. The African children taught our children to cry out, as they did, when they spied the driver turning into our road,

MONKEY
BANANA

125

COCOYAM
DRIVER!

MONKEY
BANANA
COCOYAM
DRIVER!

Joseph handed the children carefully up the steps, stood
talking and flirting with Veronica, the nurse-girl next door,
then went to his quarters for a break. At eleven he would
bring me a cup of coffee where I sat writing at the long
dining table, would lean on his broom and accept an offered
cigarette (or rush off to a neighbouring road, if we were
both out, and buy two "Job" or "Tusker for Man" for a
penny from a woman he knew). He wouldn't sit down but
would stand there, barefoot, in the worn khaki shorts and
an undershirt reduced almost to the consistency of gauze,
and he would tell me things. Compound gossip. So and so's
wife was a bad woman, she could not keep a servant. Veronica was a bad girl, or as he put it, "no good at all." He was
negotiating for a new wife, the daughter of one of the market women; he brought gifts of chocolate and money, but
still the mother scorned him. What did I want for dinner?
He had had a wife, and a child as well, but the wife was
carrying on with someone else in her village and when he
went to challenge and accuse her she put something in the
soup that poisoned him—he was sick for a long time, sick
proper. His stomach burned and his mouth was covered
with blisters. He was not lucky with women—in general
he felt that they were no good at all. His wife kept the child
as was the custom here. Now he wore a magic charm around
his neck although he was a Christian. (And sometimes, on
his day off, he would come home late, laughing and singing

126

—we could hear him from our open bedroom windows, stumbling down the steep gravel driveway, another Joseph, a stranger. But always alone, never with a woman. If a Revolution came, would he protect us?) But most of all he told me about his brother. Joseph's brother was a lorry driver on the Cape Coast–Accra road and a great hero to Joseph. The boss of the lorry park was a brother as well, but by a different mother, and much older. It was a good job, if a dangerous one, and the brother had nearly enough saved to buy a sheet-iron roof for his house.

"How is your brother, Joseph?" I would say if the conversation lagged.

"Hey! Madame!" and he would tell me of the latest near accident or adventure. Like Joseph, his brother could read and write and was a fairly regular correspondent. Travellers also arrived from time to time at the kitchen door, asked for Joseph, sat on the back steps eating kola nuts and gossiping before they picked up their loads and continued. To Joseph, his brother lived a life of adventure and thrills. As he told his new tale, our steward's hands would clench with excitement. He would grip an imaginary wheel or use the broom as a stick-shift. The name of the lorry was "God is Backin' Me." The Cape Coast road was the sweetest road in the country, paved proper and with a fine breeze blowing across from the sea. To drive such a run was a prize. Joseph imagined himself up front in the driver's seat, laughing with the mate, honking his horn, scattering women and children, goats, chickens, all manner of lesser creatures, passing inferior lorries on dangerous curves and at equally dangerous speeds. Then, tale ended, he would blink his eyes and laugh and go down into the kitchen to make a salad for lunch. How very unadventurous his life must have seemed, compared to that of his younger brother. Chopping fruit, preparing salad, serving, serving, serving. Servants serve, by definition. For Christmas Joseph wanted a cook's hat, tall, stiffly starched, and a mess jacket. We tried to dissuade him. The children, worried, took his side. The market woman threw his gifts to her daughter in his face. He laughed painfully, leaning on his broom. He wrung chickens' necks on the back stoop after the children had gone to school. Some of the other women had had four, five, seven stewards. They could not cook, they stole, they imported their wives and ragged children. "You don't know how lucky you are." Always water dripping through the filter, more water (already filtered) chilling in the (unlocked) fridge. Beautiful bread, beautiful curries, ground-nut soup, and salads, the children swinging their legs against the kitchen table, saying their teacher was very hard-o, begging ground nuts and stories of Anansi the trickster spiderman who could change himself into a yam, a stick of wood, a sleeping mat. Somehow, with Joseph there, the drums, the poison snakes (Joseph averting his eyes and beating, beating, beating with a stick) the soldier ants, the tsetse flies, the dangers, real or imagined, were kept in check. Joseph would take care of everything from dishes to disasters. "You don't know how lucky you are."

One morning, in his eighth month with us, toward the end of the dry season, when the land is so parched for water you swear that green has gone away forever and tempers flare like matches, Joseph came to me in great distress.

"Please, Madame. I need to return to my village." He held a letter in his hand. In spite of the three-bladed fan overhead, the sweat poured down the backs of my legs and down my arms, leaving wet marks on my paper. Joseph's eyes were bloodshot, as if he were coming down with fever. I was horrified. To leave us now! The temperature in the kitchen, with the gas cooker on, must be well over 100 degrees. I tried to sound sympathetic.

"Why, Joseph, why?"

"My brother, Madame. My younger brother."

"The lorry driver?"

"Yes, Madame. They say he is sick proper."

"Fever?" I said.

He hesitated. I wondered if he were fed up, if the letter was a hoax.

"Yes, Madame."

"What can *you* do?" My voice came out more sharply than I intended.

"Please, I must go."

I fell back on the old feminine excuse that I would have to ask my husband. Joseph agreed. I knew, however, what the answer would be and felt as if I had encountered the reality of Joseph as someone temporary in my life, for the first time.

For lunch we had the usual avocado salad, a bowl of freshly roasted nuts, bread still warm from the oven, a bowl of fruit. Never, now that I might lose it all, had it tasted so good. When the children went up for their nap we sat under the fan, drinking tea, and discussed what it was best to do. Of course we would have to let him go, and as soon as possible.

"But will he come back?" I was half-way through the first draft of a novel. Visions of thieving, incompetent stewards danced in my head.

"I think so. Anyway, blood ties are very strong here— we can't keep him."

Two weeks later he was back. (Two weeks of the gas cylinder running out on me, the children whining for mashed banana "the way Joseph makes it," of stumbling around a kitchen as hot as an inferno, of washing-up—how quickly I had managed to forget the tyranny of housework—of making my coffee break myself.)

"Well, Joseph."

"Eh! Madame!" He went to put his things away and, to my surprise, did not return for a cigarette and a gossip.

"What's wrong with Joseph?" the children asked, worried.

"Why doesn't he laugh?"

On his day off he came back very drunk, singing and stumbling. The drums seemed closer now, and louder too. "What do you think has happened?" We whispered to one another, lighting a candle against the darkness. "Has the brother died?"

On Monday I could stand it no longer. After the school bus had left I walked next door to Joseph's quarters—something I had never done before—with a package of cigarettes in my hand. He was sitting outside under the paw-paw tree, just sitting and staring.

"Joseph," I said, "I am your friend" (and yet wondering at the same time if that were so). "Is your brother dead?" He opened his eyes. We were the same age, Joseph and I, and yet for a minute I saw him as an old, old man.

"Dead? No Madame, my brother is not dead."

I sat down on the grass beside him—the tree shading us from the growing heat of the sun—and offered him a cigarette. Absently he took two and lighting one, stuck the other behind his ear.

"Eh Madame," he said, expelling a great cloud of smoke, "No-one knows the story of tomorrow's dawn."

"What is it, what has happened?"

That was ten years ago and yet I remember that moment, that morning, as clearly as if it were yesterday, this morning, half an hour ago. I remember the prickly grass on my bare legs and the heat, and the poinsettia hedge in the distance. I remember a butterfly as red as wine and the sound of some-

130

body pounding fou-fou in the distance. I remember the dress I wore and Joseph's smooth brown skin and the unripe paw-paws hanging above our heads. Was I ever there or was it all a dream?

Joseph's brother was driving his lorry from Cape Coast to Techiman on a certain Monday night. He picked up, at an intermediate town, a woman passenger. She was attractive but dressed, rather oddly, in black velvet. Joseph's brother put her on the front seat between himself and his mate. It was very late and the lorry was nearly empty. He judged her to be a prostitute and told her that he loved her. He suggested taking her on to Techiman to sleep with him. The mate said that she declined but that he nevertheless sped through the town of her destination without stopping. He let the mate out at the junction to his village and went on to Techiman where he spent the night with her in a rest-house, even though he was supposed to return the lorry to the lorry-park. In the morning, instead of returning to his step-brother as usual, he took the lorry and the woman to Dixcove, right off his beat. She left him and he returned to Techiman, giving his step-brother boss only a vague and unsatisfactory account of his behaviour. A few days later, on a holiday, some fellow villagers, also working in Techiman, approached the lorry driver and said one of them had died and they would like him to carry the corpse home to his ancestral village, a distance of about 250 miles. At first he refused for a corpse is dangerous cargo—the spirit of the dead man, if uneasy, can wreck the lorry. They begged and begged, however, and finally he consented so the funeral party set off. But on the way he suddenly stopped the lorry and told his mate that he could see the woman in black velvet. He shouted to her—"Ho! If you are going, it is I who will go with you!" No-one else could see her, yet he was restrained with great difficulty and persuaded to drive

131

on and deliver the corpse to his village. The same thing happened the following Sunday on his usual run. He told the mate he saw the woman in black velvet; again he called out, "If you are going, I will go with you!"

When an elder of the family was consulted (for the mate could not keep the story to himself and reported to the step-brother) the old man said that the spirit of the corpse was troubling Joseph's brother and that such a young driver should not have been made to drive such a heavy load. He made some medicine for the young man to bathe in.

The next morning he appeared quite well and set off on the regular run between Cape Coast and the capital. Past yellow taxis and rickety tro-tros, walking figures, enormous head loads like strange crowns upon their heads, the palm trees bowed down, the silver backsides of their leaves gleaming in the sun. Copra set out to dry. Billboards advertising Club beer, the Weekly Lotto, Queen Elizabeth gin, Agip gas, the Atomic-Paradise Nite Club. Past the town of Elmina with its castle-cum-fort where 200 years ago the Director General (Dutch) had drunk himself mad out of boredom and locked his chief merchant in a cage, like a wild beast, throwing bones through the bars, from time to time, for him to chew, while the civet cats prowled in the courtyard (Kaatplaz) down below. Yet just beyond the town he again saw the woman in black velvet, shouted, stopped the lorry and be-gan to weep. The mate found another driver in the next town and by the time they reached Cape Coast Joseph's brother was talking "basa-basa" or crazy, and the step-brother took him to the mission hospital. They could find nothing physically wrong with him and he was taken home to his village. That is when Joseph received the letter. He sighed.

"He did not know me, Madame. A tall."

For the past week Joseph and his step-brother had taken the younger brother from shrine to shrine, to a succession of fetish priests and medicine men, but there seemed to be nothing that anyone could do. Sadly, Joseph had decided to return to us.

Things were never the same after that day. Although he was as kind and attentive as before, some spark had gone out of Joseph. He laughed rarely and never with his old, high humour. Letters came saying that the brother was now completely mute, that another relative had taken over the driver's job on the lorry named "God is Backin' Me." On one occasion the step-brother and some other relations had taken him to Accra for a few days, in the hopes of seeing a doctor. While they were resting at their lodgings he disappeared. They eventually went to the police who had, in fact, taken him to the mental hospital. But there he made signs that he wanted a pen and paper, wrote his name and temporary address and a request to be taken home. He was pronounced not mad and sent home with his relatives. Within two months he had reverted to childhood and had to be led by the hand. Joseph, sweeping the lounge or listening to the children, brooded on the cruel fate of his brother. He stopped his search for a new wife and we did not dare to tease him.

When the Easter holidays came and I could leave the children with my husband, I offered to drive Joseph down to his village so he could see his brother for himself. I must confess that my motives were not entirely altruistic.

Early one morning we set off, a thermos of ice water in the glove compartment, a few presents for Joseph's relatives tucked in a straw basket. Down we went toward the Coast

133

Road, reversing the route of that strange journey so many months before. At the edge of a town we passed a group of men in the orange-coloured mourning cloth of the region; I tried not to see it as an omen. Joseph hardly spoke the whole way down. When we arrived the brother was sitting composedly in the yard, and I did not notice, until I went to shake hands, that he was in handcuffs and chained to a tree. The relatives stood around us in a circle, hoping we had brought some magic cure that would make the young man well again. "I hear you have been ill," I said. "How do you feel now?" Joseph translated for me, a nervous smile on his lips.

"I feel something knocking in my eyes," said the brother. "Somebody kicked my head. I have written Tamale, Accra, Takordi. One cedi is a hundred pesewas."

"Basa-basa," said the family, apologetically. "Basa-basa." They pointed to their heads.

As for the woman in black velvet, when I questioned him, he said he did not recall her.

I left Joseph there for a few days and returned alone, hurrying to get through the forest before dark and the drums began.

One other thing Joseph told me. His people believe that sexual intercourse with a ghost results in death.

KILL DAY ON THE
GOVERNMENT WHARF

"I only wish," she said, refilling his coffee mug, "that it was all a little more primitive."

The man, intent on his fried bread and tomato, did not hear or chose to ignore the wistfulness in her voice. Mouth full, he chuckled, and then, swallowing, "All what?"

"All *this*," she said impatiently, gesturing toward the inside of the little cabin. They were sitting by the window, having breakfast. It was nine o'clock on a Sunday morning and the sky outside bulged and sagged with heavy bundles of dirty-looking clouds. He wanted to get back out on the water before it rained.

"I thought you liked it here," he said, challenging her with a smile. She was playing games again.

"I do. I love it. I really don't ever want to go back. But," she said, looking at him over the rim of her mug, "seeing that the old man died only a few months later, don't you think it was rather unkind of Fate to have suggested plumbing and electricity to him? I mean," she added with a smile, "also seeing as how we were going to be the reluctant beneficaries of all that expense."

"You may be reluctant," he said, wiping his mouth, "I'm not. I think we were damned lucky myself."

She shrugged and stood up to clear the table, rubbing the small of her back unconsciously. She had acquired a slight tan in the ten days she'd been away and he thought how well she looked. There was a sprinkling of pale greeny-coppery freckles across her nose and along her arms. She looked strong and self-reliant and almost pretty as she stood by the window with the stacked plates in her hand. It was not myth, he thought, or a white lie to make them feel better. Women really do look lovely when they're pregnant. Sometimes she would say to him, quite seriously,

"Tom, do you think I'm pretty?" or

"Tom, what would you say about me if you saw me across the room?"

Her questions made him impatient and embarrassed and he usually ended up by returning some smart remark because he was both a shy and a truthful man. He wished she would ask him now, but he did not volunteer his vision. Instead he got up and said,

"Where's Robert?"

"Right on the porch. I can see him. He has a dish full of oysters and clams and a hermit crab in a whelk shell. He's been fascinated by it for two days now. I didn't know," she added, "that barnacles were little creatures. They've got little hand-like things that come out and scoop the water looking for food."

"Yes, I believe those are actually their feet," he said. "My grandfather told me that years ago. They stand on their heads, once they become fixed, and kick the food into their mouths for the rest of their lives. Now *that's* primitive for you." He drew on his pullover again. "How would you feel if I had another little fish-around before it rains? Then I'll take Robert for a walk and let you have some peace."

"Oh he's all right, except sometimes when he wants to crawl all over me. He's actually better here than at home. Everything excites him. He could live here forever as well."

"You must go back soon," he reminded her gently, "whether you like it or not."

"I don't want to. I hate the city. And I like it better here now," she said, "than later on, when all the summer people come."

"You don't get lonely?"

"No, not at all." She was embarrassed to admit it and irritated he had asked. "I walk and sit and look and read my books at night or listen to the radio. And there's Robert of course. He's become afraid of the dark, though," she said thoughtfully, "I wonder why. He wakes me up at night."

"Weren't you?" he challenged. "I was."

She turned, surprised. She had been of course, but she was a very nervous, sickly child.

"Yes." She stood at the sink, soapy hands held out of the water, poised over a plate, remembering. "I used to lie very still because I was absolutely sure there was someone in the room. If he knew I was awake, or if I should call out, he would strangle me or slit my throat."

"Footsteps on stairs," he said, rolling a cigarette.

"Faces outside windowpanes," she countered.

"And don't forget," he added, "the boy may actually have seen something. A deer, or even the Hooper's dog. I've seen him stand up and pull that curtain back after his nap. Leave the light on." He put the tobacco tin back on the window sill and got up. "Leave the bathroom light on. It won't break us."

"Won't that make him weak?" she cried, "Isn't that giving in to his fears?"

"Not really. He'll outgrow it. I think maybe that kind of strength comes from reassurance." He kissed the back of her hair. "See you later on."

"Bring us back a fish," she said, reminding him of his role as provider, knowing in her heart it was all one to him whether he landed a fish or not. She was jealous of his relationship with the little boat, the oars, the sea. He would

137

come back with a look of almost sensual pleasure on his face.

He went out, banging the door, and she could hear him teasing the little boy, explaining something. She left the dishes to dry and poured herself another cup of coffee. The baby kicked and she patted her abdomen as if to reassure it. Boy or girl, dark or light, she wondered idly but not very earnestly. It was out of her hands, like the weather and the tides. But would she really like to have it out here, maybe alone, with Robert crying from the prison of his crib or huddled at the foot of her bed, marked and possibly scarred forever by the groaning and the blood? Robert had been quick, amazingly and blessedly quick for a first child; the doctor had told her this indicated a rapid labour for the second. In her own way she was shy, particularly about physical things. Could she really go along to old Mrs. Hooper's and ask for help, or accept the possibility of being taken off the Island by one of the local fishing boats, observed by the taciturn, sun-baked faces of the men to whom she would be, if known at all, simply another of the summer folk.

It was easier in the old days, she felt, when there were no choices. She smiled at herself, for Tom, if he had been listening, would have added "and childbed fever, and babies dying, and women worn out before they'd hardly begun." He called her a romantic and accused her of never thinking things through. *He* was the one who could really have survived here without complaint, in the old days. He was the one who had the strength to drag up driftwood from the little rocky beach, and saw it up by hand, and the knowledge that enabled him to mend things or to start a perfect fire every time. He hauled his rowboat down to the wharf below their place on a triangular carrier he'd made from old wheels off a discarded pram, pulled it down the narrow ramp, which could be very steep when the tide was out, lowered it over the side, stepped in carefully and rowed away. When he was around she was jealous of his strength and his knowledge—he had grown up in the country and by the sea. She was a city girl and forever yearning after the names of things. She dreamed; he did. Her hands were clumsy, except when loving her husband or her son, and she often regretted that she had never learned to knit or weave or even to play an instrument. She liked to read and to walk and to talk and felt herself to be shallow and impractical.

Yet since they had found the cabin she had experienced a certain degree of content and growing self-respect. She had learned to bake good, heavy bread in the little two-burner hotplate/oven which she hoped to replace, eventually, with an old, iron, wood- or oil-burning stove; she had learned about ammonia for wasp stings and how to recognize the edible mushrooms that grew in profusion near the abandoned schoolhouse. She could even light a fire now, almost every time.

She had bought a booklet on edible plants and was secretly learning something about the sustaining nature of the various weeds and plants that grew so profusely around her. She had started an herb garden in an old bureau drawer and already had visions of bunches of herbs drying from the kitchen ceiling, jars of rose-hip and blackberry jam, mushrooms keeping in brine in heavy earthenware crocks. Things could be learned from books and by experiment. She got a pencil and jotted down on a piece of drawing paper a list:

cod	thistles	pick salal
salmon	stinging nettles	?maybe sell some of our apples
oysters	blackberries	?my bread
mussels	apples	
	mushrooms	
	dandelions	

plant a garden, make beer, ?a goat and chickens for Robert and the baby.

Then she laughed and crumpled up the paper and threw it in the potbelly stove (her pride and joy and a present discovered for her by Tom) which heated the little kitchen. The fire was nearly out. She would set some bread and then take Robert down on the dock until Tom returned.

"Robbie," she called, knocking on the window, "d'you want to help me make bread?" From his expression she could tell he hadn't heard so she went to the other side of the room—Tom had knocked most of the wall out to make one big room out of two—and opened the front door. It was chilly and she shivered. "Hey, d'you want to help me make some bread?"

He nodded, sturdy and solemn like his father, but with her light skin and hair. She undid his jacket and kissed him. His cheeks were very red.

"Your ears are cold," she laughed, holding his head, like a ball between her hands. "And you smell like the sea. Where did you put your cap?"

" I dunno, I want some juice." He wriggled away from her and she thought with a stab of regret, "So soon?" and tried to fix him as he was at just that moment, red-cheeked and fat, with his bird-bright eyes and cool, sea-smelling skin, to remember him like that forever.

"Come on," he said, tugging at her skirt, "juice and cookies."

"Who said anything about cookies?" she asked in mock severity.

"Juice," he repeated, quite sure of himself. "And two cookies. I'm allowed two cookies."

"Says who?"

"Juice and two cookies," he said, climbing onto a chair by the kitchen table.

Afterward, after they had smelled the yeast and kneaded the dough and made a tiny loaf for Robert in a muffin tin, she covered the bread and left it near the still-warm stove and took the child down to the wharf to watch the fishermen. There were three boats in: the *Trincomali*, the *Sutil* and the *Mary T* and they jostled one another in the slightly choppy water. She looked out toward the other islands for Tom, but couldn't see him. Then carefully she and the little boy went down the ramp to the lower dock, where most of the activity was taking place. A few of the Indians she knew by sight, had seen them along the road or in the little store which served that end of the Island; but most of the ten or so people on the dock or sitting on the decks of boats were strangers to her and she felt suddenly rather presumptuous about coming down at all, like some sightseer—which was, of course, exactly what she was.

"Do you mind if we come down?" she called above the noise of the hysterical gulls and a radio which was blaring in one of the cabins. Two young men in identical red-plaid lumberjackets were drinking beer and taking a break on the deck of the *Mary T*. They looked up at her as she spoke, looked without curiosity, she felt, but simply recognizing her as a fact, like the gulls or the flapping fish, of their Sunday morning.

"Suit yourself, Missus," said an older man who seemed to be in charge.

"But mind you don't slip on them boards."

She looked down. He was right, of course. The main part of the lower dock was, by now, viscous and treacherous with blood and the remains of fish gut. The men in their gumboots stepped carefully. The kill had been going on for at least an hour and the smell of fish and the cry of gulls hung thick in the heavy air. There was an almost palpable curtain of smell and sound and that, with the sight of the gasping

141

fish, made her dizzy for a moment, turned the wharf into an old-fashioned wood-planked roundabout such as she had clung to, in parks, as a child, while she, the little boy, the Indians, the gulls, the small-eyed, gasping fish, the grey and swollen sky spun round and round in a cacaphony of sound and smell and pure sensation. She willed herself to stóp, but felt slightly sick—as she often had on the actual round-abouts of her childhood—and buried her face in the sweet-smelling hair of her child, as if he were a posy. She breathed deeply, sat up, and smiled. No-one had seen—except perhaps the two young Indians. Everyone else was busy. She smiled and began to enjoy and register what she was seeing.

Everywhere there were fish in various stages of life or death. Live cod swam beneath the decks of the little boats, round and round, bumping into one another as though they were part of some mad children's game, seeking desperately for a way out to the open sea. Then one of the men, with a net, would scoop up a fish, fling it onto the wharf where it would be clubbed by another man and disembowelled swiftly by a third, the guts flung overboard to the raucous gulls. Often the fish were not dead when they were gutted. She could see that, and it should have mattered. The whole thing should have mattered: the clubbing, the disembowel-ment, the sad stupid faces of the cod with their receding chins and silly Chinamen's beards. Yet instead of bothering, it thrilled her, this strange Sunday morning ritual of death and survival.

The fish were piled haphazardly in garbage cans, crammed in, tails any old way, and carried up the ramp by two of the men to be weighed on the scales at the top. The sole woman, also Indian and quite young, her hair done up in curlers under a pale pink chiffon scarf, carefully wrote down the weights as they were called out. "Ninety-nine." "Seventy-eight." Hundreds of pounds of cod to be packed in ice until the truck came and took them to the city on the evening ferry boat. And at how much a pound, she wondered. Fish was expensive in the city—too expensive, she thought— and wondered how much, in fact, went to these hard-working fishermen. But she dared not ask. Their faces, if not hostile, were closed to her, intent upon the task at hand. There was almost a rhythm to it, and although they did not sing, she felt the instinctual lift and drop and slice of the three who were actually responsible for the kill. If she had been a composer she could have written it down. One question from her and it might all be ruined. For a moment the sun slipped out, and she turned her face upward, feeling very happy and alive just to be there, on this particular morning, watching the hands of these fishermen, hands that glittered with scales, like mica, in the sunlight, listening to the thud of the fish, the creaking and wheeling of the gulls. A year ago, she felt, the whole scene would have sickened her—now, in a strange way, she understood and was part of it. Crab-like, she could feel a new self forming underneath the old, brittle, shell—could feel herself expanding, breaking free. The child kicked, as if in recognition—a crab within a crab. If only Tom—but the living child tugged at her arm.

"I'm hungry."

"Ah, Robert. Wait a while." She was resentful. Sulky. He knew how to beat her.

"I want to pee. I want to pee *and* poop," he added defiantly.

She sighed. "Okay you win. Let's go." She got up stiffly, from sitting in one position for so long. A cod's heart beat by itself just below the ramp. Carefully she avoided it, walking in a heavy dream up the now steeper ramp (the tide was going out already) and up the path to her cabin.

Still in a dream she cared for the child and wiped his

bottom and punched the bread, turning the little oven on to heat. After the child had been given a sandwich she put him down for a nap and sat at the kitchen table, dreaming. The first few drops of rain began to fall but these she did not see. She saw Tom and a fishing boat and living out their lives together here away from the noise and terror of the city. Fish—and apples—and bread. Making love in the early morning, rising to love with the sun, the two of them —and Robert—and the baby. She put the bread in the oven, wishing now that Tom would come back so she could talk to him.

"You only like the island," he had said, "because you know you can get off. Any time. You're playing at being a primitive. Like a still life of dead ducks or partridges or peonies with just one ant. Just let it be."

"What's wrong with wanting to be simple and uncluttered?" she had cried.

"Nothing," he had replied, "if that's what you really are."

She began a pie, suddenly restless, when there was a knock on the door. It startled her and the baby kicked again.

"Hello," she said, too conscious of her rolled-up sleeves and floury hands. "Can I help you?"

It was one of the young Indians.

"The fellows say you have a telephone Missus. Could I use it? My brother-in-law wuz supposed to pick us up and he ain't come."

"Of course. It's right there." She retreated to the kitchen and sliced apples, trying not to listen. But of course there was no wall. Short of covering her ears there was little she could do.

"Hey. Thelma. Is that you Thelma? Well where the hell is Joe? Yeah. All morning. Naw. I'm calling from the house up above. Oh yeah? Well tell him to get the hell up here quick. Yeah. Okay. Be seeing you."

She heard the phone replaced and then he came around the big fireplace, which, with the potbelly stove, divided the one large room partially into two. "Say," he said, "I got blood all over your phone. Have you got a rag?"

She looked at his hands, which were all scored with shallow cuts, she could see, and the blood still bright orange-red and seeping.

"You're hurt."

"Naw," he said proudly, standing with his weight on one leg, "it's always like that when we do the cod. The knives is too sharp. *You* know," he added with a smile, as if she really did. Little drops of blood fell as he spoke, spattering on the linoleum floor.

"Don't you want some Band-aids, at least?"

"Wouldn't last two minutes in that wet," he said, "but give me a rag to clean up the phone."

"I'll do it," she said, bending awkwardly to one of the bottom cupboards to get a floor cloth. She preceded him in to the living-room. He was right: the receiver was bright with blood, and some spots of blood decorated an air-letter, like notary's seals, which she had left open on the desk. Snow White in her paleness. He became Rose Red. "What am I thinking of?" she blushed.

"I sure am sorry," he said, looking at her with his dark bright eyes. "I didn't mean to mess up your things." She stood before him, the cloth bright with his blood, accepting his youth, his maleness, his arrogance. Her own pale blood drummed loudly in her ears.

"If you're positive you're all right," she managed.

"Yeah. Can't be helped. It'll heal over by next Sunday." He held his hands out to her and she could see, along with the seeping blood, the thin white wire-like lines of a hundred former scars. Slowly she reached out and dipped two fingers in the blood, then raised them and drew them across

145

her forehead and down across each cheek.

"Christ," he said softly, then took the clean end of the rag and spit on it and gently wiped her face. She was very conscious of her bigness and leaned slightly forward so he would not have to brush against her belly. What would *their* children have been like?

Then the spell broke and he laughed self-consciously and looked around.

"Sure is a nice place you've got here," but she was aware he didn't mean it. What would his ideal be? He was very handsome with his coarse dark hair and red plaid lumber-jacket.

"Well," she said, with her face too open, too revealing.

"Well," he answered, eager now to go. "Yeah. See you around. Thanks for the use of your phone."

She nodded and he was gone.

When Tom returned the little house was rich with the smells of bread and rhubarb pie and coffee.

"Any luck?"

"Yes," he said, "and no. I didn't catch anything—but you did."

"I did?" she said, puzzled.

"Yeah. One of the fishermen gave me this for you. He said you let him use the phone. It was very nice of him, I must say."

And there, cleaned and filleted, presumably with the knife that had cut him so, was a beautiful bit of cod. She took it in her hands, felt the cool rasping texture of it, and wondered for an alien moment if his tongue would feel like that—cool, rough as a cat's tongue, tasting of fish.

"What did he say?" she asked, her back to the man.

"He said 'give this to the Missus.' Why?"

"Nothing. I thought he was kind of cheeky. He made me

146

feel old."

Later that night on their couch before the fire, she startled him by the violence of her lovemaking. He felt somehow she was trying to possess him, devour him, maybe even exorcise him. And why hadn't she cooked the cod for supper? She had said that all of a sudden she didn't feel like fish. He stared at her, asleep, her full mouth slightly open, and felt the sad and immeasurable gulf between them, then sat up for a moment and pulled the curtain back, looking vainly for the reassurance of the moon behind the beaded curtain of the rain. The man shook his head. There were no answers, only questions. One could only live and accept. He turned away from his wife and dove effortlessly into a deep, cool, dreamless sleep. The rain fell on the little cabin, and on the trees and on the government wharf below, where, with persistence, it washed away all traces of the cod and the kill, except for two beer bottles, which lolled against the pilings as the two young Indians had lolled earlier that day. The rain fell; the baby kicked. The woman moaned a little in her sleep and moved closer to the reassuring back of the puzzle who was her husband. And still the rain fell on, and Sunday night—eventually—turned into Monday morning.

TWO IN THE BUSH

"So," said Mr. Owusu-Banahene, "you are off to meet the man from Yamoussoukro." He inclined a half-smile in my direction, then picked up a small bone and sucked it thoughtfully. Five of us had gone to the City Hotel for Sunday lunch. Now we sat, stuffed and lethargic, around a small metal table on the verandah. The table was littered with beer bottles and the remains of chicken curry. I had just announced my plans to visit the Ivory Coast.

"You make him sound," I replied, "like the Wonderful Wizard of Oz. But," and here I too picked up a bone and sucked it, "the wizard turned out to be a fake."

"Did he indeed? Are you so sure? Oz was a happy place; he gave the people what they wanted."

"At any rate," I said, "I doubt that I shall meet him. I don't travel in such exalted circles." He shrugged. "It's not impossible. Do you know what he is always sayin'? 'I am only a peasant.' 'I am only a peasant'! The foreign reporters eat it up." His handsome aristocrat's face expressed disdain.

"Perhaps you will meet him in the market. Perhaps you will see him haulin' nets or pickin' cocoa. 'I am only a peasant'!" He ground the remains of bone between strong teeth.

"They say he has accomplished miracles," I offered, in the pause that followed. The other three at the table watched with interest. Two of them, husband and wife, were friends from long ago. One was a dull botanist named Les who

149

wore a yellow and black striped jersey and had black, fuzzy, close-cropped hair. He looked like a wasp and had contributed nothing to the conversation except a long and boring tale about his defective Omega watch. He had been brought along to keep me company I guess. Jimmie Owusu-Banahene I had known since Nkrumah's time and then after the coup and now again after five years and how many coups (was it two more?) in between? Not one of Busia's men. His own man. There were rumours, now, of yet another plot. I wondered what he knew.

"Miracles!" he said. "You'll see miracles, no blinkin' fear."

"Oh *don't* let's talk politics any more!" said Mollie in her shrill, rather affected, English voice. I agreed, nodding.

"You're wasting your time on me. I'm not political." Jimmie laughed, then raised his voice a little so that people at the other tables stopped talking.

"Not political! Nobody in this world is not political. When you are born you commit a political act, changin' the census in your village, town or state. When you die you do the same. Two unavoidable political acts and many more political acts in between. For some," (his voice went louder still, took on his best courtroom manner) "even curry lunch at the City Hotel is a political act." He waved his arm at the manager of Barclay's Bank DCO, at the new Secretary of the Town Council, at a fat black priest surrounded by a tableful of female parishioners. He broke into loud, happy laughter, then wiped his forehead with a dazzling white handkerchief.

"Listen," he said softly. "Busia is a sick man. His wife goes everywhere with him to give him his injections. And the country is sick too—sick proper! In the north they are callin' for Osaygefo again—the price of yams is terrible. Everyone steals and I don't blame them. So perhaps we too will have a peasant again as president." He laughed. "Do you know, just before the coup, whenever Nkrumah made one of his rare public appearances the vans would go ahead of him with loudspeakers: 'When Osaygefo appears, the crowd will cheer and applaud.' "

"Do you think he will come back?"

Jimmie shook his head. "No. Never."

"Ah," said Mollie, her eyes sparkling (she loved to be "in on things"), "Jimmie *knows* something." She was wearing an olive-green jersey with a sergeant's stripe on the sleeve and a cartridge belt around her middle. Across the chest had been printed, in black ink, "Let's go US Army" and an eagle. She told me she had bought it in London on her last leave. It was the "latest thing" there and she wanted something "right up to date." I thought it was terrible. She leaned forward on her plump white arms.

"Tell us what you know!"

"Go to the market and ask the market-women. It is the women who decide."

"Do you really believe that?"

"Of course."

"But it is the men who will act."

"It is the men who will act. But only with the power of the women behind them. We have a sayin' here. 'The hen too knows that it is dawn, but she leaves it to the cock to announce it.' " He got up. "You must excuse me." Paused for a minute by my chair.

"When do you go?"

"On Saturday. By lorry." He nodded. "But of course. You too want to be known as a peasant."

I ignored this.

"Can I bring you something?"

"A bottle of good French wine. A pound of butter. A miracle."

Several heads on the verandah turned carefully to watch him walk away. Did he know something? What? They watched his stride. They looked for tiny, infinitesimal signs of nervousness or elation. Something was up. It was in the air, along with the terrible heat and the lingering smell of spices from the abandoned buffet table.

"There goes the most attractive man in the country." Mollie gave a dreamy sigh.

"Jimmie told me," said John, "that one reason Nkrumah was so successful in the beginning was that he used as his ministers and officials men who were the sons of slaves and had a grudge against society."

"Oh *don't*. Please. No more politics." Mollie was restless; she had seen and been seen and was ready to go. Les, who had come with them, would, I hoped, return the way he had come. I had had enough and wanted to be alone. Which was very ungrateful because they were treating me to lunch. All around us there was talk and laughter. We sat on in a little island of silence—it was as if Jimmie had taken the talk and the laughter with him.

Then Mollie said suddenly, "Darling, how would you feel if I went along with Isobel? Felicity could see to the children—I could do with a little holiday." Mollie ran a small catering service from their bungalow—incredible English birthday cakes and fancy hors d'œuvres and petits fours. These were much in demand at the fashionable birthdays and weddings in the town. She had just catered an enormous reception for the Star Brewery—a huge success. John was an artist who taught design at the university. A small quiet man who had at least one African mistress. I looked at him in despair.

"Maybe Isobel wants to go alone."

"Nonsense darling. It's much more fun to have a companion. You don't want to go alone, do you?" All three looked at me. I knew I should say yes, that's exactly what I want to do. Yet this would be, at best, misinterpreted; at worst an insult to Mollie who had, after all, been so kind to me since my return. Jimmie's words came back to mock me: "Every act is political." Or politic at least. I contemplated the American eagle. It would be Mollie's trip. But after all, why not? She was already going on about how she knew someone who knew someone who knew someone who knew a Peugeot taxi. She would find out when it was going to Abidjan. It would all be arranged; we would simply go to the lorry park and get in.

"It sounds good," I said. "Come and let me know this week what you find out." My chair made a nasty scraping noise on the concrete floor of the verandah.

"I'll need a visa," Mollie was saying. "Darling I'll have to pop down to Accra."

Outside I walked past the boys selling Pioneer biscuits and wrapped sweets, past a stout woman in an incredible pale blue chiffon dress and pale blue chiffon cartwheel hat. The doorman, in white gloves, was handing her into a taxi. High up in the sun-faded sky two vultures circled lazily, like scraps of black paper or bits of soot. A big Mercedes full of musicians and their instruments came fast and arrogant down the long semi-circular drive. Later on there would be an acrobat from the capital and dancing to Afro-beat, the latest craze.

"Who's Makin' Love/To Your Old Lady/While/You're Out/Makin' Love" The number one hit song across the nation.

And yet in the *Graphic* this morning: "A five-inch baby alligator is alleged to be haunting the lives of an Accra market-woman and her family." The woman was receiving spiritual treatment from the Prophet Tawiah. "I believe this reptile to be the work of a witch." What was it Blake said?

"Without contraries there is no progression?" Perhaps so. Jimmie Owusu-Banahene with his beautiful Ashanti face and beautiful Oxford accent; John with his Cape Coast mistress; Mollie with her funky jersey; the vultures wheeling up above the most fashionable hotel in the city. I wanted to find Africa. Was this it? Was this the real Africa? Maybe it will be different in the Ivory Coast, I thought. I was depressed and out of sorts. A chain of small children formed behind me. "Hey Bronie Bronie, you give me pesewa!" Five years before the same children—or their brothers—had danced behind me to only a slightly different tune: "Hey Bronie Bronie Bronie, you give me a penny-o." I gave up and hailed a taxi. The children laughed and waved as I went past. One of them stuck his tongue out; I stuck my tongue out back. . . .

The Hotel Ivoire was called the "Pearl of the Lagoon." Outside, a smooth symmetry of concrete, steel and glass with a tall unfinished tower growing at one side.

We had gone there to find a man—an Angolan Freedom Fighter whose name I had been given in London. Marques Kakumba, B.P. 388, Phone 37–40–99. Which I did. A woman's voice, speaking rapid French, assured me that he either lived (or worked) at the Hotel Ivoire. We had spent the night at a brothel in the Adjamé district. The man Les had given the address to Mollie—he was either a simpleton or a practical joker. The Hotel Humanité. At one o'clock in the morning, stumbling through the darkness. No-one had heard of it. "Hey, Madame!" "Hey, Madame!" But we had found it on a side street—Rue des Ecries—the proprietor most unhappy to see us. In the tiny lounge there was a very beautiful old-fashioned wall clock with roman numerals and filigree hands and a large sepia etching of a Perseus type wrestling with a hairy monster, Humanité herself perhaps. We had been misinformed. There were no rooms. A young woman in a torn red velvet dress came in on the arm of a fat, drunk, middle-aged man. They did not even stop at the desk but headed on down the narrow corridor. I looked at the proprietor; he looked at me.

"Nothing?" I asked. "*Rien?* We are very tired." I handed him a two-dollar Canadian bill. He put it in the drawer and sighed.

"You will have to lock your door. And there is only one bed. *Non-climatisée* you understand." We said we understood.

The room was tiny and the mosquito netting over the single window had large three-cornered tears. The wardrobe was full of mops and buckets and on top of the wardrobe a sign said "HOTEL," only back to front—"ℲƎTOH" Another sign over the exposed and dirty toilet said *"Défense d'uriner dans la salle de bain."* As there wasn't one this seemed gratuitous. I spent the night holding myself away from Mollie's plump, hot, sticky body. The mattress sagged terribly in the middle. In the night there was several times the sound of laughter and once the sound of someone retching in the next room. The proprietor informed us proudly the next morning that he had sat on a chair outside our door all night. *"Vos protegées,"* I said, and made him laugh. I wanted to burn everything I had on and scrub myself with something powerful and antiseptic. Cockroaches were scampering across my feet when I awoke. Mollie, undaunted, looked at the addresses I had and charmed the proprietor into lending us a few thousand francs until we could cash a cheque. We left our suitcases as security; he was most upset to think we might return. Obviously the protection of the virtue of two white women was not an honour he took lightly or easily. He hoped we would find something on the Plateau. He recommended the Hotel du Parc. We embarrassed him—perhaps we even threatened him. What if something happened? He sent out his eldest son, a ragged boy of about eight, to find us a taxi.

"Hotel Ivoire," I said to the driver grandly.

"Eh! Madame!" He grinned at me in the mirror.

"Hotel Ivoire."

He laughed and laughed and started the meter ticking. There was a small crowd gathered on the pavement.

"Hotel Ivoire!" they shouted back. "Bye-bye." We drove off in a cloud of thick red dust.

At lunch over the pool we sat and ate smorgasbord and drank white wine and looked at the flat bellies of the young men who, wearing only the tiniest of bikinis and espadrilles and perhaps but not always a smart terry-towelling jacket, helped themselves to cold beef and cold pork, salads, sausage rolls, hot rolls and fresh fruit.

"Good," said Mollie. "But not that good." She flicked a sausage roll with her finger.

"D'you think he works here?" I said. Mollie had unbuttoned the top two buttons of her blouse and her eyes darted like goldfish around the terrace.

"What? D'you think so?" The wine was going to her head. "*Garçon*," she called. "*Garçon*." A waiter appeared. She explained about our *ami*. He thought he had heard of him. *Kakumba*. Yes. He had heard of him. Kakumba, did he work here? A beautiful young Frenchman blew us a kiss. *Oui. Absolument*. He worked here. Kakumba. We wrote out yet another note. "Dear João, you don't know us but we're friends of Grethe's, in London. . . ." Gave it to the waiter, who put it in his pocket. Our money was almost gone and it was Sunday.

"*Excusez-moi*," I said to the waiter. "Where can we cash *les travellers cheques*?" But the desk was not interested. Unfortunately, we were not staying at the Hotel Ivoire. If, on the other hand, we knew a guest. . . I felt we couldn't mention Joao Kakumba in case he turned out to be a waiter. "Let's go and ask in the Tour Ivoire."

They knew him, by God. He was a guest—he lived there. Room *trois cent quatre*. We left another note. "We have enough for a drink," Mollie said. "Let's sit and wait awhile and then give up."

A small dark man was standing at the other end of the corridor. "Excuse me," he said, in heavily-accented English. "You would like to see something *interessant* perhaps?" He placed a small white box on the marble counter.

"What is it?" I asked. The small man held up a hand.

"Wait." He took off the cover very slowly. Mollie and I and the desk clerk leaned forward to peer into the box. A huge black beetle was there. Black and highly lacquered—like a child's pull toy.

"Cochineal," he said. "I found it."

"I thought cochineal were very small," I said.

"African cochineal," he said. The insect gave off an angry clicking sound. "I will sell it," he said, replacing the cover. "Very rare." Even with the cover on the angry clicking noise could be heard. "I have other things," he said.

"*Très interessant.*" He pinched my elbow. "You would like to see?"

"No," I said. "No thank you. No."

He shrugged and tied up the box with green waxed ribbon—like florists' ribbon. Mollie and I looked at each other and moved off down the long, thick-carpeted corridor that connected the main body of the hotel with the almost-completed tower. She suggested we have a drink and wait around to see if Joao would come back and find our note.

"I don't think he exists," I said. "The waiter thought he was a waiter—the desk clerk thinks he's a guest. He doesn't exist and I'm not sure I want to hang around here."

A man in a white tropical suit and an incredible red tie

was passing as I said this. He turned around.

"Say, are you girls American?" He was very excited.

"English," said Mollie in her most English voice.

"One-time American," I said. "From Canada."

"That's just swell. Would you like to join me in a drink?"
I hadn't heard anyone say "swell" in years. We explained
about the fugitive Angolan; he said it didn't matter: he'd
be pleased to keep us company for a while. Mollie did not
seem too keen. Perhaps she thought he would cramp our
style. She wanted a no-hipped French boy, maybe, not a
rather sad-looking middle-aged American. She suggested
we find the ladies' room and then join him. It was as I suspected. "We don't want to get stuck with that man!"

"There's no reason why we should."

"Just one drink."

"That's fine with me. No drink would be fine too. Why
don't we walk around the city for a while?"

But the Hotel Ivoire obviously had its charms. Pouting
her lips at the gilt-framed mirror she applied a thin glaze of
lipstick and then, quite unself-consciously, placed her hands
under her breasts and pushed them up and out. She wore
only the best French bras and fancied herself quite sexy.

I wanted to take a bath—the smell of the Hotel Human-
ite seemed to have followed me here, and while I was
smoothing out my long skirt a cockroach fell out and skit-
tered away into the corner. Only Mollie and I were in the
powder room and she hadn't noticed. I imagined some
wealthy lady from the States sitting in her cubicle when the
cockroach hurried in. If there was one—! I knew I should
probably look for it—the repercussions could be incredible.
And such disgusting creatures, even to one not unacquainted
with them. Years before, when I lived out here, I had picked
up a big and seldom-used coffee pot off the top shelf in the
kitchen. We were packing up to go home and I stood there

158

with the thing in my hand, debating whether I would ever serve sixteen simultaneous cups of coffee back in Canada. Then I became conscious of a movement and opened the lid. It was full to the top with cockroaches. Maybe dozens of them. The big old coffee pot, high up on the warm shelf, must have seemed a castle to the breeding insects. Probably the first two came down the spout. I flung the thing across the room and cockroaches exploded everywhere. Later I put the coffee pot back and left it there—I knew I could never use it again. What if "my" cockroach—or the cockroach of the Hotel Humanité—had been pregnant? Why were they so disgusting—for they were. I shook out the folds of my skirt again—I wanted to rip it off, to strip completely and take a bath in one of the delicate marble washbasins. Wondered if the American Man had a room with a bath and would he mind?

"Let's go," I said. Mollie was dabbing Countess Somebody-or-other's perfume behind her ears. I was afraid some elegant ladies would come in, the cockroach would be discovered and we would be accused. A cochineal in a florist's box was merely eccentric. A cockroach, on the other hand. . .

"And where might you two young ladies be staying?" Looking up our "hotel" in the tourist map.

"Pardon, Madame. It appears there is no such place." Hauled off for seditious behaviour.

"But they came into this country by road, by bush taxi. A most unusual thing, your honour, for two white women to travel thus. Unusual—and, I might suggest, suspicious?" The Hotel Ivoire abandoned—deserted. The huge tropical plants in the pillared lobby are left unpruned and untended. In their search for water they grow and grow, push blindly at the heavy glass windows, crash through into the swimming pool, their tendrils waving.

The pretty French boys, the fat politicians, the beautiful

women—the rich Americans—all desert the most luxurious hotel in West Africa. The government falls. And all because of a single insect.

"Let's go," I said again.

We joined Arnie in the Rendez-Vous Bar. It was still rather early and we were the only customers. We sat in big leather armchairs and sipped gin-tonics. Arnie had been doing some inquiring.

"Your friend is real, all right. He lives in the tower and comes in here nearly every evening." After his second drink he began to tell us the story of his life. It was sad and too intimate and too painful. He owned a fleet of tuna-fishing boats; three were docked in the canal right now.

"Hell," he said. "You could anchor half the world's ships here and still have room to spare." Tomorrow we would have to come and see one of the boats, have lunch on board. The cook was terrific. We'd love it. Arnie's wife didn't love him. Her name was Lilian. She'd gone off sex completely about two years ago. "It's just terrible to lie there and watch her undress." He went to all sorts of doctors. Wondered if he had body odour or bad breath. She even tried to set him up with her best friend.

For Christmas he gave her a Mustang done up in red ribbon. The next day she went out and bought herself an XKE. We'd have to come to lunch on one of the boats. He was a millionaire but what difference did it make. Without love there was nothing. She said she loved him but she didn't want sex any more. I decided not to ask if he had a bathtub in his room.

The boy behind the bar came over with a note.

"I am sitting in the corner. João." I read it aloud. Nothing was going to surprise me any more. We turned around and looked across the room. Two men were sitting at a table. They both waved and got up. One was around 38 with a brown handsome face and shaved head. The other was fat and about 60, vaguely Levantine or Egyptian. Both had on immaculate and very expensive tropical suits. The young and handsome one was dressed in grey, the fat man was, like Arnie, in tropical white. Only Arnie's suit was rumpled— the other two could have stepped from the window of some exclusive men's shop.

"Arnie Freitas," said Arnie, then added, "tuna fish."

"João Marques Kakumba," said the handsome one, then added softly, "guns."

The third man handed me a card, reciting at the same time:

"Mr. S.M.A. Alamoody
Vice-President
African Development Bank
Abidjan (Ivory Coast)
Telephone 2256-60/69
PO Box 1387."

He smiled as he sat down. "Tuna fish," he said, "guns. . . and money."

Arnie ordered more drinks and Mr. Alamoody fished out a handsome crocodile wallet and attempted to pay the boy. Arnie, who was on his fifth whisky, shook his head.

"Naw. Put your money away Mr. Alamoody. Nobody pays when Arnie's around."

The man with the cochineal came in; he set the white box down on the bar, waving at Mollie and me.

"You know that fellow?" Arnie said. "You want to invite him over?"

"No," I said. "He showed us his beetle. That's what he's got in that box."

"How extraordinary," said João. Underneath the table his strong well-tailored leg pressed mine.

"Where are you staying?" he said. "At the Hotel here?"

161

"No—at a small hotel in the Adjamé district—a very small hotel."

The drinks had made Mollie pink-cheeked and talkative. The whole story was told. Stumbling through the hot darkness, the only hotel we knew of that was near the lorry park. The proprietor who sat outside our door all night. I wanted to add the bit about the cockroach but wasn't sure.

Arnie was horrified.

"Why, you girls shouldn't stay in a place like that!" He offered us the use of his suite on the twenty-second floor. He'd sleep on the boat. It wasn't right. "Funny things happen in this city—I could tell you things."

"But of course," said Joao, laughing a gold-tipped laugh. "We must come to your rescue."

"First we will all go to one of the truly native places and then we will bring you back here to Mr. Freitas' suite. It is very simple." Mollie was gazing wistfully around at the other people in the bar. She was not attracted to black men and somehow Arnie, although in a photograph, say, would pass for a not-unattractive man, somehow exuded unattractiveness in person. Perhaps that's what living with Lilian had done to him. All around her at other tables were beautiful Frenchmen.

"I don't think. . ." she said. I agreed, but for other reasons. I did not like to be so "arranged" by these three strangers.

"We are too tired this evening," I said. "And I think we must return to the Humanité because our bags are there. And once there, we may as well stay another night."

Mr. Alamoody offered to go and get our bags. His car was just outside.

"You'll never find it," I said. "I'm not sure we will even find it."

"I will take you," said the Angolan. The pressure of his leg was unmistakable this time. "My car, too, is just outside.

162

We will return here. Mr. Alamoody and Mr. Arnie will entertain your friend."

It was like the buddy system when I learned to swim. Stay with your partner at all times. Yet I don't think Mollie would have minded if all three had gone with me and she were left alone, plump-armed and pink-cheeked, waiting. I almost suggested it but it would sound too crazy. Finally I reached over and took Arnie's hand and spoke the truth.

"Arnie, I don't want to stay at the Hotel Ivoire. It's beautiful but it's not where I want to stay. I'm terrified of heights as well and would never sleep on the twenty-second floor of anything. I would like to come to the fish-boat for lunch and appreciate your kindness. Could we meet you tomorrow somewhere?" It was a very formal speech and he didn't argue It was arranged that we would all meet in the bar at noon except for Mr. Alamoody who had a directors' meeting—he would take us home now, accompanied by João— I can't remember why but it seemed reasonable at the time. When I stood up I realized I was drunk.

It seemed very funny as we said goodnight to tuna-fish and went off with money and guns. Tuna-fish was ordering another whisky. I wondered what he would do with the rest of his evening.

Mr. Alamoody drove a handsome car—something very dark green and smelling of real leather. I supposed he dismissed his driver at night. The car purred through the parking lot, down the hill and across the bridge. João sat in back with me, running his hand up and down my arm. If I had remembered the buddy system when they suggested we split up, I remembered now twenty years before and the back seats of a hundred up-to-now forgotten cars. I was surprised: the Angolan seemed incredibly sophisticated—not just his dress but his manner—to want to feel me up in the back seat of a Citroën. Slick bastard, I thought. And then, "Well, don't forget, you looked him up." I didn't know much about Angola except it was Portuguese and oppressed. He had been recommended as a freedom-fighter and a charming person. It didn't fit; I never figured it out.

The paving ended and we bumped, in Mr. Alamoody's beautiful car, along narrow unlighted streets. We got lost.

"I'm sorry," I said. "It seems a shame to subject such a fine car to such treatment."

"It is nothing," said Mr. Alamoody, gripping the steering wheel. He slowed down at the sight of a robed figure, rolled down the window and shouted out something in French. The reply was derisive but included some accurate directions.

In another five minutes we pulled up in front of the grimy stoop of the hotel.

"It's horrible," I said. "We can't invite you in." Even at this late hour a crowd of children and loungers had gathered around Mr. Alamoody's handsome car. He was chivalrous, concerned. João was kissing my knuckles one by one. We made our adieux. The proprietor had been very worried about us.

"Oh my God," I said, "we never cashed any money."

"We can still go to the American Embassy," Mollie said. "There's always a marine on duty, isn't there? I mean, don't they have to help you?"

The proprietor, shaking his head, sent a small boy to find us a taxi. We said we'd be back very soon.

The marine's name was Sgt. Lee Lillie and he had been asleep. He had on a white T-shirt and cotton trousers and a dog-tag. He wasn't supposed to cash our cheques but he did. Twenty-one maybe, with a crew cut and a dog-tag around his neck. He was as unreal as the rest of them. He invited us to come the next day and meet his buddies. There were four of them and they took turns. On Fridays they had a TGIF

164

party. If we wanted a cheap hotel why didn't we try Treich-ville. He pronounced it "Trashville." It was in the African, or "old" quarter. Lots of good dancin' places there.

It was two o'clock in the morning when we got back to the Humanité. Cockroaches, disinfectant, would-be custo-mers: I didn't care. We fell into bed and I, at least, was asleep almost immediately.

Just as I went off I heard drums start up somewhere quite far away. Someone had been born, or had died. Something was being celebrated or mourned. Was that Africa? Was Mr. Alamoody Africa or João Kakumba or even Sgt. Lee Lillie or Arnie the tuna-fish king? I didn't dream—why should I? Africa was a dream.

Mollie was a rather unhappy lump on the other edge of the dirty mattress. Dadada   Dadada/Dadada   Dadada—the drums didn't care about us. "Who are you?" a drunken young man had shouted at the doorman as we left the hotel. The doorman was barring his way. "Who are you?" I fell asleep.

Lunch was fresh shrimp with pasta and garlic, asparagus, fresh bread, fresh pineapple and wine. Arnie wasn't in the bar to meet us—only João. Arnie was at a meeting and would come down later. João was once again immaculately dressed. His skin shone with good health and a good diet. His fingernails were incredible, as perfect as Gatsby's shirts. He drove very fast and confidently. Mollie sat between us.

"You held his hand," she had said accusingly. "I was quite surprised."

"He held my hand." He had stuck his tongue between each of my fingers. It was very pleasant.

"You didn't pull away."

"No, I didn't pull away."

"Well, I was surprised, that's all." Mollie, whose eyes had darted to all the pretty Frenchmen.

The boat was big—I don't know what I expected. The captain was Joseph Goias, very young and handsome, a Portuguese-American with a moustache and a gold chain around his neck.

"I lie awake nights worrying," he told me. We were all in the captain's cabin waiting for Arnie before we had lunch. Two buyers had appeared—an Italian named Borghe, heavy-set, in a hot-looking blue suit and Pete, a French-Canadian who worked for one of the big companies in the States.

"They follow him everywhere," Joseph said. "We've made a big haul."

"Why do you come to Africa to fish?"

"Why not?"

His brother John, also handsome, also young, was talking to Mollie, who was rapidly growing more cheerful. She was really after a Frenchman but a handsome Portuguese-American might be a pleasant stop-gap. Pete had found a guitar and was playing the Green, Green, Grass of Home. "Hair of gold and lips like cherries." The fridge was stocked with beer and ice. Bottles of spirits lined the shelves of the bookcase. Joseph, Mollie, John and I were sitting on the oversize bunk. There were two other men in the room besides Pete and Borghe—Joao, who said nothing and stood by the door, his eyes half-shut, (but waiting I felt, waiting, and sizing things up) and a man called John, a senior member of the crew. He'd been married to the same woman for 26 years, God bless her.

"Come all you young maidens," sang Pete, "and listen to me." Everybody laughed.

Arnie had saved young John's life. That's why Arnie had a limp. Something had fallen and Arnie had seen it falling and pushed John, who was just a kid, out of the way. As Joseph talked, Arnie took on new dimensions.

"Are you married, Joseph?"

"No! Not me. I nearly was once though. The boss's daughter, just like in the movies. We got half-way to Las Vegas and I changed my mind. Got cold feet or something. She was crying and yelling 'I hate you, I hate you' and I said 'Half an hour ago you were saying I love you.' That's the closest I ever got."

"You?" he said.

"Yes."

Drunken John, the older John, picked up on this.

"Are you faithful to your husbands, girls? Tell me, are you faithful to your husbands? I been married 26 years and never cheated on the wife, God bless her."

"Arnie's been really good to us," Joseph said. "When we were just little kids our old lady took us both to Portugal. I was thirteen and John was eleven when we came back. We couldn't speak any English. The kids at school were terrible to us—terrible. Beat us up, called us 'wetbacks,' laughed at our pronounciation." He got up and grabbed my hand. "C'mon, I want to show you somethin'."

We went out to laughter and whistles. Up some stairs to the deck above. Joseph opened a little concealed door in the ship's frame. Inside a tiny cupboard space was a triptych of Mary and the Baby and two saints. A small velvet cushion was placed in front of this tiny altar and there was also a votive candle and a fresh hibiscus flower, voluptuous and blood-coloured, floating in a clear glass bowl.

"Every day I thank Our Lady for sending Arnie into my life." He crossed himself and closed the door. "I'm the youngest tuna-boat captain of a registered ship," he said. "Pretty good for a wetback, hey?" He showed me the great tank where the fish were kept alive and then, in port, dynamited to the surface and caught up with a gaff. He was sure-footed and sure-brained, full of technical knowledge.

167

"Arnie started out as nothin'," he said, "same as us. Now we're a team."

"Do you know his wife—Lilian?"

"That bitch." He spat and made no further comment.

As we came back up, Arnie was coming down.

"Seen everything? After lunch I'll show you the bridge and the engine room." Joseph put his hand on Arnie's arm. "How're ya doing, sport?" The three of us went in to lunch. João had disappeared. . . .

We moved to a new hotel, in Treichville. Lebanese, and the proprietor owned the restaurant next door. We were supposed to meet Joao and Mr. Alamoody in the Rendez-Vous Bar at nine PM. Our new room had two beds and a shower and was clean. The proprietor of the Humanité was not sorry to see us go, although it was obvious he liked us. He warned us to stay away from sailors and take only taxis with meters. In the courtyard behind the hotel his wife was pounding fou-fou with a long pole. A small child sat at her feet and reached her hand in quickly between strokes, to turn the soft glutinous mass. Then the pole came down again. Thud. Pause. Thud. Pause. Thud. Like a great heart beating. Later they would dip the soft balls of yam into a communal pot of ground-nut or palm-nut soup while the elegant ladies in the Rendez-Vous Bar sucked thoughtfully at the imported olives in the bottom of their glasses.

"Why not," I thought. "Why not just stay on here?" I was romanticizing, of course, but the life of the woman in the courtyard seemed as simple and as regular as the thud of her fou-fou pounder. Mr. Owusu-Banahene had told me another of his people's sayings—"The Sky-God pounds fou-fou for the one who has no arms." Could that really be true? What about for the one who has no yams?

In the Treichville market I bought cloth and cowries and beautiful shirts. Everywhere was colour and bargaining and laughter. I wished we had asked Arnie to come with us. Just as the proprietor had warned us against sailors so had I warned him, for no real reason, just a feeling, against João Marques Kakumba. Arnie had arranged to meet him and Mr. Alamoody one hour before we were supposed to show up.

"Suppose," I said, "he wants the *Cape St. Vincent* to carry guns?" We were up on the bridge and Arnie was signalling to other ships—a small boy showing off. Mollie was very drunk and had gone off somewhere with John.

Arnie was busy at the transmitter. He was unconcerned.

"He better not forget he's dealin' with a pro!"

"There's something about him. His eyes maybe."

"Hello," he said. "Hello. *Cape St. Vincent* to *Tana Maru*. *Cape St. Vincent* to *Tana Maru*."

I gave up. I was not political. It was none of my business anyway. Yet these people had a kind of innocence or naïvete. Joao and Mr. Alamoody looked at me with disillusioned eyes, what James saw, nearly a century before, in the eyes of Europeans. Now it included the new African politicians, the Lebanese, the Egyptians. Someone like Arnie could be a godsend. And Joseph, although younger and more cynical, would do anything Arnie asked him to.

A woman selling manioc from huge plastic garbage bins snapped the palm leaves shut. The market women were professionals too. I would pay five times as much for whatever I wanted—the price of my white skin. And bad French too. Maybe six times as much.

Mollie was upset because she had screwed with John and she wasn't on the pill.

"Why did you do it then?"

"I got carried away. He took advantage of me." It was like a Victorian novel. We had gone to a chemist's and asked for a douche. I wondered if I would sleep with João that night and what it would be like. I had decided I didn't like him but he interested me. A freedom fighter with perfect fingernails. Perhaps he wouldn't try. He was smart enough to see my sympathy for Arnie. Perhaps I would end up a headless corpse in the lagoon. That such things didn't happen was nonsense. The veneer of civilization is never more than a few inches thick. Jimmie Owusu-Banahene had told me about the murder of the new secretary of the town council six months before (he'd been stealing funds). Found with a nail driven through his head. Rushed to hospital but he died. The nail had been removed, apparently, before he ever got to the hospital and it was given out that he died of cerebral hemorrhage. The first week I was here, so many long years ago, I had seen the picture of a severed female head in *Drum* magazine. It had been placed at a crossroads and no-one came forward to claim it. If Joao wanted me to sleep with him I would. A political act. Or so I would call it later.

But he never appeared: nor did Mr. Alamoody nor Arnie. We sat in the Rendez-Vous Bar and accepted drinks from Frenchmen and Americans and rich Lebanese. It was my birthday, only nobody knew but me. Mollie disappeared with a young Lebanese boy, no more than eighteen or nineteen, who wanted to take her dancing. She obviously didn't believe in the buddy system. I was too drunk to be surprised when Joseph and all of the crew of the *Cape St. Vincent* suddenly appeared. Joseph sat down at my table and the others pushed a number of tables together and sat a few yards from us.

"You didn't say you were coming here," he said.

"We were supposed to meet João and Mr. Alamoody, a banker. It's my birthday," I said, sounding like Mr. Toad.

"Happy birthday."

"Thanks."

He was not as attractive in his American floral sports shirt as he had been in his old grey shirt on the *Cape St. Vincent*.

A girl came in and sat down at the big table. She was very pretty and wholesome-looking in a white lace blouse and long skirt. She could have been on a tourist poster.

"Ghanaian," Joseph said. "She's a whore." He pronounced it "hoor." "All the best prostitutes here are Ghanaian."

"Why's that?"

"God knows. But they come here by the hundreds. D'you want to know something else? Have you seen all the high-rises on the Plateau?"

"Yes."

"Pretty, eh? Very modern and smart, like this place, eh? But the Africans will only live on the ground floors, they're too used to living in huts."

"Is that so?"

"Absolutely so. There's 300,000 people in this crazy city and 200,000 of them are foreigners." He shook his head. "Is this Africa? I ask you, is this Africa?"

"I don't know Joseph. Probably. It's France too. And Portugal too and everything that's gone before."

The girl got up and went out and one by one the men followed her. They came back tucking in their shirts.

"4000 CFA a time," said Joseph.

"Don't let me stop you," I said. He shook his head.

"They use Arnie's suite. She's really cool, that one. D'you know what her name is?"

"What?"

"Comfort." He looked miserable.

"Listen," I said. "Why don't I go?"

"No. Please. Let's go to the Casino. It's your birthday, I'll buy you a pass."

"I don't like gambling."

"Never mind." We got up and left. Back down the long corridor where we'd first met Arnie and through a door. Down a sort of outside arbour and into the Elephant D'Or —"No Ivoirians allowed," said Joseph.

I have the card still:

Carte d'admission valable trois jours
Du Saison 71–72
Elephant D'Or Casino

Joseph told me what to do. Pete and Borghe were there, Pete's eyes reptilian when he gambled. I won $3,000 in half an hour at twenty-one. An Indian boy no older than eighteen, with silver bangles and a silver ring in his ear, blew me a kiss whenever I won. I thought how much Mollie would have liked him. Pete, Borghe, the Indian, the pretty Frenchmen, everybody was watching me.

"Joseph," I said, "I'm going home." He tried to get me to keep the money but I couldn't. The bored, intense faces of the players had defeated me.

"Will you come back to the ship with me?" he said.

"No. You're beautiful but no." He got me a taxi. "Joseph Goias you've come a long way. I like you." And added as an afterthought, "Take care of Arnie."

The hotel room was locked. I walked through the narrow streets of Treichville. Bought a chicken wing and pepper brochette from an old woman in an alley. I ignored the sailors who followed me. I was 35 years old—happy birthday to me—and knew nothing, nothing at all. And where was João? And Mr. Alamoody? And Arnie? I curled up in a doorway and put my cloth over my head and tried to sleep. Africans are night people—it wasn't easy.

The next day Mollie apologized for locking the door. She got carried away. She had thought I'd be with Joao. I took a shower and told her it was time I went back to Ghana.

172

"Really? We've seen nothing." I said I didn't care what she did, I was going back. Finally she said she'd come with me—petulantly; she didn't want to stay alone.

We went to find Arnie at the Hotel Ivoire. He invited us for lunch and seemed preoccupied. We all had club sandwiches stuck together with nasty little cellophane-decorated toothpicks.

Across the room an incredibly skinny, incredibly beautiful African girl was feeding bits of fruit salad to her lover. He would open his mouth and she would pop in a bit of paw-paw or pineapple and then run her finger around his lips. They were oblivious of everyone else.

"We've had some good times," said Arnie.

"Sure we have, Arnie."

He gave us each a card and thought it would be swell if we ever got together in Sausalito. The sugar cubes were wrapped in papers marked like dice.

"D'you know what we do?" he said. "We play craps for who's going to pay for dinner. With the sugar cubes."

We laughed appreciatively.

We said nothing about João or Mr. Alamoody (João had phoned and said he'd been tied up by business) and I decided to let the matter drop. If Arnie ran guns that was his affair.

"Goodbye," we said, shaking hands.

"Goodbye Arnie." He saw us to a taxi.

On the trip back we were stopped first by a health van (on the Ivory Coast side) and made to line up one by one and have our necks felt. The man who did this gave no explanations, simply felt our necks and motioned us to go. There was a nasty-looking syringe in some alcohol and a thermometer in alcohol and dirty cotton wool.

"What is he looking for?" I asked Mollie.

"God knows." We were very frightened.

Later on, across the border, a jeep drew up and blocked our way. Five young army officers got out and threw down all the luggage. The driver argued with them while eight of us stood in the heat, waiting. I was eating a piece of bread and one of the officers came up—he had his cap on backwards—and whipped out a knife. He pressed it through the thin fabric of my blouse.

"Give me a piece of your bread," he said. It happened too fast for me to be frightened. The knife was there, had always been there, pointed just below my ribs.

"Feed me," he said. "Bronie woman." He spat at the roadside. I fed him the rest of my bread. The driver paid some money and we were let go. There was a tiny hole in my blouse and a scratch just below my ribs. Busia's men. Crazy. Or bored. I began to shake.

The next day I came around the corner by Barclay's Bank and ran into Jimmie Owusu-Banahene. He was dressed in an English morning suit, very correct, and with a rose in his buttonhole.

"Hello!" he said. "So you are back."

"Yes."

"And what did you bring me?"

"A bottle of good wine; a pound of sweet butter. They're at the resthouse."

"And the miracle?" The boys outside the post office were watching us carefully. I shook my head.

"No miracles."

"And did you meet the man?"

"If I did, I didn't recognize him." He put his hands on my shoulders.

"Did you commit any political acts?"

I smiled. "I released a cockroach in the Hotel Ivoire."

He smiled too. And then I added, "I know nothing about Africa, nothing."

174

With his broad thumb he traced a line on my cheek—like a tribal mark. "That's a beginning," he said. "A good beginning." Then he added, "We have another sayin' that might interest you."

"Yes?"

"Once you have stepped in the river," he said, "there is no time to think of measuring its depth."

GREEN STAKES FOR THE GARDEN

His voice came first, by itself, propelled by the lazy afternoon which twitched like a sleeping dog and made a quick, spasmodic statement of how it felt about having the summer stillness interrupted; irritated, it flung his words out of the deserted street and over her garden gate—"Lady, can I cut the grass?"

Long before, or what seemed long before, his head and neck declared themselves over the top, tense and with as-yet-unexplained desperation, as owners or desperate keepers of the runaway voice which was saying again, perhaps had not paused at all except to take a breath—"Lady, can I cut the grass?" Faded red-plaid flannel shirt (and some part of her mind thinking flannel on an afternoon like this!) and faded skin, too, grey-, sidewalk-, city-coloured, but the eyes quite different, gas blue, flaming as the gate swung forward under his weight and a part of her mind thinking, even then, we really ought to have a latch, as he shot, stumbled, flung himself across the grass as if he, the keeper of the runaway voice, needed no apology or warrant or by-your-leave in his precipitous rush to recapture such a desperate and dangerous thing. "Lady, can I cut the grass?"

She was startled and not startled, said automatically, "Mind the teacups;" without raising her voice, and hardly her eyes after that first, automatic, glance—behaved much as she would if one of the children had rushed in slightly off-balance with excitement, explosive with news of a dog fight, a dead bird or the imminent possibility of an ice-cream cone, "Mind the teacups," in her professional mother's voice. So that for—how long?—five, ten, fifteen seconds they remained silent, their bodies confronting one another, but she not yet acknowledging his existence as stranger and intrusion, holding determinedly to the scene in the garden before his abrupt and apocalyptic entrance, thinking to herself, if I don't look maybe he'll go away, while her companion, who had been stretched out lazily in the other deck chair, sat up with a "What the hell?" And at the sound of *that* voice, slurred, rough, as if wakened abruptly from a sleep, she became aware, really aware, of the stranger's presence and regarded him dismayed, not because she was really afraid, but because his precipitous entrance had indeed smashed something as delicate as her grandmother's flowered cups and saucers; and the thread she had been spinning so carefully between herself and the young man sprawled beside her dangled now forlornly from her fingers (and a part of her mind said isn't that just my luck!).

She adjusted the chair two notches forward so that she could sit up straight and with one hand reached forward, palms outward, toward the stranger, warning him that he had come (gone) quite far enough. With the other she unconsciously pulled her skirt below her knees.

"Are you accustomed to come barging into other people's gardens uninvited?" (Yet even as she said it she knew she had adopted the wrong tone, could sense rather than see the young man look at her, puzzled, as if she had picked up, somehow, the wrong script. This made her even more resentful; why should *she* be in the wrong! While the strange man simply stared at her as if she had replied to him with gibberish.)

"Listen," he said, "I gotta have work. This grass here,"

178

he made a wide proprietorial sweep with his arm, taking in the tiny garden. She noticed his nails had been bitten down so low the tips of his fingers extended, naked and greyish, a quarter of an inch; so that he looked deformed, spatulate —with those naked pinky-grey pads at the ends of his fingers instead of nails. Horrible. "This here grass, I could cut it real nice for a coupala dollars." He swayed back and forth a few feet from the end of her chair while she gave him another long, careful look, still taking him in as a visual fact—a drastic rearrangement of the landscape of her afternoon. (And why should she feel bothered when *he* said what the hell in that funny tone of voice? Because that too was out of place.) The back yard seemed to have contracted so that they were practically on top of one another—she, the young man and the stranger—were eyeing each other, panting, and would soon leap forward with a snarl, the three of them rolling over and over in the hot dry grass. Over and over, crashing into the border and crushing the flowers underneath them in their terrible animal-like resentment. Even the temperature seemed to have shot suddenly upward ten degrees, although she and the young man had been saying to each other (only five minutes ago?) that this must be some kind of record.

The two chairs underneath the apple tree, the teacups, the plate of little cakes, the sprinkler moving slowly, gently across the border—it had all been so carefully thought out; had given her such *aesthetic* satisfaction. No-one, she thought miserably, would ever understand that aspect of it. How, for instance, she had carefully selected just those little cakes and no others—and just that number—to go on just that plate. And even remembered to buy three over so there wouldn't be any trouble at lunch. And how the whole day had seemed (until now) inspired, each little detail working itself out so beautifully that it was only natural to think in

179

terms of plays and paintings. Even the green stakes had been a stroke of genius.

Yet now it was all animal-like, smouldering; she could smell the stranger's sweat from where she sat. What was she supposed to do? Get up and offer him a cup of tea? (She thought of those queer spatulate fingers curled around one of her grandmother's teacups and for the first time felt afraid.)

"There's no work for you here. Please go." He never moved, never changed his movement, stood swaying back and forth and back as if he had a pain, or was still recovering from his incredible journey through the garden gate.

Her companion spoke. "You heard the lady, didn't you?" He swung one lean brown leg over onto the grass, but she motioned him back.

"No," she said softly. "It will be all right." (And a part of her mind thinking it's all very well for you to play Sir Galahad now! And again that slow smouldering resentment flickered between them.) She arranged her face in a smile.

"I'm afraid this isn't a very good neighbourhood for yard work. We all do our own. Why don't you try the church two blocks over? They might have something you could do." The smile hurt and she put her hand to her face in an effort to keep it in place. What time was it?

The children would be back soon; the afternoon was nearly over. And it had all been so perfect after the first awkward moments, hers not his, for she had never seen him awkward, had thought of him to herself as somehow lacquered or varnished—always shining, always "ready for company" as it were. And there she was, her voice fluttering around him as if he were some lacquered brass lamp and she a moth impatient to embrace her doom. But the green stakes had saved her.

"How would you like to lend me a hand with the garden?" And he amused, skeptical: "I'm not much of a gardener."

He had held out his lean brown hands and she had marvelled at the nails, so regular, a faint pencil line of white above the smooth shell-pink. But strong hands, a golden brown of a colour that made her think of chickens roasting slowly on a spit. She had a sudden impulse to reach over and bite into one of his hands, was quite dizzy with the desire to simply take one up and bite it; they looked delicious.

"Oh, neither am I," she cried. "But I bought some stakes to prop up the snapdragons this morning. I feel terribly guilty about them, poor things. The children said they'd help but I really hate putting it off another minute." She had literally run into the garage for the stakes and garden shears and twine, cried gaily, busily, "I'll hold them if you'll tie," thrusting the ball of twine into his skeptical golden hands.

They had moved slowly up the narrow border, careful not to step on the other plants and flowers. The snapdragons were bent over or lying flat. They appealed to her: strange little puffs of colour, lemon, mauve, raspberry pink, like summer sweets or summer dresses. Cool. Reminiscent of childhood. And yet their paradoxical shape, labial, curiously exciting, swollen and stretched. She lifted the stalks carefully, holding them tight against the stakes as he snipped and tied, snipped and tied, the sun strong on his golden arms and hands.

"Look how twisted they are," she mourned, caressing the tip of a blossom with her finger. "I've been promising for weeks—and now I'm afraid they're crippled for life."

She really meant it, bent over her poor, pastel invalids, felt genuinely guilty about the thing. What was so beautiful was that he had understood, had kept silent and snipped and tied, looking quietly into her eyes as they reached the

181

end and she took the garden things from his firm, brown, polished hands. "I'll get the tea."

"I'll wait under that nice apple tree of yours." Then it had all been understood between them, just like that; so that she had run up the back stairs like a girl and giggled when she nearly dropped the sugar bowl.

And she had lain back gracefully in the long chair, sipping lemon tea, surveying the border through half-shut eyes, her heart reaching out to those brave, brave snapdragons, so desperately erect—like old and wounded warriors on parade. While his firm brown fingers moved lazily up and down her leg and she had felt at any minute she might begin to purr.

So that she was actually smiling at him, lips parted, when the stranger started in again, holding onto the picnic table now, bent over as if over a basin and she became quite terrified as she used to be as a child in the midst of a nightmare knowing she was dreaming, straining to wake herself up. He spewed forth words and cries, not looking at her—looking instead, if looking at all, down through the slats of the table at the grass below as if it were personally responsible for his fate.

"You never give a guy a chance you bastards think you're all so goddamn smart she said and don't come back until you pay at last for what I've given out for free I must have been a nut and them in the corner laughin to beat hell you gotta give me what's a coupala dollars. I'll trim the hedge real nice for free your hedge needs trimmin too and she just layin there with nothin underneath saying where'd you think the money came from? Why don't you listen to me lady why..."

So that the silence was even worse when for a brief moment sound was shut off and all she could hear was a dull thud as if something overripe had fallen, quite near her, off the tree; and all she could see was a blur and thought my

God I'm going even deeper. When her vision cleared and the stranger gave her one last pleading look out of the blood grotesquely red against his face, unreal, outrageous as if some spiteful child had scrawled a crayoned obscenity across her pastel world.

And then her would-be lover's hands reached out and caught the stranger once, grasping his shoulders hard, the knuckles white, so that all she saw was the back of his head as he went back out the way he burst in, muttering and sobbing to himself out of the garden gate and up the outraged street.

And she, "My God, my God," giving the flowers one last despairing glance as she picked up the tray and headed for the stairs. All along a part of her saying isn't that just my luck!

INITRAM

Writers are terrible liars. There are nicer names for it, of course, but liars will do. They take a small incident and blow it up, like a balloon—puff puff—and the out-of-work man who comes to ask if he can cut the grass ends up in their story as an out-of-control grey-faced, desperate creature who hurls himself through the garden gate and by his sheer presence wrecks a carefully arranged afternoon between a married woman and her intended lover.

The truth is I was reading an old friend's manuscript. The truth is I thought the man hadn't gone but was lurking in the back lane just beyond the blackberry bushes.

The truth is I only thought I saw him there—flashes of a red-plaid shirt beyond the green. (Writers also lie to themselves.)

The truth is that when the police came and I was asked to describe this man I was overcome with shame and embarrassment to suddenly notice him, half a block away, moving a neighbour's lawn mower up and down in regular and practical stripes.

The truth is I still insisted (to myself, after the grinning policeman had gone) that the man had been sinister, menacing, unpleasant. And of course he is, in my story.

But what do writers do with the big events in life—births and broken hearts and deaths—the great archetypal situations that need no real enhancement or "touching up"?

Surely they simply *tell* these, acting as mediums through which the great truths filter. Not at all—or not usually or maybe sometimes when they happen to other people.

That is why I decided to call Lydia when my marriage broke up. I was living on an island—felt I needed a wider audience, an audience that would understand and accept my exaggerations for what they were. It had to be a fellow writer, preferably a woman. I called her up long-distance. One of her daughters answered and said she wasn't there could I leave my number? I put the phone down, already planning the ferry trip, the excitement of the telling of my terrible news. Lydia was perfect. Yes. I couldn't wait for her to call me back.

I didn't, in fact, know her very well. I had done a review of her first published book and then later, when I went to visit her city, had on a sudden whim called from a phone booth and identified myself. She had told me to come right over. I had my husband and three kids with me. That seemed too much of an imposition on anyone we didn't know so I took the littlest and he agreed to take the others to the Wax Museum. We drove up a very classy road, with huge houses—some were really what we used to call mansions—on either side. I began to get cold feet.

I had visions of a patrician face and perfect fingernails—drinking tea from her grandmother's bone china cups. We would talk about Proust and Virginia Woolf with a few casual remarks about *Nightwood* and the diaries of Anais Nin.

As we drove up to the front door of a big, imposing, mock-tudor residence I thought of "Our Gal Sunday," a soap-opera I had loved when I was a kid. It always began with a question as to whether a beautiful young girl from a small mining town in the West could find happiness as the wife of England's wealthiest and most titled lord, Lord

186

Henry Brinthrop.

It was her stories, you see. They were about life on the prairies—about farms and poverty (both spiritual and material) and, very often, a young girl's struggle against those things. Yet here was this house, on this road and a statue in the garden.

"Wait for me," I said to my husband, "If a butler or maid answers, I'm not going in."

But Lydia answered—in black slacks and an old black sweater and no shoes. She gave me a hug and I went in with my littlest child and didn't look back.

Through the hall into the sitting-room, then the dining-room (an impression of a piano and lots of books, of a big antique dining table covered with clutter generally, now that I think back on it. Somewhere upstairs a small child was screaming), through another narrow hall and into a big kitchen. She asked if my little girl wanted some orange juice. She wouldn't answer so I answered for her as mothers do on such occasions.

"Yes please."

When Lydia opened the refrigerator a great pile of things fell out on the kitchen floor. Frozen pizzas, a dish of left-over mashed potatoes, the bottle of juice, something unidentifiable in a glass jar. We looked at each other and began to laugh.

"The house," I said, "I was terrified."

"I *hate* this house," she said. "I hate it."

Then talked and talked while our two little girls (we each had three, extraordinary! We each had the same dinner set bought on special at the Hudson's Bay Company years before, "Cherry Thieves" it was called—she used one of the saucers for an ash tray) played something or other upstairs.

She was older than I was (but not much) and very beautiful with dark curly chaotic hair and the kind of white skin that gives off the radiance a candle does when it has burnt down at the core and the sides are still intact. Her book had brought her fame (if not fortune) but she was having trouble with her second one, a novel.

She hated the house and couldn't keep it up. Her husband was a professor—he loved it. It was miserably cold in the winter—sometimes the furnace stopped altogether. What did I think of Doris Lessing, of Joyce Carol Oates, of *The Edible Woman*? Her daughter had made a scene in the supermarket and called her a "fucking bitch." Did that kind of thing happen to me? Her neighbour was a perfect housewife, perfect. She was always sending over cakes and preserves. One day she took one of her neighbour's cheesecakes and stamped all over it with her bare feet, she said. An aging Canadian writer (male) had told her drunkenly, "Well, I might read ya, but I'd never fuck ya." Did I think it was all right to send a kid to day care when she was only three?

And even while I was talking with her, marvelling at her, helping her mop up the floor, I kept wondering why she didn't write about all this, why she had stopped at twenty years ago and written nothing about her marriage or this house or her child who had been still-born and how the doctor (male) and her husband couldn't understand why it took her so long to get over it. I wondered about her husband but he was off somewhere practicing with a chamber-music group. He liked old instruments, old houses, things with a patina of history and culture. His family accepted her now that she'd won awards.

I only saw her a few times after that—we lived in different cities and there was a boat ride between us. But we wrote (occasionally); she had large round handwriting, like a child's.

Her novel was not going well—it kept turning itself into stories—she was going to Ireland with her husband for a holiday. How was I? Not literary letters: we were both too busy, too involved in our own affairs. Just little notes, like little squeezes or hugs which said, "Sister, I am here."

We read once, at a Women's Week, or rather I read, with two others, while Lydia sat on the blue-carpeted floor with a Spanish cape over her head and let somebody else read for her. She and I were both scared and had gotten drunk before we went—by not reading she had somehow let me down. We four ladies all had dinner together and talked about what it was like to be woman and writer and egged each other on to new witticisms and maybe a few new insights but I did not feel close to Lydia that evening. I was still sore about the way she'd plonked herself down on the carpet and pulled her shawl over her head and let somebody else read for her. It was very clever, I thought to myself, and very dramatic. For there was Lydia's story, unrolling out of the mouth of another woman (whose story it was not), and there was the author herself sitting like an abandoned doll, on the floor beside the reader. The audience loved it and sent out sympathetic vibrations to her. I thought it was a con. And almost said to her, "Lydia, I think that was a very clever con," but didn't because I realized that maybe I wished I had thought of it first and why not store it away for some future date—it was a nice piece of dramatic business.

And once we had lunch in her city—at a medieval place where we swept in in our capes (I had a cape too by then) and ate and drank our way through a rainy West Coast afternoon. I wasn't staying overnight so I still hadn't met her husband. Her novel was out and she was winning more awards. I was a little jealous. My books came out and vanished into the well of oblivion. She just went up and up and up. "I've been writing for twenty years," she said, "don't forget that. Two books in twenty years."

She had pretended she was making the sitting-room curtains when her neighbours invited her over for coffee. She always worked in a basement room. Now her secret was well and truly out.

"How does your husband feel about it all?"

"Oh, I never write about *him*," she said. She lit a cigarette. "He's probably my biggest fan."

Now I waited for her to call me back. My husband (correction, my ex-husband) was coming over to be with his children. I had a whole day and a night off. Whether I wanted to or not, I had to leave this place. And I wanted to, I really wanted to. What was the point in hanging around while he was here, in crying over spilt milk, in locking empty, horseless barn doors, in trying to pick up nine stiches, or in mopping up all the water under the goddamn bridge. I baked bread and cleaned the cabin and got supper for the kids and still she hadn't called. My ex-husband called, however, and said in his new strained, estranged voice, was it all set for tomorrow and I said sure but began to feel sorry for myself because there was really no place I wanted to go except this one place—Lydia's—and I'd got it into my head that if I couldn't go there I couldn't go anywhere and would have to end up going back to the city I had left behind and getting a room in some cheap hotel down near Hastings street, and drinking myself into oblivion with cheap red wine. Or going back and forth all day on the ferry, ending up at midnight on one of the neighbouring islands, getting a room at the inn. A stranger in a brown wool cape. Going into the public room and ordering a drink. Did they have a public room? Would there be local characters sitting around and playing darts—a handsome stranger whose sailing boat was tied up because of the storm? There was not even a small craft warning out but never mind—the weather was almost as fickle as friendship—it was not inconceivable that a sail-boat-disabling storm could blow up by tomorrow night—

"I'll always care what happens to you," he said.

We were teasing wool on the floor in front of the potbelly stove, the three of us—the youngest child was asleep. There was only the oil lamp on and the CBC was broadcasting a documentary about Casals. "The quality of a man's life is as important as the quality of his art," the old man said. Our hands were soft and oily from the lanolin in the wool. We touched each other's faces with our new, soft hands. Yes, I thought, yes. And maybe I'll be all right after all. The fleece had been bought by my husband's lover, my ex-best friend. It was from New Zealand, the finest wool in the world. I paid for it, the wool. I had left a cheque on the table the last time I was in town. On the phone my ex-husband mentioned it wasn't enough, she'd mistaken the price or the price had been incorrectly quoted. But it was all right, he'd make up the difference.

"I bet you will," I said.

I was seeing everything symbolically. Lydia phoned and I said, "Just a minute I have to light a candle." The room with the phone in it was in darkness. I stuck the candle in the window and picked up the phone again with my soft lanolin-soaked hands.

"Hello," I said, "Can I come and visit you tomorrow and stay overnight?" Her voice sounded a bit funny but that could be the line, which was notoriously bad.

"Sure," she said, "Of course. But I'll be out until suppertime. Can you find something to do until suppertime?"

"Can I come a little before? I want to talk to you."

"Come around four," she said. She sounded as though she had a cold.

"I'll bring a bottle," I said.

"Fine."

I had to be away on the first ferry—what would I do all day? I rubbed lanolin into my face. Sheep shed their old

191

coats and went on living. Snakes too. I could hear Casals'
child laughing in the background. Someone had lent us a
spinner and it stood in the corner of the front room. Not a
fairytale spinner which would turn straw into gold. Very
solid and unromantic—an Indian spinner without even the
big wheel. Nothing for a Sleeping Beauty to prick her finger
on. It worked like an old treadle sewing machine but I didn't
have the hang of it yet—my wool always broke. Whirr
whirr. There was something nice about just pressing down
on the treadle.

I took the candle into the kitchen and wrapped my bread
in clean tea towels. I put out a jar of blackberry jam and two
poems folded underneath the jar. That would have to do.

When I got to Lydia's house she was frying chicken in the
kitchen. Same black slacks and old black sweater. Same bare
feet and clutter. There were two enormous frying pans full
of chicken wings both hissing and spitting away and Lydia
had a long two-prong kitchen fork in her hand.

I took off my cape and sat down, unwrapping the bottle.
"Good," she said, "pour us a glass." Her voice didn't
sound as if she had a cold any more; it sounded harsh and a
little loud, as if she were talking to someone slightly deaf.
She was jabbing the chicken wings as if they were sausages
in need of pricking. She couldn't leave those chicken wings
alone and after my second glass I began.

"Listen," I said, "I've got something I want to tell you."

"I've got something I want to tell you too," she said, and
then, rather absent-mindedly, "did you buy only one bottle?"

"Sorry. But have some more, it doesn't matter."

"It's all right," she said, "we'll drink the dinner wine.
Tony will just have to bring some more."

I was anxious to begin. I wanted to make it funny and
witty and brave—to get rid of the pain or to immortalize it
and fix it—which? I don't know, I never know. I took

192

another drink of my sherry and wished she'd stop poking at those chicken wings.

"I don't actually live here any more," she said, waving the long-handled fork. "I only come back to cook the dinners."

"You what?"

Turning all the chicken wings over one more time, she lowered the heat under the pans and came to sit down next to me. She kept her fork with her, however, and laid it on the tablecloth where it left a greasy two-pronged stain.

"I've left him," she said, "the bastard." Her voice was very harsh, very tough. I felt she'd put something over on me, just as I'd felt the day of the reading when she sat on the floor and pulled her cape over her head.

"I wish you'd told me over the phone."

"I couldn't. It's too complicated. Besides, I come back here every day in any case."

It was both moving and bizarre. He had been supposed to move out, she had even found him an apartment only a few minutes away. But at the last minute he panicked, said he couldn't live in an apartment, talked about his piano, his collection of old instruments, the upheaval. He suggested she move out instead.

"But what about the children?"

"That's the trouble. I have to pick Ellen up from school —he can't do it of course and so I just stay on and make the dinners. The other two are all right, it's only the little one who still needs to be looked after."

"But that's crazy."

"Is it? What would you do?"

I admitted that I didn't know.

"But how can you all eat together—how can you stand it?"

"I can't," she admitted, "but he won't move out, and find-ing a house big enough for me and the girls is going to take time." She got up and rummaged in the pantry. Came back with a bottle of wine.

"I think we'd better start on this," she said. I undid the cork while she got up to turn the chicken wings.

"He brought her right to the house," she said. "When I was on that reading tour. Brought her right here and the children were here too."

The name of the wine was Sangré de Toro.

"At least she wasn't your best friend," I said.

"I knew her, I knew her, she's one of his students. I used to think she was mousey. I encouraged her to do something with herself. Ha. And I think the lady next door too," she said.

"The one who bakes cakes."

"That's the one. The perfect mother."

"Maybe you're just being paranoid."

"Maybe."

We began the Sangré de Toro.

"What's your big news?" she said.

The two older girls were out somewhere for the evening so there was just the youngest child, who must have been six or seven, Lydia, her husband and myself. She and I were pretty drunk by the time we finished the Sangré de Toro but she had insisted I call her husband at the University and ask him to bring home another bottle.

"Tell him specifically what you want," she yelled at me from the kitchen. "Otherwise he'll bring home Calona Red."

I told him. Now he sat opposite me with two huge plates of chicken wings between us. I didn't want to look at his baffled eyes, his embarrassed smile.

"He still wears a white handkerchief in his breast pocket," she had said. "Irons them himself."

The vegetable was frozen peas and there was bread on the table because Lydia had forgotten all about potatoes.

The child was raucous and unpleasant. I wondered what happened when she woke up in the night with a bad dream and whether he went in to her or whether her teenage sisters did. I wondered if she had been the one to tell about the student. Kids will do things like that and not always out of innocence.

Lydia ate one chicken wing after another. We were all going out as soon as the dishes were done and the babysitter came. My real self didn't want to go but my drunken self thought what the hell it's better than staying here with these three miserable people.

While Tony was doing the dishes Lydia hauled me upstairs, pulled me up after her like an older sister a younger, or a mother a reluctant child. I understood the fierce energy of her anger. It was like someone who is hurt during an exciting game. While the excitement is there the pain is simply not felt. She hurled me into their bedroom.

"Look," she said.

I don't know what I expected to see. Stained sheets piled up in a corner or the student stark naked and manacled to the bed or what. But everything seemed all right. No shattered mirrors or blood-stained bedspreads, just an ordinary pleasant-looking bedroom.

"I don't see."

"Look." She was pointing to the walk-in closet.

"I've left all my shoes here except one pair. Crazy isn't it? I just can't seem to take my shoes away."

"Maybe you don't really want to go."

"Oh no, I want to go. I have to go. Or he does. One of us anyway. It isn't just the girl."

"It never is."

On his side of the closet the tweed jackets and neatly pressed trousers were hung with military precision. On her side there were only empty hangers and a large heap of shoes piled any which way. Was that significant, the order/disorder? Was it an attempt to break through this orderly self that made him bring his student to this bed? Or had he just been lonely? I didn't want to think about that for after all, wasn't he the enemy?

We went back downstairs.

The babysitter came and we went out. Lydia had put on a filthy white crocheted wool poncho. Tony objected mildly. "Are you going out in that? It's dirty."

"That's tough," Lydia said.

They were playing to me, an audience of one. Maybe that's why we were going out—to gain a larger audience. I panicked—what if I had too much to drink and began to cry? Lydia looked witchy and wicked with her uncombed hair and dirty poncho. I felt she was quite capable of doing something terrible to her husband—mocking him or humiliating him in some way, and I was to be her accomplice. He had a heavy projector in his hand.

"We had arranged to show some slides," he said, "before we knew you were coming."

"Slides of our European trip," Lydia said. "One of Tony's colleagues is going this summer—he wanted to see them."

I thought it was strange they didn't invite him over here, but maybe Lydia had refused to actually entertain. I found the whole thing strange—sitting between them in the car, following them up the steps of their friend's house, saying hello and taking off my cape, patting my face to keep the smile in place, the way some women pat their hair before they go into a room. Our host was shy and pale and had a club foot. There didn't seem to be any hostess. But there were two other people in the sitting-room, a tall, lean man in a bright blue shirt, string tie and cowboy boots, and a plump woman in a black crêpe dress, black pointy fifties shoes and a rhinestone brooch. Both the man and the woman had nice faces, expectant faces, as if they expected that whoever walked through the next door was bound to be cheerful and interesting and good. Innocent faces, almost the faces of small children. We were introduced and asked what we would like to drink and Tony began to set up the projector.

Lydia was talking to Tony's colleague in her strange new brassy tough-gal voice, flirting with him, making him smile. "Does he know?" I wondered. He had introduced her as Tony's wife. I sat down next to the man in the blue shirt.

"What do you do?" I asked.

"I'm a bee-keeper," he said.

"You might say he's a bee-baron," said his brother. I could see they were brothers in their smiles and something to do with their ears, a strange extra little fold where the ear joined the head. Other than that they didn't really look alike, the one small and dark and with the pallor of the academic, the other tall and fair and with what we call a "weathered" skin.

"A swarm of bees in May," said Lydia, "is worth a load of hay. I remember hearing farmers say that when I was a kid. I grew up on a farm," she said and flashed a smile at the bee-keeper's wife.

"Do you like it," I asked, "keeping bees?" I had thought of buying one or two hives for the island. I already had hens and a fleece for spinning and would have my nine bean rows in the spring. Lydia had laughed when I told her my real dream was to have a little farm.

"Ha. Only city people yearn to live on a farm. I hated it."

"Why?"

"I'm not even sure why any more. The constant work—the catastrophes—the exhaustion—the women always in the kitchen—something always being butchered, beheaded or skinned or pickled or preserved."

"Maybe it doesn't have to be that way?"

"It has to be that way. If you really live off the land you live off the land. Nothing can be put off or wasted or ignored. I always felt the kitchen smelled of blood or sugar or vinegar or manure or all of these. I felt I went to school stinking of all of it."

"Those are good smells. Honest smells. I worked in an asylum once—I got that smell on me. I used carbolic soap and tried to get it off."

She shook her head and changed the subject, only adding, "They weren't good smells when I was going to school."

Had she been teased, then? Had the boys pulled chicken feathers out of her dark curly hair—had her dresses been too long—were her hands all wrinkled from washwater? I realized how little I actually knew about her except through her stories. I guess this conversation took place before her novel came out.

Tony asked in his apologetic manner if we were ready to see the slides. Lydia and the bee-keeper's wife were sitting in easy chairs on the other side of the room, where the screen had been set up, so they had to move. Lydia came and sat cross-legged on the floor by my feet. The bee-keeper and I were on the couch and we shoved over to make room for the bee-keeper's wife. Tony was next to me, behind the projector and his friend was next to him on a kitchen chair. He got up and after offering us another drink (only Lydia and I accepted) turned out all the lights.

I don't remember much about the slide show. Tony projected and Lydia commented. Ireland, England, Scotland, Wales and then across the Channel into France and down through Spain. They were all "views"—that is to say they told me nothing about the two people who had taken that trip. Alone. Without the children. Was that when they first suspected they had nothing to say to one another? Had they

198

set off with high hopes and become more and more disenchanted? What had finally driven that orderly controlled man to introduce that student into his bedroom? Not secretly but openly, "in front of the children." From where I was sitting I could see that his hands shook every time he put in another slide.

"You've got that one in backwards," Lydia said. We all came to attention and studied the screen—it was a bull fight scene and looked perfectly all right to me.

"I don't think—" Tony began.

"Look for yourself. Look at it. Can't you see it's back to front?"

"I sure don't see anything funny," said the bee-keeper.

" 'Initram'," Lydia said in her bold brassy voice. "Look at the advertisements and tell me what kind of a drink is Initram."

"Oh," he said. "Sorry."

"Ha."

His hands shook a little more as he carefully pried out the offending slide and turned it around.

"There," he said. "Is that better?"

"Oh God," said Lydia. "You've done it again." And sure enough he had. There was "Initram" being advertised again.

"I'd like another drink," said Lydia, "Initram on the rocks."

Tony switched the projector off and for a minute we were in a complete and tension-filled darkness before his friend had enough presence of mind to reach up and switch on the lights.

"That's all folks," he said, trying to sound like Woody Woodpecker, trying to be funny.

"Don't you want to show the rest of the slides?" Lydia said.

"No, I think that's enough."

"Well, tell us about bees then," she said, turning around and facing the sofa, backing away a little bit so she could gaze up at the bee-keeper, her pretty head cocked on one side.

"What do you want to know?" he said, smiling. But uncomfortable too for he was not so dumb or naïve that he didn't see what she was doing to her husband.

"Oh. Everything. Everything." She waved her hand. "Their mating habits for instance. Do they really only mate once? The queens, I mean."

"No, they can mate more than once, maybe two, three times. But usually only once. It's funny," he said, "when you stop to think of it. From a human point of view the drone that wins is the loser really."

"I don't follow you," I said. I really knew nothing about bees. Whereas I had a funny feeling about Lydia. Would a kid who had a grandfather who kept bees—? Or maybe she never did have such a grandfather. Maybe her grandfather just said that whenever he saw a swarm—the way my father used to say, "Red sky at night, sailor's delight" when he'd never been near the ocean.

"Fun, frolic and death," he said, "fun, frolic and death. Those drones are the laziest devils you'd like to see. Waited on hand and foot by their sisters—don't have to do nothing except eat and lie around and take the occasional look-see outside. Then one day the queen just zooms up into the blue with hundreds of those drones dashin' after her. A fantastic sight—fantastic."

"And the race is to the swift," said Lydia, taking a long sip of her drink as if it were some strange nectar, then parting her lips and looking up at the bee-keeper with her new bold look.

"The strongest and swiftest catches her," he said. "Sometimes she even zooms back toward 'em, because she wants

200

to be caught you know. That's all part of it."

"She wants to be caught," repeated Lydia. "She has to be caught." She took another long sip of her drink. The bee-keeper's wife just sat back against the cushions and smiled.

"She has to be caught."

"So she is caught."

"And then?"

"And then he clasps her to him, face to face—there's a little explosion as all his male organs pop out and they fly together like that face to face, while he fertilizes her."

"Then he dies?" I asked.

"Then he dies. You see, they fall to the ground together, outside the home hive of the queen, and when she tries to pull away, he's stuck so fast to her she pulls most of his abdomen away."

"Ab-*do*-men," said Lydia, lightly mocking him. But not in the way she said, "Initram."

"My brother probably knows more about bees than any man in North America," said the man with the club foot. "He could write a book about them."

"It's my job," he said simply.

"Oh don't," cried Lydia. "Don't ever write a book about them." She gave a mock shudder. "I wonder what it feels like," she said. "To fly out like that after the darkness of the hive into the blue sky and the green trees and to feel the sunshine on her back. To know that her destiny is about to be fulfilled." Then she turned toward the bee-keeper's wife. "And you. Is it your life too? Bees?"

She nodded her head, serene in her black dress and rhine-stones. She had a strong Southern accent.

"It's my life too."

Then the bee-keeper did a beautiful thing. He just reached over and put his lean brown hand over hers.

"We try to study the bees," he said. "We try to do what

they do."

"Fun, frolic and death?" said Lydia, flirting, slyly mocking.

"No," he said, but not angrily. He didn't swat at her any more than he might swat at a bee who flew a little too close to his ear.

"They are true communists—the bees. No-one works for any profit to himself. Everything is done only for the good of the colony. If we could live like that—"

"Ah yes, Utopia." Lydia sighed. "Perhaps if we all ate more honey?" She was mocking him again, circling back. She smiled at the three men in the room. All she needed was a yellow sweater.

"Who knows? That's where our word honeymoon comes from, you know—the old belief in the magical powers of honey. Germany I think it was, or Austria. The newly-married couple would drink mead for a month after the wedding."

"What was it supposed to do for them?"

"Now that I'm not sure of. Make 'em happy and industrious I guess."

"Is it true," said Lydia, "that the queen can sting over and over—that she doesn't die when she stings? I read that somewhere I think. Tony, do you remember reading that somewhere or somebody telling us that the queen could sting over and over?"

"I don't remember."

"Well, it's true, isn't it?" She appealed to the bee-keeper.

"It's true. She has to defend herself. It's her nature."

"There, you see Tony, I was right. It's her nature."

"There is usually only one queen," said the bee-keeper, "she kills off all the others."

"Why not?" Lydia said, "it's natural."

Then we were all leaving—I can't remember who stood up first. We said goodbye to the bee-keeper and his wife. I

202

wrote down the name of a supply house where I could get supers and bee suits. I wrote down the names of two books. He (the bee-keeper) went out to his van and came back with a little jar of honey for each of us. Alfalfa honey, clear and thick and golden.

"Jim Ritchie and Sons," it said. "Abbotsford, BC," and "Unpasteurized" underneath. "Mary Beth designed the labels," he said proudly.

I slept downstairs in a little parlour with a fireplace. They had coal and started a fire for me. Made up the Hide-A-Bed and went off upstairs together. I lay in the darkness under Lydia's grandmother's Star of Bethlehem quilt and smelled the smell of the coal fire and was back fourteen years under a quilt in a big double bed in Scotland. On my honeymoon. The maid had come in with a stone hot water bottle but we were already warm from drinking a strange mixture in the public bar—something called Athol Bross and now that I thought of it, I seemed to remember that it was made of porridge and honey. Or maybe I just had honey on the brain.

What had happened to us? What had happened to us all? I began to cry while Lydia made noisy love upstairs. I heard her—she wanted me to hear her. It was the last line in the last paragraph of the story she'd been writing all evening. I wondered if she'd come down the next morning with Tony's abdomen irrevocably stuck to her front.

We don't see each other very much any more. She lives in a distant city. But once a year we meet—at the Writers Union annual general meeting—and compare children and lovers and ideas for stories, usually in that order. We flirt, we get drunk, we congratulate ourselves that somehow miraculously we have survived another year, that we each have money and a room of one's own and are writing fiction. This year I told her (lying) that I was thinking of writing a story about her.

"I'm calling it 'Chicken Wings'," I said.

"Chicken Wings?"

"The night I came to see you, and you and Tony had just split up."

"And you wanted to tell me about your break-up."

"*Sangré de Toro*," I said. We began to laugh.

"Do you remember the bee-keeper and his wife?"

"Of course, they're in the story."

"Fun, frolic and death—oh God."

We laughed until we cried.

"What name d'you want?" I said. "You can choose your own name."

"Lydia," she said. "I always wanted to be called Lydia."

"All right," I said. "You can be Lydia."

"But I don't like your title," she said. "I think you'll have to change it."

A MONDAY DREAM AT
ALAMEDA PARK

Coming down to Mexico had been the best thing they could
have done. Laura was afraid of nothing, nothing, and her
strength was infectious. Although he did not have her youth
or her cast-iron stomach (perhaps the two went hand in
hand) and his minor attack of *turista* became, in San Miguel,
cramps and diarrhea of such intensity that he took himself
off to the hospital, not surprised at all to hear it was somehow, in spite of all precautions, dysentery. He had not taken
all precautions, no indeed. His old self would have taken
all precautions—his wife would have seen to that. It was as
if after that first lack of caution or precaution which led to
her pregnancy and later to their marriage (a miserable affair
in a Registry office) she had settled down to make sure that
nothing would ever happen by chance again. Laura came to
the hospital with great bunches of flowers, sat on his bed
and held his hand and he forgot to be afraid. He was
ashamed of his sickness—losing control of his bowels—
there was something very humiliating about that. As if the
neat bandage of skin which so tightly binds in all the necessary nastiness of the human body had suddenly slipped and
revealed things that are best kept hidden.

Laura did not spend all day at the hospital—oh no. She
was her own person (they had made a pact before they left
Vancouver) and besides, he wouldn't have expected it. He
read Octavio Paz and Oscar Lewis and slept—the sickness

had taken a lot out of him. At five o'clock the bells would begin to ring and the roosters to crow. It was the first time he had slept away from Laura since their marriage. He thought of her waking up in the pension, her long naked body stretching and turning and settling down again. When she walked down the street with him he understood for the first time the sense of pride a man can feel at the side of a beautiful woman. Yet knew she would be displeased if he told her that and knew himself it was not an acceptable (any more) way to feel. If men brushed against her she grew angry and cold. Not frightened but contemptuous.

He was the one who had wanted marriage—he told her it gave him some protection, some security, although he wasn't even sure what he meant by that. The bells rang, the roosters began to crow—he imagined his wife turning over in the double bed.

Last year she had taken acid with her younger sister and a friend. And masturbated. Had her first masturbation orgasm. She told him this with the same frankness she told him everything. He and his first wife had been so shy, so horribly reticent about their bodies. It had nearly killed him. It would, in the end, have killed him. She had written him long, hysterical letters, proclaiming her love, her unhappiness, her desire to try again. Or presenting him with past hurts like unpaid bills.

He had never loved her, that was the worst discovery of all.

"Fourteen years as vegetables," he said. "What are you crying about?"

When Laura made love to him she made sounds, very low at first and then louder, louder, never words, just a strange babble or tide of sounds, crooning to him and touching him all over with her long restless fingers, igniting him, giving him life.

She was the first woman who had ever caressed his nipples; he loved it.

And she loved him—in spite of the dystentery stains on his trousers.

For twenty years he had been a teacher—at first young and eager and with ideas as fluffy and tentative as the hair on a new-born chick. Student, graduate-student, lecturer, assistant professor and so on. His mind toughening, reaching out. He had chosen the Metaphysicals because of their intelligence and acrobatics. He loved teaching them—it still, after twenty years, amazed him that anyone should pay him for what he liked doing best. But where had his body been during all that time?

His wife said, "It was dope that turned you on, not Laura."

"That may very well be," he replied. "But why couldn't you?"

Love's not so pure, and abstract, as they use
To say, which have no Mistresse but their Muse

With all his degrees and metaphysics he had never known before what it actually felt like to be his foot. His foot in his sock in his shoe. At first he was frightened, but the dark-haired girl sitting opposite him smiled and leaned over and touched his face. Over the weeks everything hard and cold within him began breaking up, like winter ice. He wrote a letter to his wife.

"The real meaning of Easter, it now seems to me, is that resurrection is a possibility for us all." He applied for a leave and got it.

On the fourth day the doctor said he could go home. That is to say, back to the pension. They celebrated by having a drink at La Cucaracha although the noise made him feel a little dizzy. Laura began talking to a woman who had been a nurse in World War II. She was at the *Instituto* taking a course in batik. She was telling Laura about S.I.F., "Self-Inflicted Wounds."

"You could always tell the S.I.F.s," she said.

"How?"

"They always shot themselves between the first and second toe."

"To get out of the fighting?"

"To get out of the fighting."

They strolled arm in arm across the street and into the *jardín*. Everywhere was the sound of birds and bells.

"The first night you were in the hospital," she said, "I was feeling a bit lost so I came here to sit for a while. There was an American lady on one of the benches. Dowdy, late middle-age. Sitting there and trying not to cry. Every so often she would put her head down and dab at her face and then sit straight up again. Finally I went over and asked her if I could help. She was ill, she said, with high blood pressure and was going home the next day. She's been coming to the *Instituto* for six years, ever since her husband died. She said her blood pressure attack came on because someone 'tampered' with a package—that was her word, 'tampered.' It contained her dead husband's stone-working tools. 'I can replace tools,' she said, 'but I can't replace *his* tools.' Now she hates Mexico and doesn't think she'll ever be coming back."

"I can understand that," he said.

"I'm trying to," she said.

They decided they were glad to have seen San Miguel but it was time to move on. Laura had put flowers everywhere in the bedroom. And had scented the sheets with some sweet, pungent herb. They had to get up with the roosters if they wanted to catch the early bus.

"This afternoon in the church by the market I saw this

sign," she said.

"It was written on a blackboard and I copied it out for you—"

Misas Rezadas:
Una por María de los Angeles Rodriguez
Otra por Crescenciano Rivera
Otra por Victoriano Muñoz
Otra por Soledad Ortíz
Otra por Julian Zalasar
Otra por Felepa Soto
   Tres misas Rezadas por todas las ánimas apuntadas.

"Three masses for all the damned souls. Is that right?"

"I think so. It reminded me of Lowry's virgin for them who have nobody with."

He thought briefly of his first wife. No. Souls damned themselves. And saw himself once again as a man miraculously saved. As if he had been literally held down or held under. And then had somehow broken free and swum away. Must he now light candles for the ones who didn't make it? For "todas las ánimas apuntadas?" Let the dead bury the dead. He handed her back the piece of paper.

"I'm glad I have 'somebody with.' "

But it still seemed a strange thing to copy down.

That was a week ago. And they were beginning to find out, to their surprise, that they liked Mexico City, in spite of itself, in spite of that first sight of it, coming in on the bus, terrifying—a haze over the city as if it had been bombed about a week before and the dust was just beginning to settle. One expected to hear faint cries for help from underneath the rubble. And the traffic! He was glad again that they had decided to leave their car back in Canada. They found a little hotel within walking distance of the Anthro-

209

pological Museum and after a day or two began to settle in. They got up late and went down together to the café connected with the hotel. Orange juice and rolls and coffee. His insides were still not quite right and Laura would count him out the *Lomatil*, "how do I love thee, let me count the ways." Teasing him, but not maliciously. Often they did not meet again until late afternoon or evening. He had to take things more slowly because he had been ill, and besides they were very liberated, very liberal, in their attitude to one another. What was the point in their always being together?

Some mornings he simply walked to the Anthropology Museum, taking his lunch with him in a basket—bread tortillas, yogurt, cheese, an avocado, a tin of juice—ate outside in the courtyard and then walked home again. He would take a nap (somehow he never mentioned this to Laura), setting the alarm so that he would be up and washed and downstairs in the café sipping a chocolate when she breezed in. She loved the markets and loved bargaining—bought cloth and ceramic flutes and spinning tops and papier maché masks for her nieces and nephews. Her Spanish was minimal but she always made herself understood, got where she wanted to go, had only positive adventures. She assumed that people would like her and so of course they did. In the evenings they wandered around hand in hand until they found a place to eat, then went to a movie and home to bed.

One night they met some people in a bar and were invited to a party. Americans and Mexicans and he and Laura sat in the back of a taxi with a Mexican they called "the pole." The pole kept going on and on about mushrooms. When they arrived at the party no-one was there but a boy and a girl making love in an old brass bed. Their new friends said it didn't matter, wrong address, and offered the lovers some beer and some tequila. They all got stoned and slightly drunk and he kept telling Laura that this was a far cry from the Museum of Anthropology. But the next day his guts were very bad and he felt the whole thing wasn't worth it. He began to envy Laura's energy and good health. She was thinking of staying on in Mexico for a while—he had to go back in two more weeks and see his sons. He tried not to be hurt that she might stay on—after all, that had been the agreement, they were both free to come and go. He met a girl in the bank that afternoon and invited her to a movie that night. She was from Chile and very beautiful.

"I can practice my Spanish," he said and Laura smiled and nodded.

"If I were your wife," Inez said, "I wouldn't allow you out of my sight."

"That's ridiculous," he said, and then looked up and saw she was teasing him. She was a psychologist at the institute for drug research. She would introduce him to her boyfriend, Rosario, who was doing workshops with LSD. Donne and Marvell seemed very far away.

Laura wasn't too sure about going—"maybe I'm jealous," she said.

"Do you think so?" He couldn't help feeling pleased. "She says her boyfriend will be there." They were all to meet at Inez' apartment and then go out for a drink.

Rosario was small but beautifully made. Inez had on white jeans and a tiny crocheted top. Her apartment was large and full of rugs and soft furniture. She kissed Laura and offered drinks. It was the apartment of a wealthy woman—she said she lived alone except for the maid. "A Chilean refugee." Rosario was running a marathon acid session at the institute beginning Saturday morning. There would be participants and attendants and observers. People were coming from as far away as Harvard, would they like to come? Inez put her arm around Laura. "Your skin is incredible." They were all a little drunk.

"What about this movie?" he said.

"Oh!" said Inez. "Do we really want to go to a movie? We cannot talk in a movie and we are all just getting to be friends." There were white curtains of some beautiful thin gauzy stuff and brilliant woven cushions on the sofa. Rosario smiled at him and began to talk about the expanding consciousness. Inez got up and offered to show Laura the bedroom.

"All of us," she said, "let us all go and see the bedroom."

It was the biggest bed he had ever seen. A coarse-woven cloth and more bright pillows, dozens of them. Who suggested it? Rosario? Inez? That they should all make love together. Rosario sat on the edge of the bed and rolled a joint. Inez put her arms around Laura and kissed her. He had never seen one woman kiss another like that before and it excited him. But Laura pushed away. Why?

"I don't want to stay."

"I'd like to."

"That's fine."

"You don't mind?"

Inez looked from one to the other. How old was she? Thirty? Thirty-five? It was hard to tell. She was small, like Rosario, and had to reach up to kiss Laura. Had reached up and pulled her head down, a gesture both childlike and erotic.

"But Laura, it will be great fun. We will all become really acquainted, really friends."

Laura shook her head.

"I'm sorry."

Inez shrugged and turned away, dismissing her.

"And you?"

Laura had told him he must always be honest.

"I want to stay."

Laura came over and kissed him on the cheek and then

was gone. He told himself he felt no guilt, she was a big girl and if she'd wanted him to come she would have said so.

They took off their clothes and Inez lay down on the bed between the two men. They just lay there smoking, nothing happening, until suddenly she pulled him over on top of her. Rosario began caressing his back and buttocks, harder and harder so that when he finally came he wasn't sure whether it was because of Rosario or Inez and that frightened him a little. Rosario and Inez both began to masturbate, with their eyes shut and then he was pushing her hands away and licking her while Rosario got down behind and began licking him. He was totally out of his senses, totally. It was just pure sensation and violence, too. And nothing loving about it at all. Inez screamed and pushed him away and Rosario rolled over on top of her. The sight of Rosario fucking Inex excited him again and he felt lost, left-out and frustrated. Inez came and then asked whether he wanted her or Rosario to suck him off. He said "both" so they took turns.

"Now we are very close," she said, "very close. I am sorry your wife wouldn't stay. She has a beautiful body, beautiful skin."

He arranged to meet Rosario for the acid marathon and went out into the street. He did not feel close to those people at all and was terrified by his response to Rosario. Things would have been different if Laura had stayed.

She was sitting up in bed waiting for him when he got back. He told her everything.

"That's why I left," she said. "I felt we were somehow being set up for their amusement. They're cruel people, sophisticated and cruel."

"I was frightened," she said. "When I got to Reforma I began to run—it was ridiculous. I just didn't want you to come after me and drag me back there. I went into one of the hotels, I don't know which one. There was a mariachi band and all the tourists were whooping it up. I met a man, older, who'd been sitting in that hotel for four days afraid to go out. His brother was supposed to join him and was delayed. He hadn't been *outside* of the hotel."

They wept in one another's arms.

"Were you attracted to Inez?" he asked.

"No, because I felt I was being manipulated."

"Have you ever made love with a woman?"

"Yes," she said. "Once, but it was someone I loved. I don't think I could make love with a strange woman."

"Yet I was turned on by Rosario."

"You were being very carefully manipulated."

"*Todo el mundo es loco loco.*"

"What?"

"It's a movie sign I saw today, with Ethel Merman."

"I love you," she said, "even if you are loco loco."

He began to cry again.

"Let go of it," she said. "Let it go."

The next day he felt very tired and convalescent. He decided to go back to the Anthropology Museum once more and she would go to the Museum of Modern Art. They agreed to meet for a picnic lunch at two. The walk seemed very long and the broad avenue of Reforma crowded and unpleasant. "Let's take a bus," he said, "I still feel a bit woozy."

They stood at the bus stop together and she leaned up against him.

"I feel very close to you," she said. "I just wanted you to know." It came over him that if he died right then, that instant, he would have known more happiness in his few months with this girl than he had in all the years of his former life. What about never going back? What about staying down here and finding a little village somewhere. All for love and the world well lost. Laura got off at her stop

214

and blew him a kiss.

"Two o'clock."

"I won't forget."

She asked nothing of him except that he be himself. If he weren't there at two she would not be jealous or hurt (although he would like to think she might be a little concerned). She would assume that something had caught his interest and he couldn't make it. "Loving," she had said to him, "is letting go, of yourself and of the other person, the 'beloved' as your old poet-pals might put it."

It was not a lesson he learned easily. For if she stood *him* up?

And then of course his museum was closed. Monday. Why hadn't he noticed that before? He stood there at a loss. It was only eleven and the Museum of Modern Art would not excite him a second time round. However he began to wander back in that direction—to find Laura. To tell her he was going on to something else. A man and a woman were setting up a little stall of glass figurines outside the children's playground. He smiled and bought a fragile giraffe and three babies which were carefully wrapped in grey lint. They were not very expert examples of glass-blowing but they pleased him all the same. Laura was sitting on a bench in the children's playground watching two monkeys feed a bird.

"Hey Señorita." She didn't turn around. "Laura!" Turned and saw who it was and waved. There was a high fence between them.

"How did you get in?"

"Keep going. Around the other side."

Her museum was closed too. Maybe everything? He wanted to see the stuff at the Palace of Fine Arts, she was easy, didn't really care. They walked back toward the en-

215

trance to the park and found a phone booth. Someone assured him the Palace of Fine Arts was open.

"Let's go."

Then just as they were about to cross the boulevard she saw a balloon man.

"Wait a minute, I want to buy a balloon."

"What colour? I'll treat you to one."

"Red," she said, "yellow, I don't care."

In a sudden rush of delight he bought them all. Eighteen, twenty, he wasn't sure how many. The balloon seller thought he was crazy. Loco loco. He went away shrugging his shoulders.

"Here," he said, embarrassed now. "A special bouquet."

"You will become a legend in some small street in this city. The crazy gringo who bought up all the balloons."

They crossed over and began a slow leisurely walk along the boulevard, Carlotta's boulevard, arm in arm, the balloons bobbing in the air above them. Why had he thought the street unfriendly, cold? Laura gave a balloon to every child, to old people, to a laughing policeman. She did not expect to be snubbed and no-one snubbed her. They walked like this for about three miles, slowly, ceremoniously, arm in arm. Laura had on a long dull-red skirt and a black T-shirt. He wanted to photograph her but did not have his camera. She was colour and life and delight. When they reached Alameda Park it was afternoon and they sat amongst the statues and shoe-shine boys and ate their lunch. Laura tied a balloon to the bench where they had sat. He felt quite dizzy when he stood up to go and thought for a minute of his usual afternoon siesta. He could go back now, Laura wouldn't care. No. It was just the late night and the dope and the drink and of course the altitude. The altitude slowed almost everybody down.

A boy came up to them, carrying his brass-decorated shoe-

216

shine stand.

"Shine your shoes, Señor?"

He held out his sandalled foot and laughed. The boy laughed too.

"Cut your toenails?" Laura gave him the last balloon but one.

The Palace of Fine Arts was closed—only the office (with the phone) was open. He was terribly tired. The secretary suggested the Rivera murals at the Ministry of Education. They walked round and round. His head ached, his back ached, his whole body ached. Yet still he felt the power of Rivera's vision.

"I read somewhere," Laura said, "that at one time they wanted him for President of the Republic."

His people were as solid as mountains. The calves of the peasant women bulged. Freedom. The women handed out machine guns. Liberty. Everything was made simple. The truth shall make you free. His back ached horribly.

"There's one more place I'd like to go while we're down in this area," she said.

"Where's that?"

"It's a hotel with a big Rivera mural. The Hotel del Prado."

"Do you know where it is?"

"I know it's near the Alameda Park—where we ate lunch."

They went back the way they had come. Laura had kept one balloon, a red one, and now, because he was tired and felt ill, because he really didn't give a damn about seeing another mural, because all he wanted to do was go back to the hotel and go to bed, it seemed to him that people were laughing at her—stupid American woman carrying a balloon. He wished it would break before they got to the Hotel del Prado, but of course it didn't.

They had walked all the way around the park before they found out where the mural was. Across the street, the traffic snarling and pouncing, up some stairs and into the lounge. It was "Happy Hour," a sign said, they could have two drinks for the price of one. He ordered two gin and tonics and when the girl came she put the drinks down and then stood with her hand out. He paid for the drinks and still she stood.

"What d'you want?" He hadn't meant his voice to come out so loud.

"You have to tip me Señor."

"What do you mean, I *have* to tip you."

"It is the custom."

He shrugged and gave her a few pesos. She looked at him with contempt, put the money down by his drink and walked away.

"Stupid bitch."

"Shh. It's beginning."

A small man with a pointer came out of nowhere and began to explain the mural. It was huge—the history of modern Mexico set in Alameda Park. That was the name of the mural—"A Sunday Dream in Alameda Park." Rivera had painted himself in the centre, a small boy with a frog and a snake in his pocket. On one side of him a woman, a skeleton in a long dress. The Plumed Serpent was a feather boa around her neck.

The gin made him feel a little better, but the mural danced like a landscape in the water and he couldn't pay attention to the little man with the pointer. General Zapata. Madero. Rivera's first wife, Guadalupe, his daughter Ruth, his second wife Freda in maroon with a yin/yang symbol in her hand. The landscape was divided into three parts. In the Colonization Period everything was smoky and unclear "because our nation was not independent." Then balloons like Laura's balloons—strength—"everythin' is shiny bright —the win' is not even blowin'." When was that? After Juárez presumably. Then the winds began to blow amongst the trees in Alameda Park—there will be a revolution— "leaves begin to get sick."

He tried to follow. Which revolution? What was the man talking about? Laura was taking notes. Good. He could ask her later.

Phrases stuck in his mind. "Forty years late on." "Lil boy." "Consider him par of the family." *Tierra y Libertad.* *"El Sueño de un domingo en la Alameda."*

The lecturer announced that he was Facundo Vásquez and that contributions would be accepted.

Laura put her notebook away and hunted for some change. She went up and stood chatting with the man. He wondered if he would faint if he stood up.

A Sunday dream. A Monday dream. Rosario and Inez. Had we but world enough and time. How old was Freda when Rivera married her? In ten years Laura would be 32 and he would be 60.

She came up to him as he was moving toward the door.

"Leaving without me?"

"I just wanted to get some fresh air."

They took a taxi back to the hotel. There was no elevator and the stairs seemed endless. Left foot. Right foot. He took off his sandals and fell across the bed.

"Got to have a little sleep. Very tired."

She smiled and shed her clothes. Stood there naked and unself-conscious in the middle of the room and he felt nothing, nothing at all. Sleep. The soft lap of sleep. The last thing he heard was the sound of the shower....

She came out towelling her hair, and looked at her sleeping husband. She kissed him gently and covered him up with a light blanket. Then she put on a dress and her sandals and checked that she had money and her keys. It was not that she didn't love him, for she did. But all around her the lights of Mexico City had come on, in the fountains, the circles, the parks, the bars, the boulevards. She tied her balloon to the arm of the single chair and quietly let herself out.

In Alameda Park the lovers walked with their arms around one another's shoulders. But let him sleep.

THE MORE LITTLE MUMMY IN THE WORLD

Oscar A. Lempe
Denver, Color U. S.   14-V-1876
                       23-XI-1958
Guanauato, Gto.
   Recuerdo de Su Esposa
   Chijas
   Perpetuidad

Louis Montgomery Allen Sr.
New York City   Dec. 6 1887
                  Feb. 12-1957
Guanauato, Gto.
   Perpetuidad

Handprints on this one—of whom? *Su esposa? Su hermosa?*
A passing, naughty, unrelated child?

Elisabeth Carnes Allen, D.A.R.

She wandered through the cemetery looking at every stone,
imagining the people, what had brought them there, what
the town had been like nearly a hundred years before. The
lure of what riches? The silver mines perhaps.

221

Everywhere there were flowers stuck in tins—Mobil Oil tins, paint tins, tomatoes, green chillies:

Chiles Jalapenos, En Escapbeche

She took out her pocket dictionary.

The wind blowing through the cypress trees rattled the tins like bones.

To My Beloved Wife
Maria Concepcion Buchnan

Although there had been a long line-up to see the mummies there were very few people in the Pantheon itself. A young couple with their arms around one another, laughing, exchanging kisses, some old women in black, a gardener. And the dead of course, the multitude of dead stacked six or seven high. The soft brown hills beyond and El Pipla, the boy hero, alone on a hill above the Jardin de la Union, his arm upraised.

Ayer (yesterday). *Hoy* (today).
Mañana

Mother
Lily Mast McBride
Born Sept. 19-1882
Died July 22-1926

A pretty blue-grey stone, this one, beautifully incised.

It was very peaceful here with the wreaths, the plastic flowers and the real—gladioli, lilies—the white ones she saw everywhere here, Easter lilies back home—geraniums, carnations. The flowers dead too of course, or dying, sucking up the last dregs of rusty water from the tins. Still, she liked this place better than the churches with their bleeding Christs, their oppressive smell of hot wax, their plaster damned pleading to her for one last chance at salvation.

Some stones were casually propped against still-occupied cabinets. (They couldn't be called tombs and she couldn't think of a beter word than "cabinet"—cabin, verb, to confine in a small space, cramp). She turned one over.

> *Naci Inocente! ...*
> *Muero Ignorante*
> *Freyre Jose E.*
> *V-7-1925*
> *Perpetuidad*

So much for *perpetuidad*!

She had been thinking of failures and of suicides and had gone to mass on Palm Sunday in the hopes of finding something positive—if only for a second, if only for an instant, if only, even, an aura or a whiff of hope for her salvation.

Buenos días. Adios.

She straightened a tin of gladioli which had fallen over in the wind.

Outside the Parroquia women and men were braiding palms into elaborate patterns. She bought a small crucifix and went in, covering her head, but the Mass was a disappointment. She stood up. She sat down. She prayed. The priest was way way way up in the chancel. Little bells rang. There was no pageantry, no music, nothing to draw her spirit up and away from the deep well of despair into which it seemed to have fallen. Over the words of the priest a poem of Yeats' kept running through her mind:

> That is no country for old men
> The young in one another's arms
> Fish/flesh/and fowl commend
> all summer long
> Whatever is begotten, born or dies

They had been going to come down here together. Had maps, dreams, destinations. Even a tape:

> *Siento molestarle!*
> *No es ninguna molestia!*
> *Salud!*

How much too much please thank you don't mention it.

Instead he took her out (at her request) the night before she left. To a Greek restaurant (again at her request). She drank a lot of wine, and crumbling a bit of bread between her fingers, told him it was she all along whom he really loved.

"Do you think so?" he said and smiled at her over his wine glass. Then in an offhand manner he asked her if she'd ever been in any of the other Greek restaurants along the street, places where you just walked in and took whatever was going, places where the Greeks themselves went, cheaper places than this. (And he, who never went into a restaurant alone, whom had he lingered with in a small café full of the smell of lamb and garlic and the whine of recorded music. Who? Don't ask, or, as he would have put it, "why humiliate yourself?") He had always been Machiavellian; had always known how to put her in her place.

Once they had been at the house of his best friend and

"I was coming in on the bus from the island," her lover said, "toward sunset—a beautiful evening. Suddenly I looked up and there was this incredible cloud formation—incredible! I said to the fellow next to me, without really thinking about it, you know, 'My God, that looks just like the Mushroom Cloud!' I saw the guy look at me and give a little frown and then I realized with a start that he was younger, younger than the Bomb—that he didn't even know what I was talking about. The only mushroom cloud he knew was psilocybin!"

Peter had laughed appreciatively. He was 35.

"It's true. People talk about the generation gap—as a metaphor I mean—but it seems to me there's a real gap—I almost see it as a physical space—between those born before or during the War and those born after it."

"Yes. There's a point at which Rachel and I just can't communicate; we were born into two different worlds." He had turned to her. "When I talk about Marlene Dietrich I don't know if you even know who I mean."

She was immediately defensive. He had wanted her to be, had set her up.

"Of course I know who Marlene Dietrich is."

"Ah yes—you know her name. But is your Marlene Dietrich the same as mine—I doubt it." Peter nodded and began singing "Lili Marlene." Her lover sat back and lit his pipe.

That night at the Greek restaurant he had given her a handsome present—a shoulderbag with three sections, or pouches, like a saddlebag.

"Now you will have three places to put all your clutter," he said, "instead of just one." ("It's not that she doesn't have a place for everything," he said once, at a party, "it's that she has several places." He was very tidy and they fought about the missing cap to the toothpaste.)

Buenos dias. Adios. No comprendo.

In one place there were freshly-dug graves, four in a row, an accident perhaps. This in a courtyard which led to a view of the city. Bougainvillaea had been splashed against the walls, the original purple and the scarlet, blood-coloured. In the distance she could hear the sound of children's voices.

Estoy esperando un paquete.
Lo tiene usted aqui?

When he came to get her at the hospital he was very brusque and efficient, annoyed that she was still in bed and crying. His sons were in the car—they were going camping. Yet still she wanted to buy him gifts—an onyx chess set, a heavy silver ring, a blanket for his bed. Things of beauty and whimsy, things that would make him think of her, remember her and want her.

Donde este? Where is?

He had told her there was nothing wrong, that maybe she should see a shrink. The gifts would only embarrass him. When she began to cry at the bus station, he kissed her quickly on the forehead and then walked away. She hated him; no, she loved him.

She had read in the guidebook that if the rent was not kept up on the crypts (yes, that was the word she had been searching for), the bodies were removed after five years and the bones thrown into a common bone-house to make room for new arrivals. But the region was very dry and some of the

226

bodies would be mummified. When they were, they were put into the museum. Directly outside the cemetery were souvenir stands—skeletons, on horseback or playing fiddles or dancing, with springy arms and legs. Postcards of the mummies, earthenware, bone letter-openers and crochet hooks (human bone?). There were mummies of pale beige toffee with raisin eyes. These were wrapped in red or yellow cellophane. As she approached a man had offered her two large ones in one packet, "*Momias Matrimonias*," and laughed at her discomfort. Now she was trying to get up enough courage to go into the mummy museum itself.

Death and disease were accepted here. Death was even made fun of, made into toffee to chew or chocolate to lick or tiny plaster figures to decorate, along with gilded pictures of miraculous virgins, the windows and mirrors of buses and cars. She knew now that almost certainly, whenever she saw a street musician, either he was blind or lame or leprous or there was a terribly deformed creature, just out of sight, on behalf of whom he was playing his music.

Her operation had been therapeutic and therefore covered by her insurance. No back streets or borrowed money— things were easier now.

Ayer (yesterday). *Hoy* (today).
Mañana

This was a very strange town to walk around in and easy to get lost. The main road ran underneath the town in places, reappearing above ground several hundred yards beyond. It was really a stone-arched tunnel and rather frightening. And there were six or seven main squares, not just one. She had already, in spite of her map, been lost several times. The night before, wandering steep alleys full of wrought-iron

227

balconies, she had stumbled upon a strange religious cere-
mony in one of the smaller lamplit squares. There were
bleachers set out and many of the people were already
seated, men, women and children, facing an old church. The
church bell began to ring and then a priest appeared high
up on the church steps, intoning Hail Marys and Our Fathers. And she understood a bit of it, the history of the week
leading up to the arrest of Jesus. Below the steps stood men
in purple sackcloth and black hoods, very mediaeval and
frightening. A lifesized statue of Christ (looking not unlike
the "Jesu Christo Superstare" she had seen in Mexico City)
was brought out of the church by more hooded men, carried
down the steep steps and put on a flower-decked platform.
There was a rope around his neck and it hung down his back,
binding his hands behind him. A child-angel and one of the
masked men climbed up and sat on either side of him.
Torches were lit and as the rest of the masked men shoul-
dered their burden the crowd gave a deep moan of pity and
anticipation. The statue had real hair and jointed, movable
arms. He terrified her, for he hovered somewhere in a
strange space between icon and the living god. The wind
blew his hair across his gentle, accepting face. His gown was
purple like the garments of the men but his was of velvet,
not hemp. A workman beat a drum and the entire affair—
Christ, angel, masked men, flowers, scaffolding, torches,
priest—began to move. A young boy followed behind, playing a simple pipe and the procession slowly moved out from
the small square into the larger one beyond. Behind came
small children, some on tricycles, the women in black, the
men, balloon sellers, a thin brown pariah dog. The bowed,
bound figure of Christ rode above them all. It was amateur-
ish in a way but very powerful; she hid herself in the crowd.

Por que? Why? *No se.* I don't know.

228

Perdone.

It was as though once she had decided she didn't want it he had washed his hands of the whole affair.

"Ruth Barnes"
Just a small stone marker with a dried-up geranium obscuring the date. Presumably to be buried in this small courtyard was more expensive than to be deposited on the shelves. The wind blowing rattled the tins like bones.

If he were here he would have struck up a friendship with the gardener, would try out the little Spanish he knew and supplement it with laughter and broad gestures. His energy was one of the first things that had excited her. And his keen intelligence, his learning, the whole sum of his life experience. He had been married (twice), had children (one as old as her youngest sister), had suffered and taken chances.

"I find it impossible to live alone," he had said to her the first night, "and yet somehow I always seem to fuck it up—my relationships with women." He showed her pictures of his sons and took her home to bed.

Dispenseme. Excuse me.
Muchas gracias.

Everywhere down here men followed her and tried to feel her up—a woman alone deserved to be treated that way. Then they gave their paycheques to their mothers and went to mass on Sunday.

Hail Mary Full of Grace Blessed is
The Fruit of Thy Womb Jesus

On the train from Nuevo Laredo she had met a middle-aged

man who lived in San Miguel. He said the happiest day of his life was the day when they nailed his wife's coffin shut. Federales came on the train looking for contraband. They wore their revolvers tucked in the back of their pants, Pancho Villa style.

"Watch for the Mordida," the American said.

She shook her head.

" 'The Bite.' To force someone to give you a bribe. It's a game between the Federales and the people coming back."

Was that what she had done by getting pregnant? Put the bite on him?

The boy-hero stood unconcerned on the distant hill, his arm upraised forever. Her first day in the town she had followed the crude signs and climbed steep stairs and back alleys until she reached the top of that hill. She had taken some bread and fruit with her and sat in a little summer house just below the enormous figure, eating slices of pineapple and writing in her journal. The boy had set fire to the granary in which the Royalists had barricaded themselves. At his feet it said, in Spanish,

"There are still other castles to burn."

She felt quite happy there, after her climb, the whole town at her feet. But in the evening, at a band concert in the Jardin de la Union, she sat on a wrought-iron bench and longed to have him with her, next to her, observing, commenting, loving. Canaries mocked her from the laurel trees around the square.

Where is? *No comprendo.*

She retraced her steps, back through the main courtyard with all its stacked and silent dead, back through the black iron gate with its simple cross on top. There were very few people in line now so there was no reason not to wait.

He had been quite calm when she told him. Just said, "Well, what do you want to do about it?" He left it entirely up to her. Had she wanted him to be otherwise? Had she wanted to bear his child? She wanted to be a writer, a poet —had he not encouraged her, sung her praises? In Chapultapec Park in Mexico City she sat on the grass one Sunday and watched the fathers spoil their children. They were immaculate—it was the mothers, of course, who saw to that. There were funny animal heads on the trash cans in the children's playground. The children laughed and squealed when they stuck their little hands in.

She paid her five pesos and went into the mummy museum.

In Chapultapec Park she had sat on the grass and wept. She wanted to be six years old in a white dress and riding on her father's shoulders, her small hands tugging at his curly hair. She wanted to be held and to be forgiven. She wanted a red balloon.

Her mother was at home making a delicious Sunday dinner.

Ayer. (yesterday). *Hoy* (today).
Mañana.

The mummy museum was really a long artificially-lit corridor with the mummies displayed in glass cases along one side. The corridor was hot and very crowded, so that for a moment she experienced a wave of claustrophobia and almost turned around and ran.

Some of the names and dates on the stones had simply been scrawled in the wet plaster.

Aristo Perez
Manuel Torres M.
Maria de los Angeles Rodriguez

So there were the mummies, in glass cases like curios—
which of course they were. Most were without clothes,
jaundice-coloured and hideously wrinkled. A few had on
mouldy shoes and there was one man who had on a complete
suit of tattered black clothes. Very few had hair and this
surprised her. Was it just an old wives' tale that the hair
would keep on growing?

He read her, one night, from John Donne's "Funerale"

Whoever comes to shroud me,
   do not harme
Nor question much
That subtile wreathe of hair,
   which crowns my arme:

and from "A Feaver"

Oh doe not die, for I shall hate
   All women so, when thou art gone,
That thee I shall not celebrate,
   When I remember, thou wast one.

She got up and cut off a lock of her hair and gave it to him;
he kissed her neck and put the lock in the back of his grandfather's gold watch.

Donde este? Where is?

The mummies' faces were full of anger and terror. Shrink-

232

age had pulled their mouths open and their hands were clutched across their empty bellies. Her Spanish was not quick enough to understand everything the guides were saying, but there were abnormalities and tumours and other curious things being pointed out as they moved along. The mummies were tall or short, male and female, the men's papery genitals still visible, the women's wrinkled breasts.

She wrote him letter after letter and tore them all up.

Quiero comprar una postal. I wish to buy a postcard.

As she crossed the street to his car and his waiting sons, she stumbled, still drugged and swollen-eyed, against the curb, and turned her ankle. Suddenly she had to sit down on the grass and put her head between her knees. She knew the boys, his sons, were watching her. What had he said to them? Why had he brought them to the hospital? What was he trying to say?

People with limps, people with no legs, blind people, lepers, pariah dogs. The country swarmed with outcasts and with cripples. The tourists bought silver rings and onyx chess sets and turned their heads away. After all, it was not their problem. Charity begins. . . .

"They hate us," the American man had said. "They want our money but they hate us. They would prefer if we just mailed it down."

Almost at the end of the corridor was a display case full of child mummies—some in christening gowns and bonnets, some naked or wrapped in tiny shrouds. In front of the smallest of these a cardboard sign was propped. She pushed closer, in order to read it, then tugged at the guide's elbow.

"Please. *Por favor.* What does the sign say? *Que quiere decir?*"

"*La Momia Mas Pequena del mundo.*" He smiled at her, showing perfect teeth.

"*Si. Si.* In English. *Habla Usted Inglis?*"

"*Ah. Inglis.*"

He smiled again.

"The more little mummy in the world."

It sat there, no bigger than the rubber babies she had played with as a child.

Where were the parents? Why had these children been removed to this terrible glass limbo? She looked at la momia mas Pequena but it refused to answer.

The American had asked her to come and spend a few days with him in San Miguel.

She pushed her way through the tourists and out the exit door. The sun struck her like a slap. She half-ran, half-walked toward the souvenir stands, rummaged quickly through the cards until she found the one she was looking for, the one she knew was certain to be there. _

Back at the apartment he had said, "D'you think you could rustle us up some dinner—we'd like to get away before dark." The boys were looking at her curiously. She went into the bedroom and began to pack, tears running down her face, the little plastic hospital bracelet still locked around her wrist.

Go. Come. Are you ready?

Don't forget.

She fumbled in her bag for the change purse, then headed back down the hill. Tonight, drinking her cho-ko-la-tay in that little restaurant near the Plazuela where she had seen the Christ, she would get out the card and address it.

"Having a wonderful time," she would write.

"Wish you were here."

THE NEW CANADIAN LIBRARY LIST

McCLELLAND AND STEWART LIMITED
publishers of The New Canadian Library
would like to keep you informed about
new additions to this unique series.

For a complete listing of titles and
current prices – or if you wish to be added
to our mailing list to receive future catalogues
and other new book information – write:

BOOKNEWS
McClelland and Stewart Limited
25 Hollinger Road
Toronto, Canada M4B 3G2

McClelland and Stewart books are
available at all good bookstores.

Booksellers should be happy to order from our catalogues
any titles which they do not regularly stock.